DUSK SHALL WEEP

ALSO BY KELSEY GIETL

HOPE OR HIGH WATER — OVER THE ATLANTIC
Across Oceans
Twisted River

HOPE OR HIGH WATER — WAR ACROSS WATERS
Broken Lines
Unsettled Shores

LARKSONG LEGACY
For a Noble Purpose
Dusk Shall Weep

LARKSONG LEGACY · 2

DUSK *shall* WEEP

KELSEY GIETL

Purple Mask Publishing
Saint Charles, Missouri

ISBN-13: 979-8-9856744-2-2
ebook ISBN: 979-8-9856744-1-5
Library of Congress Control Number: 2023900176
First Edition

Scripture quotations are taken from The New American Bible, St. Joseph Edition.

Quotations from *Swallow Barn; or, a Sojourn in the Old Dominion* (1832) by John Pendleton Kennedy, sourced under the public domain.

Chinook language from *The Northwest Coast; or, Three Years' Residence in Washington Territory* (1857) by James Gilchrist Swan, sourced under the public domain.

Cover design by Kelsey Gietl (kelseygietl.com)
Cover photos: Face of Woman used under license by Adobe Stock. "Rope" by Engin Akyurt, "Paper" by Prophsee Journals, and Poles from "White Lighthouse at a Distance" by Oliver Paaske used under free license by Unsplash. Additional images from the The Metropolitan Museum of Art, New York, Open Access Collection.
Back cover photo: "Brown Cardboard Box on White Table" by Dan-Cristian Pădureţ used under free license by Unsplash.

For my Walking With Purpose ladies. You help me stay the path.

And for all those trying to find their way.

"At dusk weeping comes for the night but at dawn there is rejoicing."
(Psalms 30:6)

KEY CHARACTERS
INCLUDED IN *DUSK SHALL WEEP*

THE SHAY/OWENS FAMILY

Coraline Owens Shay — South Carolina widow in search of hope and healing from a degenerative eye disease. Age: 24

Alice Ann Owens — Coraline's 18-year-old sister

Mercy Owens — Coraline's 28-year-old sister in South Carolina

Ned and Octavia Owens — their parents in South Carolina

Oliver Shay — Coraline's late husband

THE LARK FAMILY

Jamison Lark —Former South Carolina plantation son who now serves as doctor and spiritual leader in Larksong. Age: 27.

Daniel Lark — Jamison's 33-year-old brother in South Carolina

Tobias Lark — Jamison's 31-year-old brother

Sarah Lark — Tobias's 29-year-old wife

Martha Louis — Sarah's 31-year-old former maid and dearest friend

Garrett Lark — Jamison's 29-year-old brother in San Francisco

Cade Lark — Jamison's 21-year-old brother

Alonzo and Geraldine Lark — their parents (deceased)

Josiah — The Larks' 58-year-old former butler in San Francisco

Levi and Marie Harper —The Larks' former field hand and housemaid. Age: 30 and 29. Married with five children: Jonah (9), Marilee (7), Reeslie (6), Aphid (5), and Quint (3).

OTHER CHARACTERS

Clinton Reed — 34-year-old cattle rancher

Gabriella Reed — Clinton's 28-year-old wife, currently missing

Quea'Quim (*kway-ah-kwim*) — 24-year-old Chinook tribal member

Anwillik (*ann-will-ick*)— Quea'Quim's 22-year-old sister

Tleyuk (*tay-yook*)— Anwillik's four-year-old son

At the beginning of the eighteenth century,
in the first month of the year of our Lord,
The sailing ship Oblique
made her final stand against the sea.

After the earth moved and the waves crashed,
only seven of her crew remained.
Forever changed by God's great thunder,
their legacies carried on.

One-hundred-and-fifty-two years later,
this is but one of their stories...

1

When the threat of darkness loomed like a dragon perched on the castle keep, it made you do things you might not otherwise do and things you would do, you did with careful precision.

Going blind was curious like that. It had taken hold of Coraline Shay's life and become a gauze around her every breath, now stitched within her like the binding of her treasured novels. Every step she took across the Washington wilderness, her slim boots sunk in sand and mud, was a step closer to never seeing its landscape again. Her type of blindness crept in like a thief who visited not once, but every evening, making off with a little more each time, until one day there would be nothing left. She had known about its possibility since childhood, about its certainty since she was seventeen, and about its imminent pursuit since her twenty-third birthday last year.

There was no cure. It was as certain as it had been with her father and her grandfather before him. Her Aunt Patrice and Great-Uncle Warren. "An inescapable sin," the doctors told them. With so many affected in a single family, it must be. There was no escaping when it was trapped in the blood.

Perhaps it would be several years or twenty, but eventually, she would lose her eyesight. One physician had suggested bleeding in hopes to remove the impurities, but her father refused to allow it. Minor as they were at the time, he feared bleeding would kill her. Her current tin spectacles were only moderately helpful, having been made over two years ago in her hometown of Charleston, South Carolina. Nevertheless, she made do, lucky to have retained as much sight as she did.

Outside the cabin window, the sky painted the pale lavender of pre-sunrise as her feet whispered across the single-room cabin toward her trunk. From within its recesses, she slipped on a modest mauve day dress followed by a fresh cream apron. She knotted the strings back in front before drawing her brunette curls into a simple knot at the base of her neck with a swath over her ears on either side. No embellishments or combs. They were not needed in a wilderness such as this. Still a territory, Washington boasted barely one thousand settlers and their town of Larksong hardly contributed more to that number.

"Ready to greet another glorious day?" her friend and cabinmate Martha Louis asked as she tied her own apron over her brown and blue checkered skirt and cream-colored blouse. She reached for the matching bonnet and settled it over her coal-black braid.

A former slave, Martha had come about their wagon party by chance, fleeing Missouri with her mistress, Sarah. After a slew of deceased husbands, Sarah had been avoiding life in an asylum, while Martha ran from being sold. The girls had grown up as sisters and were now the dearest of friends. In turn, their two-thousand-mile journey together had solidified their friendship with Coraline. Although, even their kind souls were not enough to yet know of her affliction.

Coraline offered Martha a smile, which she knew her friend could see even in the semi-darkness. "I will grant you the gloriousness of the sunrise, but the day? I'm afraid a conclusion is yet to be drawn."

"You say that every morning. I don't know why I should've expected today to be any different."

"Perhaps you should stop asking then."

Martha grinned as she slipped the final loop through her bonnet's bow and tugged. "I will when you provide me a different answer."

"I'll provide you both with a glorious string of saucy language if you don't let me sleep. Honestly, Cora, the sun isn't even up."

This snip came from one of the two wood-hewn beds which contained the semi-sleeping form of Coraline's eighteen-year-old sister, Alice Ann. Her burnished locks fell across her pillow, her lightly tanned complexion as different from Martha's deep umber skin as could be. She stretched across Coraline's empty half of the bed.

"I thought sunrise was the best time for fishing," Cora said. "Papa swore his life by it."

"I run my fishing business my way."

"That would be admirable if your way worked."

With a snort, Alice Ann turned over to face the cabin's exterior wall and pulled her blanket to her chin. Without proper chinking, the cabin's half-moon cedar walls leaked and the sod shoved between the cracks was barely a buffer for the wind. The mud between the roof beams had already been replaced twice.

"This is what your father wants for you and Alice Ann," their mother had told Coraline the day they left Charleston. "This will be a better life. Beautiful land that you should see before you can't anymore." She took her middle daughter's hands. "This is right, darling." A pause and tears welled. She drew her child into her arms. "Oh, I am going to miss you."

Despite their mother's assurances, it had not been a better life. The sisters were constantly at odds, with Alice Ann unable to remain in check and Coraline afraid of when her sister would reveal her vision impairment to the rest of the homestead. She knew she must tell them eventually, but with so many hardships and so few people, the strands of Larksong were already like braided fibers having lost their finishing knot. Her blindness could not be the final tug that set the tapestry to ribbons.

Even while wearing her spectacles, Coraline had to step carefully across the cabin floor, counting her steps to avoid collision with their few meager pieces of furniture: 1...2...3...4...5... She continued up to twelve which brought her to the edge of her and Alice Ann's shared bed. She yanked the blanket off her sister clear down past her nightdress and bare feet. With a shriek, Alice Ann flew upright, grasping for the blanket which Coraline held out of reach. Martha's distinct snicker sounded as she lit a match in the table lantern, bringing Alice Ann's mussed appearance into bright profile.

Bless you, Martha, for your fine timing.

"Give me my blanket!" Alice Ann cried.

Coraline tossed it on the opposite bed. "Please get dressed. We have breakfast to attend to at Sarah's."

"I thought you wanted me to catch fish."

"Only if you're bringing them for breakfast."

Coraline spun on her heel toward the door, no longer needing to count her paces in the lantern light. She donned her cape from the wall hook and pushed the fasteners through the leather loops with shaking fingers.

How it angered her at times to think how blessed Alice Ann was and yet how terribly ungrateful. Perfect blue-eyed vision, perfect memory, and perfect feminine features even though she preferred to hide her loveliness under mussed crimson braids and bare feet. For months, her sister's petite hands had reeked of oysters, salmon oil, and sea slime, all in an effort to create her own fishing establishment. To whom she would sell remained a mystery. Larksong was at least three days' ride from the nearest settlement and several more from Astoria's docks. There were the natives, of course, but they hadn't seen hide nor hair of them since passing through Shoalwater Bay over six months prior.

Before their papa went blind, the Owens family had been of decent means. Until they spent all their money trying to bring back his sight, and nothing helped. That was when Mama and Mercy started taking in laundry as a means of support. By then the family was already long gone from the townhouse and moved into the cottage down near the shore. Alice Ann had been thrilled as it meant more time on the water, but while they all loved the ocean, its nearness only reminded Coraline of all they had lost. The beauty of God's paintbrush was nothing compared to the height of His disregard.

Before her blindness became a question of *when*, not *if*, she had treasured her role as a librarian in Charleston. All her volumes were ordered alphabetically, two trunks worth neatly arranged, their colorful bindings winking with *come hither* stares whenever she opened the lids. Even when other settlers tossed every manner of sundry belongings from their wagons to lighten the load, she couldn't bear to part with her novels. It was too close to parting with friends.

She had intended to drink them in one last time, reading in the evenings by the firelight as had been her custom back in Charleston, but every day made her more exhausted than the last. Dim light left her eyes weak, and stories which used to take mere days to finish now took weeks to muddle through. Pain settled behind her eyes and worsened until her head throbbed. It happened more and more these days, leaving her with a pit in her middle certain to remain unfilled.

The way she understood her future, there were really only three options in front of her:

First was to accept her place in Larksong as it lay and treasure each moment until darkness claimed her. With the way her eyesight had already deteriorated, however, she would estimate perhaps only another few years at most. After experiencing the strain of her father's blindness, she would not sentence Alice Ann or Martha to a lifetime of her care.

Her second option would be to leave Larksong and secure employment profiting enough to pay for a nursemaid in subsequent years. That was hardly a realistic option, nor would she return to Charleston to become a burden to her mother and Mercy. Eventually, they would resent the extra hand to hold and Coraline would commit herself to the lunatic asylum to bring them peace.

Which left but one choice—she must take another husband. It was the most logical way for a woman, invalid or not, to endure. Even blind, if she found the right partner, she could still be a helpmate in some fashion. Her late physician husband, Oliver, had agreed to it. Another would as well. Unfortunately, in a town of only fifteen residents, five were children, four were married, one had taken a liking to her sister, and Mr. Reed's wife had gone missing along the trail. Therefore, only one option remained: 27-year-old Jamison Lark who, despite his roguish exterior, was faith-filled and compassionate.

Luckily for her, he also didn't believe in divorce.

Martha met her at the door, her own cape already secured. "Ready?"

Coraline settled her bonnet, tucking the edges around her bun, and stretched her fingers. She forced a smile. "Yes. Let us find that glorious morning you so speak of."

2

Despite Coraline's earlier cynicism, the dawning day, like most others on the Northwest Coast, was indeed glorious. In a life where rest came at a premium—and new challenges around every corner—she could still take time to appreciate the sunrise over the mountains, striking veins of gold through emerald evergreens along their faces.

Like watercolors on a canvas, mauve and periwinkle seeped up from their crest, and a cool wind brought the brine of sea air as clouds floated low upon the waves. She didn't know how many steps it was to those mountains; she had never ventured in that direction and had no desire to. There were fifty-five to the ridge, however, and another seventy or so to the shore, depending on the tide. Fourteen from her front door to the garden, thirty-two to Sarah and Tobias's, and two-hundred-and-seven to the stream. It was the same trick her father had used. Every step memorized in preparation for the days to come.

Commotion rose as she and Martha entered the rear courtyard, the sound of wooden ladders being raised and tools clinking as the Lark brothers prepared for another day's work. Linking arms, the two women observed the skeleton of a roof taking shape above the outbuilding beside the stable. Having extra room would allow them to store more for themselves while also providing space for the horses, mules, and oxen. They needed somewhere to stockpile food, smoke and dry meat, and store chopped firewood along with animal feed. That didn't even include building an ice box over the stream, an absolute necessity for fresh meat and fruit preserves.

Her eyes immediately recognized Jamison's muscled shoulders as he swung a leg from the ladder to straddle the top beam. Unlike on Sundays, when he slipped into pastor mode, today he wore no vest or pocket watch, only a worn shirt with suspenders holding up his wrinkled trousers. The heels of his mud-flecked boots angled against the outbuilding's exterior wall to keep him steady. He leaned down to lift the board his twenty-one-year-old brother, Cade, handed him, swinging it around to slap atop the roof beams. On the opposite wall, his second eldest brother, thirty-one-year-old Tobias, positioned himself to accept boards after Cade ran the corner. Their cattle rancher, Clinton Reed, was nowhere to be seen, probably attempting to secure the fencing around his property, which his steers managed to break through at least once every other week.

Tobias waved as the ladies stepped over the scattering of tools upon the packed dirt. "'Morning, ladies. Beautiful day, isn't it? No rain today, so we should be able to raise most of the roof beams."

Martha glanced at the billowing clouds above. "How can you be certain?"

"Just have a feeling. It's going to be a good day for work." His expression drooped. "Say, would you mind helping Sarah with the coffee this morning? She's been awfully tired from the weather lately. It would be a big help to her."

Martha waved him away. "I'll help her if she needs it, but if I know your wife like I do, I bet the pot's already on the fire."

Tobias opened his mouth again, but she smiled before he could ask. "I'll help get breakfast too." She held up the sack of flour in her arms. "I'll make sure the biscuit basket is full."

"You're a good woman, Martha Louis. Where can I find you a man?"

"That's a pickle, ain't it? Certainly not 'round these parts."

With the tip of his hammer, Jamison gestured down to the dark-haired scalp of his youngest brother. "You can have Cade here."

Cade went pale-faced and bent to examine the logs as though they carried the answers to why the sun rose. The dismay in his expression sent the rest of them into fits of laughter and the humor in Martha's shaking stance even granted Coraline a chuckle.

Coraline remembered the day she met the brothers; the same day Oliver handed her down from the carriage outside the Larks' plantation home. Their Carolina mansion had been a romantic dream, sunlight gleaming off its white marble and Spanish moss drifting lazily from live oaks along the drive. A wagon sat before the front stairs where a young man loaded supply crates for their journey west. He had paused his task as they approached.

"Jamison!" Oliver had exclaimed. "Finally, I'd like you to meet my wife, Mrs. Coraline Shay!"

She recalled Jamison's smile, so warm and inviting, charming her every time after that until she couldn't help but return his enthusiasm. Without his hat, his musket brown hair revealed a jagged part, strands nearly to his shoulders and tied back with twine. Oliver had offered her hand into his so he could bow low and kiss it.

"You're Mr. Shay's business partner?" she asked. He didn't look like any of the doctors she knew.

If it was possible, that smile grew wider. "Sure am. I would say I'm sorry about my appearance, but I'm not really. This is just who I am, ma'am."

She hadn't minded. Truly, she hadn't. In fact, her desire had been to run her fingers through those long straight locks, an impulse which, thankfully, she controlled. She was married. Such a reaction was more than inappropriate.

So, she had released Jamison's hand and stepped closer to her husband, even as her brown eyes held his hazel ones, their set a little wider than the average man, certainly more so than Oliver's narrow features.

Those eyes met hers now from atop the outbuilding, sweeping her in, swallowing her up, without knowledge of all the ways she intended to coerce him into a legally binding union. Standing here, staring up at him, she knew he would be an easy sell. He had been her husband's business partner, but also the one who brought her solace when Oliver died. Far more compassionate than she deserved. It should be simple to pull him into a lifelong partnership.

"Let me help you, Coraline," he had said the day he offered the land, although it wasn't until months later that she accepted his offer.

His words had come too close to what Oliver told her when she answered his newspaper advertisement for a wife.

"I'm a physician, Miss Owens," Oliver had said. "Your blindness is a certainty, but I can help you. In turn, our marriage will bring Larksong the extra acreage the government is offering to married couples. Three hundred and twenty for you and three hundred and twenty for me." He took her hands between his and gently kissed her cheek, showing more affection than she had ever received from a man. "You can help me, Miss Owens. Let me help you too." So, she had.

Theirs had been a convenient marriage but a fulfilling one. Agreeing not to consummate, they created their marriage on the expectation that their contractual relationship came first and their personal one second. Even though there was no romance between them, she never doubted his devotion.

Until God, in his confusing wisdom, saw fit to take him from her, and by a snake bite no less. He died within days and left her to despair. Jamison with his straitlaced Catholicism would never understand her lack of faith. Still, since that first day in Larksong, she learned how easy it was to pretend for his sake.

"Oliver would have wanted to be here," Jamison had told her that day. "He would have enjoyed sharing this moment with you."

"With us," she clarified. "God said it's not good for man to be alone, right?"

"Nor woman." He had opened his arms and she had walked into them and although nothing else had been said, nothing else had been done—they had spent no time alone since—a plan began to form. A plan which, though delicately woven, placed both gladness and guilt inside her heart. She had simply been too cowardly to place it into motion until now.

Jamison considered himself a man of God, but she was certainly no woman of the Spirit. She was not the sort to cower, especially not before a God in whom she didn't trust. He wanted faultless, blameless, and perfect; most of Jamison's community prayers were around that very thing. How could he expect her to give up more of this world in exchange for her heavenly inheritance? There wasn't much more she could give up. Their remaining supplies were meager, their abilities to build and farm lacking, their homes in constant need of repair. Without a husband, she had been required to forfeit the entirety of Oliver's claim, succumbing to life at Jamison's mercy should he ever desire his land back. Or worse, should he marry a woman without sympathy for a blind woman's plight. The only reasonable solution was for Coraline to marry him first. Still, it wrenched her conscience to force him into the life she had seen her mother and Mercy endure.

Martha's tug expelled her from her mental wanderings, back to the side of a half-finished outbuilding and a town only partially begun. Jamison bent back over his work, his hammer a steady drumbeat with every muscled stroke, his brothers taken again to their own tasks. Coraline continued toward Sarah and Tobias's cabin, all the while realizing it was impossible to catch a husband when you never even said a word.

3

J amison heard Coraline's footsteps drift away before he turned to watch her again. Why had she come out here and then said nothing? Just to watch them work? To watch *him*?

She had been living on his land for over seven months and he still didn't have the courage to approach her as he should. What good was a man like him to someone like her? He could perform feats of medicine beyond modern science, but he hadn't recognized the signs to save her husband.

Be reasonable, Jamison, he scolded. These Gifts—this legacy—his father had left his sons didn't make them miracle workers. Jamison couldn't lay a hand on someone and cure their ailments, but he could draw the knowledge without awareness of how he came by it. Better, quicker, more efficiently than other physicians. The ability to mix medicines not yet used by any doctor in the world. How to set bones and stitch wounds so that they would heal with precision and never leave a scar. Perform surgeries most couldn't fathom in their wildest dreams. Yet, when it came to a snake bite, death had bested him.

Of course, when Oliver finally told him, the venom had already driven too far into his blood, a poisonous river rushing his veins, and the wound too high on his thigh to amputate safely. No hospital or clinic for hundreds of miles. Out on the trail, there was nothing to be done except watch Oliver fall, leaving his widow with a complicated future. No claim to live upon, no husband to protect her.

Had he secretly desired it? He thought of the adulterous lust of David for Bathsheba, the mighty downfall of a man God had called to be His servant. Jamison had never envied Oliver save one thing, and he held her in his sights at this very moment. Did he send his friend off to the proverbial war so he could have his wife?

Of course, that was ludicrous. Jamison didn't send Oliver anywhere. Clinton Reed's wife, Gabriella, had gone missing and Oliver offered to help with the search. Who could have predicted that in the process, he would trip into a snake hole?

"Jamison? Did you hear what I said?"

Jamison's head whipped around, his hammer drawing back a second before he smashed his finger rather than the board. Tobias peered at him from atop the opposite roof beam, eyeing him with annoyance. His older brother always seemed irritable these days.

Not that he didn't have a good reason. Before their time on the trail, Tobias had been Gifted in carpentry, able to build a single wall in the same time it took multiple men to do so. At his best, he could build a prairie schooner in a night and a modest two-room house in only a week's time. He had created delicate sculptures out of nothing but twigs and fashioned his wife, Sarah's engagement ring from clover and goldweed. The band remained intact even after a year on the trail and seven months in the Washington wilderness. Of course, that was before the gunshot wound which nearly claimed his life.

With Sarah's quick wits and direction, Jamison had managed to extract the bullet, but at the great cost of removing Tobias's Gift. Unfortunately, the other brothers weren't skilled builders; they always assumed Tobias would carry that load. With his Gift, they could have erected an entire town in a few months. Instead, they spent most of the winter huddled in their wagons scrounging for food, praying, and wondering if they had made a mistake in coming here. How many times since leaving Charleston had they wondered that? Jamison couldn't even count.

Even now, Tobias rubbed circles into the shoulder where the bullet once lodged, a place he often complained of pain most likely caused by nerve damage. He grimaced with the movement, but the brunt of his discomfort was still directed at his brother. "Well?" he said. "Don't you think it's time?"

"Time for what?" Jamison asked.

"Our Gifts," Cade told him. He had mounted the ladder and stood three rungs below the roofline. His elbows rested on the same beam where Jamison sat. "Tobias was saying that we should tell everyone. I think I agree."

"Do you really agree or do you just not want us to argue?"

Tobias didn't wait for Cade's response as one likely wouldn't come. He pushed his fair hair out of his eyes with the claw of the hammer. "It's time they knew. I'm tired of keeping this a secret when Sarah already knows—"

Jamison pegged him with a look. "You were the one who wanted to keep it a secret. You told me it was too risky to tell anyone." Even when Tobias knew that telling Oliver could have saved his life.

He had to push that thinking away. It did nothing good for their town, his brothers, or himself to dwell over what haunted him personally.

"What about Garrett?" he reasoned. "Shouldn't he have some say in who knows his secret?"

"Garrett's gone," Tobias snapped back. "He went to San Francisco to chase some feeling that may or may not exist. He took Josiah with him and he might never come back." He grabbed a wooden nail from his bag and swung his hammer into it so hard, he lobbed the head clean off.

Cade's voice was low, barely a whisper. "He'll be back, Tobias."

"Will he? We haven't even received a letter."

Jamison rested the hammer over his knee and met his brother's gaze. "This is uncharted country. We can't expect to ever receive one. We can only pray he returns."

"Garrett will have to trust our wisdom in this matter," Tobias said. "He isn't here to include his two bits and we can't wait for him to return. Cade even told me he'd like to tell Alice Ann, as much as that girl concerns me."

Cade blushed, red streaks rapidly rising up his neck. "Our town is small and she's my only friend close in age."

Jamison stared at him. No one bought his innocent act for a second. Between all the time Cade and Alice Ann spent alone, their hand-holding, and several times caught kissing along the Washington shoreline, no one believed they were merely friends. Jamison and Tobias both hated the situation. It was indecent and he would bet Coraline thought so too, but Cade was an adult and unfortunately, he had to make his own adult decisions. Jamison just prayed those decisions were actually his own.

Now flushed as a pink azalea, Cade added, "When my Gift predicts weather perfectly, it would be nice to share with everyone why I can."

It would be nice, Jamison thought. To not stop to think about the consequences before he stitched someone with a suture that didn't exist in the medical world or create a salve that had never been seen. It would be nice for people to know him as he truly was.

"This is the right decision, James," Tobias assured him. "Right for Larksong's future. Trust me."

It was more optimism than his elder brother had expressed in months. He wanted to celebrate the possibility that his prayers had been answered and returned Tobias to them whole and happy. But he knew his brother would never be how he was before his wounds. Garrett might never come back at all and their eldest brother, Daniel...well, they would never see him again.

'Where a lone man may be overcome, two together can resist,' he reminded himself. 'A three-ply cord is not easily broken.'

He needed his brothers; none of them could attack this new life alone. A three-ply cord was not quickly broken, but a five-ply cord would have been even stronger...six when God was present at the center. In the Lark family's cord, God was there, but too many other cords had been broken, the strand unraveled and frayed at its ends.

Jamison turned back to the roofline. With a swing of the hammer, he drove another nail in. "Fine, Tobias. I trust you. Let's tell them."

4

From the moment Sarah Lark opened the door with her pleasant blonde-haired, green-eyed welcome, Coraline and Martha were met with the bustle of a usual morning in Larksong. Their friend, Marie Harper, had already arrived with her three girls and two boys, a bundle of energy running rampant around the cabin, leaping off chairs and knocking each other down in their usual fashion. Their mother raised her eyes to heaven with a sigh, her wooden spoon stirring grits on the only fully functioning stove in their new town. It meant every breakfast and supper saw them crowding fifteen bodies into Tobias and Sarah's one-room cabin, but truly no one minded the camaraderie of gathering together. Not when so many perished every day along the trail.

Martha immediately crossed to lay a gentle hand on Marie's shoulder. With a smile, she handed Marie the flour sack she carried, then rushed toward the children with her no-nonsense face and scolding tones. All an act, she scooped up three-year-old Quint and swung him into her arms for a pleasing round of tickles. The other children pounced, tugging on their "nanny's" skirts until she took them all in a firm hand and demanded they get themselves outside and tend to the garden.

"Weeds are growing high again, so you best get to pickin'," she said. "We'll call you in when breakfast's ready."

With minimal grumblings, seven-year-old Marilee grabbed the wooden pail near the door and six-year-old Reeslie took up the trowel. The two trudged outside like they'd been asked to dig graves rather than sneak barely ripe vegetables as they were wont to do. Nine-year-old Jonah grabbed five-year-old Aphid by the hand and put three-year-old Quint on his hip, then followed them out. As soon as the door closed, Marie shot Martha a grateful smile. "I've been trying to settle them all morning, but there's been so much to attend to. Quint kept me and Levi up half the night with his tears. I'm afraid he's still not used to the place."

"He's getting to that age," Martha told her. She took the spoon from Marie's grasp and nudged her away from the stove. "Just when you think they're ready to be on their own, they're in a new place and everything is big and scary again. I bet Quint's glad to have a Papa like Levi to keep him steady."

"Where is Levi?" Coraline asked. She hadn't seen the well-muscled man helping with the outbuilding earlier. Accustomed to field hand hours in the Charleston rice paddies, he was usually one of the first risers.

"I let him sleep," Marie explained. "He'll be right furious when he learns that the boys started the day's work without him, but bless his heart, he was an angel from heaven through all Quint's fussing. He deserves an extra hour." She lifted the metal coffee kettle from the fire and strained the black brew into a line of cups on the table, one for each of the women. Back home, it was customary to bring the men their coffee first, but here they did things differently. The ladies could savor the day's first pot and let their limbs loosen a little while fixing breakfast.

Coraline brought the coffee tin over to meet Marie at the table where they scooped and ground, pressed and filled, until another pot was ready to go on to boil. Pulling out a chair, she directed Marie to sit in it and took the kettle back to the fire. "Take a rest," she told her friend. "You look like you've been up for days."

Marie gave a weak smile. "I feel like it."

"It's this Washington weather," Sarah said. "Always so dreary." She had settled herself at the table and now sorted seeds into piles, half a dozen with brown and yellow ovals ready for the freshly tilled earth. It wasn't the right time in the season to plant, but they had to do what they could when they could do it. Prior to today, they had kept their gardens within the confines of the courtyard but knew it was time to spread farther. The small plot of land wasn't nearly enough to sustain them throughout the summer, let alone long term. Hence the importance of the five children outside weeding. If weeds choked the garden, they would lose what little they already had.

"It's bound to get better once the spring showers have passed and summer comes," Martha told them. "Come August, we'll probably beg the good Lord for a thunderstorm."

Coraline drew a sip of her coffee, remembering how long it had taken her to get used to taking it strong and without sugar or cream. Now, she found she didn't mind it as much. At least they still had coffee, although for how much longer she couldn't say. If the coffee store was anything like their other supply tallies, she had better savor every sip.

A knock on the door announced Alice Ann's appearance. She hadn't brought fish, but she had at least dressed herself, however disheveled her appearance may be.

"Good morning, Alice Ann," Sarah said. "Come get yourself a cup."

The girl's bare feet slapped the wood floor as she paced across the room and collected the cup Marie handed her. She took a long draw and smacked her lips, causing Coraline to cringe. In a small way, she thanked goodness their parents would never see this unladylike side of their youngest daughter ever again. Sending her to the other side of the country was supposed to offer her a new depth of beauty, not turn her into an unrestrained savage. Yet, it seemed that a savage was exactly what she had become.

Never wearing stockings, never wearing shoes, climbing trees only to line her skirts with sap, and swimming in her underthings. Her braid was always half unraveled, frizz flying around her face. When Coraline once asked that she tame the unruly locks, Alice Ann shocked everyone by slicking it back with fish oil from that morning's catch. Then she grabbed Cade's rifle and brought home a string of squirrels for supper simply because she could. Their mama had always believed there was a lady somewhere under all that dirt and derision, but Coraline had run out of ideas on how to extract it.

Alice Ann now moved to the window and nudged the curtain away, increasing the sounds of carpentry from across the yard. Leaning her elbows upon the sill, and coffee cup between her fingers, she watched the men while they worked. They had secured the beams leading up to the central peak and Coraline could make out Tobias shimmying down the ladder to take a drink from the water bucket. He drizzled a line over his head and shook out his hair, sending droplets flying.

"Alice Ann, it isn't polite to stare," she reprimanded.

"Why not?" her sister replied with a smirk. "I notice you staring often enough. Marie, Sarah?" she called. "I think Cora's out to steal your men."

Sarah dropped three yellow seeds into the matching pile without looking up. "No one's worried about Coraline stealing anyone. I have faith in my friend and my husband. You should too."

"How touching. I suppose when you're an old bitty, you can't laugh at a joke."

"And being young doesn't allow ya to be indecent," Marie reprimanded. She folded her arms upon her chest and waited like she expected an apology, but of course, none came. Alice Ann turned back to the window without a word.

Outside, Cade raised another wood plank up to Jamison, his back muscles flexing beneath his shirt and suspenders in the process. Alice Ann released a slight sigh that garnered a worrisome glance between the other women. Ever since the early days of the trail, she and Cade had given more than regular attention to one another. Heaven only knew what they got up to when they disappeared from town for hours at a time.

Coraline wanted to trust her sister, but Alice Ann wasn't known for her demure nature and Cade wasn't known for a sense of courageous rebuttal. She remembered Jamison telling her once that the Larks' father showed no mercy when it came to punishments, even going so far as to whip Cade, leaving his back full of crisscrossed scars. Ever since, Cade had been the line-keeper, the peacemaker, too close to others' feelings and his own. "Empathic" was the word Jamison used. She hadn't known what it meant, but he used a lot of medical terms no one had ever heard before.

The short and tall of it was that Cade was meek and Alice Ann bossy and Coraline feared it would get them both into trouble.

But what could she do? Ned and Octavia Owens placed Alice Ann into her care, fully knowing that Coraline's vision would fail and the tides would turn. Alice Ann would become the caregiver and Coraline little more than the invalid sister.

All the more reason for Coraline to marry and relieve her sister of that chore. If Alice Ann hadn't her sister to worry about, perhaps she would consider a more feminine lifestyle.

Wrapping her coffee cup between her hands, Coraline joined her sister at the window. Without glass, the sea breeze blew between them, ruffling their aprons. They were far enough away that the men couldn't hear; still, she kept her words soft. "Don't string that boy along. He really seems smitten with you."

Alice Ann's eyes flashed up at her before jolting back to the men. "What'd you come over here for, just to mother me some more? I don't need that. I'm fully grown and eighteen now besides. Back in Charleston, I'd probably be planning a wedding already."

"With the way you act? Like you were raised on the docks of San Francisco? I'm surprised Cade is even interested."

She grinned but didn't turn. "He's very interested, Cora dear. He'd like to kiss me 'till my toes curl."

Coraline felt her cheeks afire even without the sound of Sarah's gasp. Thankfully, the men gave no acknowledgment that they had heard. Cade cornered the outbuilding's far edge and moved out of sight.

"Alice Ann Owens!" she hissed. "That is Sarah's brother-in-law you speak of and completely base talk for a woman your age. Or any woman."

"Oh, Cora, really. You're so delicate sometimes. It isn't as though I don't know what goes on between married people. How do you think Marie landed herself with all those children? Same way Jamison's going to get you all round the middle someday."

Coraline stepped back, reeling, and barely caught herself before she dropped her chipped china cup on the floor. With shaking fingers, she set it on the window sill and looked round at her friends who stared at her like they watched cannonfire head in from offshore.

Stovetop ignored, the sizzle of burning squirrel filled the room and turned into a putrid tang.

"Well, go on, Coraline," Marie urged. "You're not her mama, but you're all she's got. Somebody's got to put her in her place."

"She's right," Martha said. Sarah merely nodded.

Barely able to gather her wits over her embarrassment, Coraline seized Alice Ann's arm and shoved her toward the front door. "We will return momentarily."

She pulled her sister past the Harper children throwing mud clods at each other in the garden. "Back to work!" she shouted. They only stared, mud dripping from between their fingers.

She dragged Alice Ann past their shanty of a home and down the ridge, through the waving shore grass to the sand and the white foam surf washing upon it. There, she finally let that menace of a girl go. She hoped her eyes shone fire.

Alice Ann slapped a hand to either hip, jutting one to the side in a motion that made Coraline want to forcibly rearrange her sister's spine. "Why are you so scandalized, Cora? It's no secret that you've had a tickle for Jamison since Oliver died. You think I'm not watching, but I remember everything. Surely, everyone else has noticed some part of it too."

"Whether I have or whether I haven't is my concern, not yours. It is certainly not your place to share the news." How many others had noticed, she wondered? Had she truly been that transparent in her feelings?

Surely not. This was simply another one of her sister's attention-stealing tactics. Grasping at an innocent friendship and exploiting it. Even as a child, she persuaded her friends into handing over their treasured oranges and sweet treats. Coraline shuddered to think what she might do as an adult.

Like ask for kisses that curled her toes?

Certainly not.

Cade was so different from Alice Ann; it didn't make much sense why she would take a shine to him or him to her. In truth, she probably *was* stringing him along, preying on his affections and peaceable attitude to gain a partner in her fishing business. She liked men, but she didn't love them and romantic notions were never high on her list of priorities. When it came to the danger of premature courtship, Alice Ann had been easy for their parents to raise. No boys to chase off the front porch or lectures to give on keeping one's skirts well below her knees. Their father knew he had a business partner who wouldn't leave him.

At least, that was before he went blind and the business sold. The fishing boat was gone along with his—and Alice Ann's—dreams.

Their parents believed sending the sisters west granted them a gift, but it had only damaged their already tentative relationship. Trying to be both sister and mother and expecting some measure of respect in return...it was an impossible assignment.

Coraline squared her shoulders. "You will respect me, Alice Ann, and you will keep quiet about Jamison."

Alice Ann snorted. Yet another terribly unladylike movement. "Another secret, Cora? I'm already keeping your secret about your eyes, which is nonsense. They'll all find out when you trip over yourself one day and go falling off a cliffside. Who will hold onto your secrets then?"

"That has been my worry, which is why I need you on my side. We are sisters in a foreign land. We have to be able to trust one another, but how can I do that when you act as you do? You are a lady, Alice Ann Owens."

"No, I'm not."

"Yes, you are and you need to start acting like one."

"Who will force me to? You? Martha? Cade?"

"Be careful with him, Alice Ann. Don't you dare break that boy's heart like you broke our mother's. Like you're breaking mine."

"Maybe I will!" she shouted. "Maybe I'll leave this horrible place, get on a ship and sail away from here. Then you wouldn't need to worry about me stringing men along and telling all your secrets!" She spun on her heel, flinging up sand as she strode off down the beach alone.

It wasn't the first time her sister had threatened to jump on a ship and leave. She planned it out back in Charleston, too. She would bind her chest, steal their father's trousers, slice off her hair, and buy a revolver, of which she had become a talented marksman. On the way west, she had also mentioned the idea more than once, but whenever an opportunity arose to leave, she never did. Coraline prayed her threats would remain unfounded.

She counted her way back toward the cabin, but somewhere around ten lost track within her thoughts. She stood on the ridge, her back to the sea and eyes closed, anxiety against her spine like the slow hand of death. This is what life would be like someday. Dark and alone, unable to watch over her sister at all. If Alice Ann was already finding trouble, how much more would she tumble into when Coraline couldn't run after her anymore? That could be all it took for her to finally make good on her promise. To leave and never return.

Reality was a harsh demon and its slap struck like burning coals.

A sob caught in her throat, barely stifled behind her fingers. When she opened her eyes, Jamison was watching her from atop the outbuilding roof. He didn't say anything and he didn't need to.

5

It had taken more strength than Jamison knew he possessed not to slide down the ladder and race after Coraline and Alice Ann. Letting them run off in such obvious tension grabbed his gut and threatened to yank him from the roof. He held onto the structure even as he swayed in place.

A woman shouldn't wander off alone, not with animals and Indians and sheer cliff faces right outside the door. It was a man's job to secure a woman's virtue and her safety, especially when choices for a decent match were slim. If only Jamison didn't have this guilt in his chest, this pain in his heart, he would propose to Coraline himself, today. Guilt over taking what he didn't feel should belong to him, at least not the way he had received it.

Two years ago, underneath the waving Spanish moss of Larksong Plantation, its drive circling the gnarled central live oak, Oliver had introduced him to Coraline. The white-pillared plantation house stood before them, the place he called home all his life. His childhood hadn't been pleasant; their father saw to that from an early age. Still, trepidation tapped with the thought of leaving a place so familiar.

From the parlor window, his eldest brother, Daniel, held back the heavy draperies, allowing the sun to brighten his sandy hair and worried features. Unlike the rest of the brothers, Daniel wasn't Gifted, which to him meant he never had and never would belong. He had taken his heir's inheritance, offered equal shares to his brothers, and sent them on their way with a harsh conversation and even harsher insults. Jamison loved his brother, but there were some decisions he never would understand.

"Don't worry about him," he told Oliver and Coraline. "That's just my brother, Daniel. He's staying here to run the plantation."

Something behind Coraline's eyes shifted, an emotion he would only understand later as compassion. She too had left a sister behind. "Won't you miss him?" she asked.

Jamison glanced to the window, but Daniel had vanished. The draperies barely moved in the breeze from the open window. He met her gaze again. "Yes. There are many things I will miss. Others, not as much."

Handing her that piece of himself had been his first mistake. Taking a piece of her had been his second, and it occurred the very next day.

He had waited until after breakfast, when he knew Oliver and Tobias would be in town obtaining supplies and Alice Ann toured the grounds with Cade. He then invited Coraline on a tour through the house, watching her head swivel in every direction, staring into open doors and up to the ceiling. It embarrassed him to see her lips part in awe at all they had when he knew her family dwelt in a fisherman's cottage.

When he opened the door to the library, her gasp echoed across the room. Floor to ceiling, she stared at thousands of volumes his father had collected over the years. Only a handful had been removed and packed away for the journey west. Sturdy burgundy-upholstered settees and bronze wingback chairs were situated in rectangular arrangements while fireplaces filled either wall. Both sat cold in the warm weather and without servants to light them.

Jamison's heart swelled as Coraline sped with unladylike enchantment to the shelves, her fingertips pausing a hair's breadth away from the spines. She glanced back. "May I?"

He extended his arm with a smile. "You are my guest. Take whatever you'd like."

"Oh, I wish I could take them all." Her fingers landed hungrily on the leather binding before falling back to her side with a frown. "But I already brought an entire trunk's worth. I couldn't possibly bring another."

"Why not? Our town will need a library and you can be its first librarian."

She lifted a volume from the shelf and opened it, sighing when the unread pages crackled within her hands. "Yes," she said softly. "I would like that."

Allowing her freedom to choose, he paced to the floor-to-ceiling windows which overlooked the grounds. Pink azaleas bloomed gloriously along the perimeter of the veranda. Instead of live oaks, magnolias smattered the plantation's rear, casting shade over the garden path and the seating area where his mother used to take tea every afternoon. Beyond the magnolias, however, lay the true place of his coming-of-age, three hundred acres of rice paddies.

He could have had a perfectly comfortable life at his father's side, already married a lovely girl from a neighboring plantation, and settled down. He was a little young, but not horribly so. Instead, like Tobias, Garrett, and Cade, he spent those courtship years overseeing their field hands, sweating in the hot sun, and swatting away mosquitoes. Bringing in crops all so his father could profit while paying their servants nothing.

The alternative had been bleak. Either hire overseers to treat their fieldhands like chattel or take the task upon themselves and provide them with what decency they could. At least, until Daniel decided to sell their fields and their servants without explanation. Larksong Plantation was Daniel's birthright; it was his to do with as he wished. He didn't want to own slaves, so he didn't, no matter his brothers' pleading or the cost to their servants' lives.

Suddenly, Coraline was beside him, her arms stacked high with leather-bound volumes, another substantial pile upon the writing desk. John Pendleton Kennedy's *Swallow Barn* lay on top. He had never read it, preferring theology, philosophy, and medical books, all topics most ladies found dull. If she was bringing it with them, though, perhaps he would make the time to read it.

"Your property is beautiful, Mr. Lark." Her eyes swept the grounds, taking it all in, and he realized that like her perception of the rest of his home, she had probably never seen gardens as elaborate as these. Once again, the association left him uncomfortable.

"Yes, it is."

"Will you miss it?" she asked. It was the same question she had asked about Daniel the previous day.

"I will miss the beauty of this place, but Tobias says that Washington will be just as beautiful. I won't miss my father's memory or his associates, but I will long for the comfort of my mother and sisters' graves and time spent with our servants. Only three and their children will be traveling with us, but this time as friends and freemen."

"You're friends with your slaves?" So much surprise laced her words that Jamison lifted the top book off her pile, staring at it rather than at her.

"Oliver said you were sympathetic to the abolitionist cause."

"Of course. We don't own any slaves, nor had servants, but I am...sympathetic that is. I've just never known anyone to be friends with their servants before."

"We're a much different sort than you'd meet every day."

If only she knew how different. It was something that had rolled over and over in his mind since they learned of Daniel's decision. With a few exceptions such as Josiah and Levi, Jamison had never thought of labeling their servants as friends. At least not until they were gone. Then he realized that they had been. He had looked forward to seeing them every day, talking to them about their lives, and getting to know their children. Their father hadn't allowed those men and women to attend Mass, so Jamison baptized their babies and performed their marriages, all within the confines of his father's shadow.

"I think it's admirable," Coraline said. She smiled, and the expression was so pure and lovely, that he did too. Each of them held onto the other's smile for longer than was proper and for some reason neither wanted to—or could—acknowledge at the time.

Now here they were, two years later, and he had distanced himself so far, they barely spoke. He had always believed himself a man of God, determined to preach love, truth, and forgiveness. Yet it was a terrible burden trying to convince himself of his own worthiness.

Even with the daily scripture study and pleading with the Lord, his feelings for Coraline never vanished. He let his covetous thoughts drive his friendship with Coraline, and now that she was widowed, all his mind could envision was how he could turn those desires into reality.

He couldn't, though. His brothers were counting on him for support. Coraline was grieving a husband and a sudden loss of financial stability. Without Oliver to lay claim with, she needed to know where her roots would be. She didn't need romance; she needed a spiritual guide to reinforce her faith and a physician to help heal her soul. Those things he could give her without compromising his integrity or his brothers' mission.

Perhaps someday God would align their paths. For now, it was enough to ensure her protection in this new uncharted land, even if he could not yet claim her heart.

6

That evening, Jamison stood by as Tobias revealed all to their friends and family. Their Gifts were rattled off one by one like a list of groceries at the market, then as was logical, they were asked for proof. Garrett, of course, was hundreds of miles away and while Cade could tell them what the weather held that evening—absolutely nothing of importance—he couldn't prove it until it happened. Tobias also couldn't demonstrate with his Gift long gone, although he mentioned how he used to be able to build a schooner wagon in a single evening. Then came Jamison's turn to fill in the gaps.

Since they didn't have anyone in need of dire surgery—thankfully—and he refused to harm someone simply to prove he could fix them, he discussed how to perform an as-yet-undiscovered technique called cardiopulmonary resuscitation. The process couldn't be found in any published manual, not even the basic theory behind it, yet he had performed it successfully on a patient in his Charleston operating room. Jamison never told the man or his wife what occurred behind the privacy of those wooden doors and bloodied sheets. Thankfully, none of those listening now seemed disturbed by what he could do. Only that they hadn't known he could do it.

"Why wouldn't you share something like this with us?" Levi asked. The light from Sarah and Tobias's fireplace danced across his drawn expression, his deep ebony skin barely standing out from the shadows behind him. He crossed his arms upon his chest, casting his muscle ridges into deep shadow, his usually full lips pulled tight between his teeth.

"We've known each other for a good long while now," he accused. "Always thought it was more than servant and master, but I suppose not."

Beside him, Marie rested a hand on his arm, all five of their children asleep in their own cabin next door. They would find a way to explain the situation to them one day, when they were older and their minds able to comprehend. "Course it wasn't like that, Levi. Can't say much for their Pa, but the Lark boys always cared for us right."

Levi didn't appear so easily convinced by his wife's words. He rubbed the stubble on his jaw and narrowed his eyes at Tobias. He wouldn't speak ill of his former master in front of Alonzo Lark's sons, but the scowl upon his lips did the speaking for him. He was well aware of the whispers surrounding Geraldine Lark's suicide, strung up in the attic for her eldest son to find. She had never been herself in all the years she was married to Alonzo. He had held her every whim within his commands until he had no further use for her. That one final demand was all it took to end their marriage with the snap of a rope.

Jamison never told anyone, but it had been his mother's suicide that almost stole his faith. The Church had forbidden her a Christian burial and Tobias literally screamed his demand for the reason.

"Show me where it says she's condemned!" he had shouted. He then grabbed his Bible from the side table and threw it at his brother, leaving a bruise on his shoulder where spine met skin.

Jamison spent the next months scouring his Bible for any proof of their mother's fate, whether that landed her in heaven...or in hell. Late nights burning candle after candle to a stump proved fruitless. With eyes blurry from fatigue, he finally had to admit that there was no definitive answer. Only God knew His judgments and who was man to know better? He only wished the acknowledgment made him feel better.

"You've always been our friend," he told Levi. "But we couldn't tell anyone. It would have been too dangerous for all of us."

"What about Josiah?" Levi asked. "Did he know?"

A pregnant pause followed where the three brothers looked to each other. Who would muster the courage to answer the question? Josiah, their second father more than a servant, knew about their talents before they were born. A secret both Josiah's father and grandfather had known of before him. He was the only one of their servants trusted enough by their father to be allowed within the inner circle, but it was widely known that if Josiah had loosened his lips, it would have also cost him his life.

"Yes," Tobias finally said. "He knew." He turned to his wife seated at the table with Martha, Coraline, and Alice Ann, but her eyelids lowered to the scuffed tabletop. He looked back to Levi. "Sarah knew too, and she told Martha about a week after we arrived."

Martha had known for months and Tobias hadn't said anything to his brothers? Jamison wondered if Tobias knew from the beginning or if Sarah had defied his wishes and chosen to share their secret with her friend. Either way, what was done was done, but he hated to think that his brother might be keeping more from him than this.

"Anyone else?" Clinton demanded. He had been relatively silent since they gathered, but now the rancher braced one hand upon the fireplace mantle, gripping it with a mysterious gleam in his eye. His dark hair fell across one dark iris, skimming the edge of his neck and curling out at the ends. He shifted his weight away from the mantle and his spurs clicked together, unnecessary for a man with no horse to his name, but required for the devilish rogue persona he preferred to exude.

On the trail he had tried tirelessly to become a trusted second, going so far as to take down Tobias's attempted murderer, only to then hole himself away on his claim for weeks at a time. Until Tobias threatened to take his share of the outbuilding space, Clinton barely managed to drag himself over for more than daily supper and church service on Sundays.

"No," Tobias said. "No one else."

"Hmmm." Clinton peered into the fire for a long moment while the rest of them stood idle, eyes shifting from one to the next and quickly away again. The brothers had told everyone as they intended—as they should have—but now no one knew what to do with this information.

Even the brothers hadn't gotten far enough in their plans to know what this would mean for the group. In an ideal world, nothing would change. But when after Eden had they ever lived in an ideal world?

"All my twenty-nine years I've worked for you," Levi said finally. His voice deflated like a collapsed lung. He too turned his eyes to the fire rather than them. "Wouldn't we have sensed something?"

Tobias, of course, had the answer for that too. "We only used our Gifts in small doses and made sure we left enough room for minor errors. I could have fixed things faster. Jamison could have prepared wounds for quicker mending. Garrett never needed a search party to find the Morrows' daughter. He could have found her within minutes on his own."

Marie met Jamison's gaze, her fingers still white-knuckled around her husband's arm. "What about poor Gabriella? Garrett couldn't find her."

"We can't explain that. I suppose all we can assume is that for some reason she didn't want to be found."

"Or she's dead," Alice Ann muttered.

Tobias cleared his throat and glanced at Clinton who still stared into the fire. "Yes," he said. "Or that."

"All the same," Levi continued. "Wouldn't something have slipped? Some small thing. How could our eyes be blind to whatcha had?"

Coraline jerked at his question. She pushed her chair back from the table and walked to the window, sweeping the animal hide aside to allow a breeze through the house. "They were good at hiding it," she said softly. She looked back at them over her shoulder, her fingers still clutched upon the curtain. "As a physician, Oliver had to hide things from his patients all the time. How dire their prognosis was or acting like he had all the answers when he didn't."

Her eyes sought Jamison's from across the room, intent, questioning, wanting answers he couldn't provide. Outside of Oliver's death, however, he didn't know what the intensity of her gaze could mean. Perhaps she simply wondered like the rest of them, how she could know the brothers for two years without any indication of their differences.

Leave it to Alice Ann, however, to find the knife her sister discarded and plunge it into his conflicted emotional constitution.

"Your Gift could have saved Oliver!" she exclaimed. The force of her accusation jolted Jamison back to the center of the discussion and a round of eyes planted firmly on him, including Alice Ann's glare. No, her glower. Demanding the explanation Coraline refused to ask for. Why her brother-in-law was deceased and the sisters left to take refuge upon Jamison's land rather than the one promised to them by Oliver Shay.

A smooth stream of crimson rose up Alice Ann's cheeks, bright enough to match her hair, even in the dim firelight. "What about Ephram Tull, the boy who got crushed by the wagon? For goodness' sake, he was only two years old. Why didn't you help him?"

"For goodness' sake, Alice Ann," he said, throwing her words back at her, "Oliver was poisoned, Ephram was already dead, and I'm not God." The Lord knew how the toddler's death still tore him up inside. Despite all the good his Gift could bring, there was still so much it couldn't. No amount of talent could restore the dead.

"What about your brother?" Alice Ann looked at Tobias whose gaze was ever-narrowing. His lips pressed into a thin line as though weighing the wisdom of their announcement. "*He* didn't die," she sniffed. "Why don't you heal his Gift?"

"I can't. Our Gifts don't work on other Gifted. Never have. We're lucky I was able to save him at all."

"It doesn't seem like much of a *Gift* then," Alice Ann replied, "if you can't do much more than normal doctors can."

"Alice Ann," Martha said gently. She placed her hand on the table between them and offered a smile clearly forced. "It's more complicated than what we can understand."

From the corner of the cabin came a creak and a groan as Cade rose from where he perched upon the edge of Tobias and Sarah's mattress. Threading one thumb through the end of his suspender strap, he stepped forward and placed a trembling hand on the table beside Alice Ann's shoulder. The ever-shifting shadows reflected his anxious energy and soulful expression.

"She isn't entirely wrong," he said slowly. His sights were

anywhere but focused on the rest of them. "I've often wondered myself why we were chosen for this. How can we be extraordinary, yet still so limited in our skills?"

"Are there others?" Coraline asked. The breeze teased a lock of hair from her bun, letting it fly loose against her shoulder. She tucked it back and turned fully from the window, letting her sights fall to Jamison's. "Others like you?"

"I don't know. In the beginning, there were seven Gifted families. Our father, however, told us they're all dead now."

"Shouldn't we find out? If there are more of you, it would benefit us all. There's safety in numbers."

"We intend to find them," Tobias cut in, "but not at the expense of our town. Our family comes first. Once everything is established and Garrett returns, then we can address where the others might be."

"So, it's just us?" she asked.

"It's just us."

Tobias released a chuckle then that sounded more like a stifled sob. He leaned against the edge of the kitchen table and reached for Sarah's hand who immediately obliged. His expression seemed like a thousand years had passed and Jamison felt the same.

Although the brothers had argued their fair share about the likelihood of other Gifted, Jamison was still the rock, the Simon Peter of their family who held the keys to keeping them together. There was only room for one Lark brother to lose his wits and it couldn't be him. At least not in front of everyone.

With the next bout of silence, it was clear that the discussion was over for the night, although not likely the last it would be spoken of. After a round of goodnights, and Cade whispering that he was taking a shoreline stroll with Alice Ann, Jamison crossed the courtyard to his cabin alone. He latched the door and pulled off his boots, setting them against the wall and his damp jacket on the hook above them. His rifle was propped near the bedpost, ready if need be, but he hadn't needed it yet, so why would he need it now?

Tossing another couple logs on the fire, he watched the flames lick the bark as he took to his knees. His clasped hands found his chest and he bowed his head, praying for a sense of reason to pass over him. Had they made the right decision by telling everyone? His heart and soul said yes, but his mind wasn't so certain.

Lord, a definitive answer would be mightily appreciated.

He raised his eyes back to the flames then cast about the small cabin, cluttered with his and Cade's belongings. He tugged at his vest, casting it from his shoulders and across the kitchen chair, then let his suspenders fall to his sides.

Lord? What's next?

A knock on the door shot him to his feet, his heart racing like a cardiac patient.

"Jamison?" came the feminine voice on the other side of the door. "It's Coraline."

He pressed a hand to his chest, letting its paces slow. He pulled his suspender straps back up and stepped to the door. Coraline met him on the opposite side, hands in her apron pockets as she peered up at him with doe-eyed desperation. Her dress sleeves were rolled to the elbows, revealing once tanned skin now faded to pale peach under Washington's grey skies.

"I need to know something, Jamison," she said softly. "I need to know that what you can do is real."

"My Gift? It is. It's real." He reached for her then stopped himself. "But I couldn't have saved Oliver. By the time I knew what happened, he was too far gone."

"I'm not asking for Oliver. I'm asking for me." With a simple smooth movement, she removed a kitchen knife from her apron and held the point to the outside of her wrist.

"Cora, what are you doing?"

That time, he did reach for her, at the same moment she slashed the knife upward.

7

A red gash bloomed upon the back of Coraline's arm, a trickle
of blood quickly oozing its way around to her wrist. She
dropped the knife with a dull thud in the dirt and drew a
deep breath to keep from fainting. She hadn't been this woozy when
Tobias was bleeding from a gunshot wound, but she supposed, with it
being her own blood...?

"Woah, stay with me." Jamison grabbed her arms before she could
fall over. Snatching up the knife, he directed her into the cabin and
kicked the door closed behind them. He pulled a wobbly wooden
chair out from a table barely big enough for two and settled her into
it.

Dipping a washrag, he pressed it to the wound and slapped her
palm over it, applying pressure. "Hold this there. Don't move." Then
he crossed the room to retrieve his black medical bag from the floor
beside the bed.

Coraline let her attention roam around the room, anywhere but at
the blood seeping through the washrag upon her arm. With only the
firelight to guide her, most of what she saw came in bursts of clarity,
the shadows causing her to squint into their depths. Unlike her cabin
with Alice Ann and Martha, Jamison and Cade didn't live in homey
comfort. The fire sputtered sparks over a mound of ashes and along
the ceiling, jerky dried in strips. For two men who lived on a
plantation all their lives, she had expected something more refined.
Although, they didn't have servants waiting on them now either.

She winced when Jamison lifted her hand and the washrag along with it. He held her arm over the washbowl as he poured water to flush the wound, followed by a brown tonic whose cool liquid stung rather than comforted. With gentle strokes that still felt like stabbing needles, he dabbed the wound with a fresh washrag, starting in the center and moving to its edges. First, down one side then the other.

His eyes remained fixed on his work while she observed how his shoulder-length hair curled behind his ears and his long lashes dipped toward his cheeks. After months of building the town, she had grown used to seeing him in only his shirtsleeves and suspenders, but for some reason, it seemed more intimate alone in his cabin. He wasn't even wearing shoes.

The stab of a needle through her arm, however, returned her thoughts to reality quickly enough. She couldn't silence the hiss that passed her teeth as the black thread drew up from her arm, looped, and passed back through again.

Jamison glanced up at her from beneath heavy eyes. She expected him to ask how she fared or if she needed something for the pain, but he simply lowered his lids again. He drew another stitch before asking. "You couldn't simply take me at my word?"

He didn't need to explain what he meant. He had been in Tobias's cabin. He knew that the entire notion of Giftedness sounded unbelievable. What he didn't understand was how the thought of his Gift had tantalized her every moment since he spoke the words.

She kept her eyes on the fire, where in its glow, her vision was best. "I had to know for sure."

Another stitch drove through her arm. "Why did you need to make such a large incision? A smaller one would have healed the same."

"I knew you could fix it."

"But what if I couldn't? You could have bled to death." He drove another stitch through her arm and this time he wasn't kind about it. He was irritated with her. She supposed she couldn't blame him. What *had* she been thinking? What if his Gift didn't work as he said? The others would see what she had done and know she was unhinged.

"I knew you could," she repeated. "Am I wrong?"

"No." Tying off the last stitch, he returned the needle and thread to a small leather pouch within his medical bag and exchanged them for a swath of rolled bandage. Once white, its color had dulled to a milky tan after being boiled many times along the trail. She knew it wasn't the way either Jamison or Oliver preferred to treat their patients, but they had to make do with what they had.

He lifted her wrist, allowing her elbow to prop upon the table, and laid the end of the bandage upon her palm, folding her fingers over its edge to hold it in place. Then with tender movements that belied the seriousness of his gaze, he wound the fabric around her arm until right below her elbow. Tying it in place, he gently rolled her blouse sleeve down and buttoned the cuff.

"All finished. In a few days, you'll be as good as new. By week's end, there won't even be a scar."

"No scar? It seems too good to be believed."

"It isn't; however, please don't test my skills again."

"I won't."

She expected him to release her hand, but he kept it between his, running his thumb along the lace at her cuff. She could just feel the pressure between the gaps in the lace, the warmth of his touch whispering across the bandage.

When she met his gaze again, he was already staring at her. "I know you're concerned about losing Oliver's claim," he said. "Alice Ann has found ample opportunities to remind me of as much. But I assure you, Cora, you'll be cared for here. You don't need to go to such lengths for me to prove it."

His word should have been enough, except that his promises were based on a woman he only knew one side of. He was promising to care for her when he didn't know what that meant. He wouldn't take her from her land. She was part of the community even without Oliver at her side. But what good would those promises be when he learned how worthless she would truly be? Only marriage would force Jamison to keep his promises. To him, marriage was a sacrament, a binding vow to God, and as such, he would never break it.

Maybe he would restore her eyesight if she simply asked—or begged. The brothers said their talents weren't magical, and Jamison couldn't heal outright, but had he ever tried? He had demonstrated exceptional skill on the trail, being able to treat with an ease she had never seen. Not from Oliver, not from anyone. He had always claimed to be naturally gifted and laughed it off as medical studies being put to good use, but what if it was self-preservation rather than limitation? Once he healed one person, everyone would desire an easy way out.

As the wife of a physician, she should have suspected. Had Oliver known and never said? In their platonic marriage, they had kept much of themselves from each other. But if he did know, that also meant he chose not to tell Jamison in time and die instead. That didn't seem like the Oliver she knew.

Slashing her arm to prove a point wasn't like her either, though.

"These healing abilities you possess," she asked. "Are there any ailments they can't fix?"

Jamison swallowed, pushing his visible worry past his Adam's apple. She knew that expression. She had seen it often from Oliver. They may not have been intimate, but there were some things a wife couldn't help but learn about her husband. That look said that he was a doctor and she was a patient. Inner thoughts did not overwhelm bedside manner. A doctor never revealed a dire nature to a patient in distress.

"A few," he told her. "Shall I assume you're not only asking for curiosity?"

"No, I..." Another pause followed, only interrupted by the staccato crash of the flapping window skin and the occasional childish screech from the Harpers' cabin. Quint must have awoken and wanted to play.

Prying one hand from Jamison's, she lifted her fingers to touch the metal rim of her spectacles. "I..." she again faltered. Her grip lost its place upon her brow. Letting her fingers grip her skirt instead, she diverted. "There are no opticians in Washington. What will happen when my eyesight worsens and there are no resources to craft another pair?"

Guilt stabbed with his subsequent smile and relieved exhale. She should have told him the truth, but after his next words, knew that such admission would be impossible.

"That is an easy situation. Natural degeneration can be improved with a variety of ointments and perhaps surgery. It will never be as it was, but we can delay its progression."

"Natural degeneration?"

"Yes. The normal stages of vision loss that occur as we age. Now things such as cancer, milky eye, or the deterioration of the retina are more complex and often a patient is too far gone to reverse...at least with the tools currently available in this world. Maybe someday we'll be able to..." He shook his head. "Oliver and I shared patient notes. He would have told me if you had anything to worry about." He squeezed her hand. "We are still men. We are in the hands of our Creator, and our own hands can only do so much. Sometimes His will does not match ours and it is wholly frustrating."

Like with Oliver's death. She could see the thought in his eyes, but that's where they both kept it.

She wanted to weep. He couldn't help her just like he couldn't help Oliver, but he had no way of knowing that. He thought her vision loss was "natural degeneration" not a sinister disease slowly stealing her life. And Oliver—bless her husband's soul—had shared nothing to the contrary because Coraline had begged him not to.

Jamison thought he could help her and she would let him believe the lie. She would let him give her ointment and surgeries until the last flicker of her sight was gone. And when none of those worked, she would let him take her into his care out of obligation, to fulfill his duty as a physician. He had wanted to be a priest once, to tend his flock. He was too kind a man to leave one of his sheep wandering alone.

"Is something else the matter?" he asked. Concern etched his brow, ignorant of her inner conspiracy. "Your arm will heal. No scars, I promise, and we'll keep your eyes as they are for as long as we can. You're young. You have years yet."

She shook her head, but he couldn't understand that it was from refusal at his final statement rather than acceptance of his first. Her lips lifted into a smile and she squeezed his fingers, placing her other hand over his. "I'm only so relieved you can help."

After Jamison escorted Coraline back to her cabin safe and sound—or as safe as she could be with stitching down her arm—he returned to his own to stoke the fire and put on a pot to boil. He dumped a handful of mint leaves into a tin cup.

What was he going to do with Coraline? He had never known her to be so unwise as to go about harming herself to prove a point. She had always been sensible and full of insights which he adored. She retained human emotions, of course. Fear, despair, sorrow, but he admired that she kept them in control. She wasn't flighty or unmanageable like some women could be. Nothing like so many frivolous plantation ladies back in Charleston.

Now she had twelve stitches down the back of her arm.

The wound would heal and heal perfectly, but neither of them would ever forget that it had been there. Just as Jamison never forgot the scar running parallel to his seventh and eighth ribs. Not deep enough to damage any major tissues, but close enough for their father to express his point.

It happened shortly after Jamison told their father that he didn't only want to heal people's bodies; he wanted to heal their souls too. Remembering it now, he couldn't believe his sixteen-year-old self had dared to tell Alonzo Lark he wanted to become a priest, a profession that paid no salary and produced no Gifted grandsons.

"That is not a profession for men such as us," Alonzo told him. "But if you wish to be like Christ, I will oblige." Then he grabbed the fire poker from the hearth and slashed it across his son's ribs, deep enough to cause crimson, but not enough to break the bone. It was the same fire poker that would catch Tobias unaware after he helped free one of their slaves years later. His calf still bore the scar.

For a week after, it hurt Jamison to draw breath. As expected, however, he made a full recovery. Like Tobias, only the scar remained.

He could have gone into the seminary once his father died. No one would have stopped him. If not for his brothers, he probably would have.

He ran a palm over his face, scuffing across weeks' worth of scraggle. At least, unlike him, Coraline wouldn't carry the scars of her decisions like inked tattoos.

As he poured water over his tea, the door opened and Cade stepped through, latching it securely behind him. He dropped back onto the bed with a sigh.

"Rough night with Alice Ann?" Jamison asked.

Cade's fingers ran through his already tousled curls, clenching them as he closed his eyes. He groaned. "I think I could use some prayers."

Jamison released a sigh of his own. "Believe me, brother, I could too." He grabbed another cup from the shelf. "How about I offer you some coffee and we don't think about women at all?"

When Cade's eyes opened, a smile edged his lips. "That sounds perfect."

8

Coraline pushed the hoe through the soil, slipping her boots backward to draw another line for planting. Marilee and Reeslie matched her pace, dropping the last of their seeds from Carolina into the trench, while Martha followed along behind, sweeping the dirt back over to cover their new crop. When they reached the end of the row, all the lines now secured beneath the soil, she hastened the children off to the stream, wooden buckets swinging, to collect more water. Without their laughter and rollicky footsteps, the sound of progress from the men atop the outbuilding became more apparent. Although Coraline couldn't see them from her vantage point, she knew that, rather surprisingly, Mr. Reed had begun assisting them over the past week, and the exterior structure was almost complete.

It seemed the Larks' Gifted announcement had affected a change in them all.

Removing her spectacles, she wiped her apron across the sweat upon her brow, then rubbed the dirt from the glass lenses. Without them on, the world blurred, and the edges of her vision turned grey. She hated how things appeared through her eyes alone; it only served as a reminder that they would continue to deteriorate. It did, however, provide an excuse to rest her injured arm from the effort of the hoe. All along the line of sutures, the muscles throbbed.

She had expected the wound to be completely healed by now. Jamison promised it would be. Without even a scar. It *was* healing quicker than normal, but the laceration remained red and the surrounding skin slightly purpled. Likely, she had worked herself too hard these past days and the strain delayed her recovery. It had been extremely foolish doing what she did, especially when it didn't even yield the results she desired.

What did Jamison truly think of her now? He said he would care for her. He said he would help restore any measure of her eyesight that he could. Those promises seemed genuine, despite her crazed episode outside his door. The way he held her hands certainly implied more possibility than a doctor-patient relationship. Then there was the matter of finding a priest or a preacher in these remote parts. Jamison had married Tobias and Sarah along the trail, but he certainly couldn't marry himself.

The proposal came first. Then she would deal with everything else.

Approaching footsteps turned her head, but without her spectacles, the figure was no more than a blur of white and brown. Quickly, she returned the lenses to her face and the image came into greater focus, enough to make out her sister's lean figure.

Crimson braid swinging, Alice Ann plucked one of the half-ripe snap beans from the bush beside her only to receive a hand swat and a reprimand from Marie.

"Ya don't let 'em ripen and they won't multiply neither," she tsked. "We're low enough on food stores as it is."

Alice Ann responded by plucking another and slipping it between her lips with a naughty smile. She was like a child who needed a good spanking to put her in her place, but she was too old for such punishments and Coraline wasn't her mother besides.

"What brings you back from the shore so soon?" Martha asked her. "You told me this morning, you planned to be off all day."

"I would have been, but the fish were plenty today. I caught us a feast." She lifted a stringer, hooked with five redtail surfperch on either side. "I figured I'd ask Cora if she'd come down to the stream and help me wash and prepare them for supper." Unfortunately, the stream ice box still wasn't ready, so anything they couldn't smoke or dry, they had to eat quickly lest it spoil and poison them all.

"You're speaking to me now?" Coraline asked her. "I thought you were angry with me for dragging you across the country and ruining your life."

"That was yesterday, Cora. I'm over that. Now, I'm cross with Jamison."

"Jamison?" Martha asked. "What did he do?"

"Nothing. That's the reason. He had the ability to save Oliver this entire time and he didn't just so he could keep some stupid secret. We could have had a claim to ourselves, an entire claim, not just a corner of it. Instead, my poor sister's widowed and we're borrowing land until Jamison decides to toss us off. How selfish."

"It wasn't that simple," Martha told her. "Those brothers had their reasons for doing what they did."

"Selfish reasons."

"It isn't for us to judge."

"And remember," Marie said gently. "Levi and I cannot claim land either. We are also at the Larks' mercy. There's no choice but to trust them."

"Hmph," Alice Ann sniffed and plucked another bean, tossing the entire thing in her mouth. "Well?" she asked Coraline, crunching on the green pod. "Will you help with supper?"

Coraline looked to Martha who nodded and shooed her with a wave. "Go ahead. I'm growing hungry and fish sounds delicious," which really meant, *It will be good for you two to spend time together.*

It wasn't far to the edge of the stream, only about a quarter-mile walk along a path cut through the trees. They had chosen the area specifically for its easy access to both fresh water and the sea. The chilled stream gurgled across rock obstacles, descending into a near-silent flow at its deeper points, before its mouth opened wide into Willapa Bay. A downed log had been placed at the stream's edge, its top sheared flat to provide a makeshift workspace. Dark stains covered its surface from Alice Ann's previous cleanings as well as the men slicing their hunts into manageable portions. The ice box would be built upon the water with a footbridge to allow easy access to the food stored within. Once the outbuilding was complete, the ice box would be next.

Marilee and Reeslie ran past on their way back up the hill, hefting their wooden buckets in both hands and sloshing more water on the ground than they carried. They smiled and laughed when they saw the women, barely managing to keep the remainder of their buckets upright.

"Careful, ladies," Coraline scolded as they slipped around her. She called after them as they disappeared beyond the tree line. "If you lose all the water, your mama will only send you back for more!"

"We'll be careful, Miss Cora!" they shouted, but Coraline could swear she heard another splash of water hit the ground. She couldn't help but smile though. Except for nine-year-old Jonah, who was old enough to understand some of the town's plight, the other children were mostly ignorant of adult concerns. After a life enslaved and six months on the trail, they enjoyed their newfound freedom. Being able to run along the beach and up through the forest, to feel the sand and evergreen needles between their toes and call to the birds if they so desired. They could hunt for shells in the surf and help Alice Ann "rescue" oysters from between the rocks. When they planted seeds, they also had the pleasure of eating their harvest. To the adults, much of day-to-day life looked like work, but to the children, even work became a great delight.

Coraline followed Alice Ann to the log table, watching as her sister dropped the stringer upon it and separated the fish. Their wide eyes and open mouths screamed in a silent plea. Even though Coraline had also been raised a fisherman's daughter, adept at dressing and cooking all manner of seafood, she had still never cared for the sight before the creatures lay cooked and garnished on her plate.

With deft movements, Alice Ann lifted her skirt to withdraw the knife attached to her calf in their father's worn leather holder. She laid out the first fish and slid the knife tip into its center, guiding the body with her left hand while her right circled the filet. Meat went into a pile on her right, valuable scraps into a greased hide-skin bag on her left for future bait. The rest she flung back into the stream as food for whatever might be hungriest that day. Several oval mouths popped to the surface, tiny fish nibbling at the chum as it floated downstream.

Meanwhile, it was Coraline's job to take the cut filets and wash them clean in the stream, picking away any remaining bones and sluicing excess blood and oil. Making certain each was ready for frying over the fire. As much as she detested the feel of the slimy creatures, the task didn't hurt her arm like most other chores, and she didn't have the slick oil and stink all down her front like her sister did.

"Do you plan to wash before we eat?" she asked as she laid the final fish onto the pile of cleaned ones. She dipped her hands in the stream, but scrubbing alone wasn't going to remove the feel of fish grit from her finger pads.

Alice Ann shrugged. "I'll rinse my hands. I'm not eating with anything else."

There was no hope at all of transforming her into a lady. The wilderness had thoroughly claimed her for its own.

"Might I suggest you take the fish back to Sarah's? Ask her to get the fire hot, then fetch the soap bar from our cabin. I'll wait here." After a morning full of screaming children, gardening, and fish scouring, Coraline—and her tired muscles—could use a few moments alone before heading back to it.

Thankfully, her sister didn't fight the suggestion. With a nod, Alice Ann collected the quartered fish into her apron and headed back toward the homestead, her bare feet sweeping away leaves and pine needles in her path. Pretty soon she was out of sight and Coraline was left with the break of the stream, the soft rise and fall of spruce branches, and her many thoughts.

Turning round again, she quickly realized, however, that the forest was not her only companion.

She pressed her palm to her mouth to stifle her scream, the potent scent of fish guts causing her to gag and nearly lose her assets on the stream bank. The copper-skinned Indian peered at her from the shadow of the trees, his low frown half-seeped in darkness. He wasn't doing anything dangerous and didn't appear to even carry any weapons, at least none that she could visibly acknowledge. But he must, for she had never known a man, native or otherwise, to not carry some form of protection.

He wore no shirt and his trousers were no more than a pressed cedar bark breechcloth and tan hide leggings. So unlike the full animal garb of the natives along the westward trail and certainly more skin than she had seen of any man to this point. A string of salmon slung over his shoulder which would make even Alice Ann envious. His long black hair was parted center and tied back, although contained no adornments. The harder she squinted to observe him, the more unfocused his form became. She fluttered her eyelids until he returned to better vision.

He stepped from the shadows with raised palm outstretched. With each step forward, his bare feet tread lightly upon the forest floor, making none of the disturbance Alice Ann had with her departure.

Where was her sister? Would she return soon with the soap? Alice Ann was a crack shot and had likely instructed herself in knife throwing as well. Would she attack the Indian? Would he attack her? Could it lead them all to war? This was her first Indian encounter outside of the trail. Every scenario suddenly seemed likely, even the most remote.

He stilled on the opposite bank of the stream, only forty feet away. His dark eyes floated over her from head to toe, drawing a line between each feature like a student studying a diagram for the first time. Finally, his hand lowered. "Greetings," he said and she stepped back, startled. She had expected him to speak in his own language.

"You can speak English?"

He cocked his head to the side in confusion. "English?" he said. "No."

He must not know the word as she knew it. "What do you call your language then?"

"Chinook. The name of my tribe. With the Boston People and the Passaieux, I speak the Jargon."

The Jargon? She had never heard of it. That must be what they called English out here. "Who are the Boston People and the Passaieux?" she asked.

He lifted a hand between them, pointing at her with all five fingers extended. "You are either Boston People or Passaieux. Americans hail from Boston. We call them Boston People. Passaieux come from land of France."

"I am American, but not from Boston."

"They are all from Boston."

Was it safe to tell him anything more? What if he was inventing words, using what little English he knew to lead her into a trap? She had heard the stories all along the trail. Abductions, rapes, mutilated bodies left for family members to find...or sometimes not. Taking women and children and adopting them into their tribes as wives, sons, and daughters. No one would know where she had gone, and Garrett wasn't here to seek her out. She would simply vanish like so many others.

Before she could speak another word, Alice Ann's indelicate approach caused the man to turn and flee into the woods, his footsteps crossing the forest like a whisper of the wind.

Coraline ran up the path to meet her sister as she stepped from between the trees. "Did you see...?"

Alice Ann peered around her then straight into Coraline's wide eyes. "See what?"

Coraline whirled back to the stream. She strained to see the place where the Indian disappeared, searching the trees for a flash of his blush-inducing wardrobe or the salmon string upon his shoulder. There was nothing to indicate he had been there or spoken to her. No broken branches or definitive path. Were her failing eyes playing tricks? An unexpected symptom of her impending blindness? If so, how had she spoken with him? She might be going blind, but her hearing was as sound as it had ever been.

Or at least she hoped so.

"It was nothing. I saw two squirrels playing."

Alice Ann handed her the soap with a roll of her blue irises. "You always wind yourself up over everything, Cora."

Coraline scrubbed in the creek, determined to banish the rest of her insecurities, knowing full well that would be impossible to do.

Coraline remembered when her eyesight first started to fail. The fall before they moved to the cottage by the shore. When her friends still visited the townhouse parlor and dreamed of debutante balls and enchanting beaus, even though none of **their** parents were wealthy enough for such parties. Still, there would eventually be courtships and fine dresses with laced fans and swishing petticoats. More than anything, she had wanted to wear her grandmother's blue lace wedding gown. Grandma Owens had been married during the Revolution, placing the dress squarely out of 1840s fashion, but there was nothing more romantic to Coraline than two people married amidst a war, fighting against injustice, pledging love when they didn't know what may come tomorrow.

Then in a snap, she was seventeen years old, having the optician set spectacles on her nose like a very old lady. Even older than her grandmother long since passed.

She had squinted into the foggy looking glass at the metal curving around her eyes and thought how awful she appeared. Her father said the spectacles made her look intelligent, like the men who attended the university, but Coraline didn't want to be like the men. She was a woman and she wanted to look like one. She wanted to be approached by dozens of suitors, fall in love, and have a wedding surrounded by lilies and bluebells. Then children. So many little ones running about her ankles at home, but perfectly behaved when at church, and who would wait patiently upon the dock while their Aunt Alice Ann navigated the fishing boat into shore.

Those spectacles meant a different image of her life now, one where she had no images to look forward to. Men would no longer want her for love or companionship, but for her father's dowry or to save face from moral ambiguity. Many a whisper had been heard about men who took lovely brides to conceal their masculine affections.

Not long after that day, the Owenses packed their belongings in crates and carpet bags and closed the townhouse door for the last time. Moving closer to the sea, to her father's failing business, where there would be fewer expenses and fewer neighbors to gawk as Coraline and her father stumbled into doorways and over furniture. One blind family member was pitiful enough. Two was too many to bear.

There were no more girlish imaginings after that, no parlor visits or frivolous dreams to giggle over with her friends. Like so many wasted days, she hadn't realized the significance until they were gone.

For years, her grandmother's wedding gown lay folded at the bottom of her mother's cedar chest. On her and Oliver's wedding day, she never even opened the lid.

9

The first day the sky cleared, although it still cast a grey sheen, the women flocked down to the shore. For the last week, rain had splattered the area, fine for the newly planted crops, but harmful to their tender emotions and progress on the outbuilding. Thankfully, after a few days, the men completed the last of the exterior construction and now focused on making the inside suitable for storage. Meanwhile, the ladies, weary of being cooped up in their cabins, needed both fresh air and a place to wash the laundry. The sea salt would help remove the toughest grime then the stream water would rinse the salt granules away. Finally, they hung them on the outside lines to dry in the sunshine, the fabric's resulting stiffness overcome by the scent of ocean air.

Now, it was on to the mending.

Situated on a quilt spread upon the sand, Coraline drew another stitch in the skirt she held, unable to cast the stitches evenly in the glare off the water. She raised a hand parallel to her forehead to create a shadow. Sure enough, the patch she had been working on was crooked. Tugging the last two stitches loose, she shifted it a quarter inch so it made a diamond rather than a square. Now no one would be the wiser.

She sighed. So many pieces were falling to tatters, it was difficult to maintain a proper wardrobe. The men had purchased three new fabric bolts when they filed their claims in Astoria last month, but there hadn't been time to craft any new outfits since. It was difficult just to keep up with the mending. The bolts sat in the back of Sarah and Tobias's cabin, waiting for their chance whenever that may be. Coraline knew that her halting pace wasn't helping.

Beside her, Martha laid another set of trousers into the finished basket, their patchwork, as usual, perfectly square. Even Sarah, with her slow and steady stitching, had managed to complete a fair number and while Marie's pile was smaller, it was only because she demanded only the finest results.

Coraline knew she should tell someone about her encounter with the Indian, especially with the women and children left exposed to the elements. It would be easy enough for any warrior to swoop in and carry one of them away, easier still if they returned with a band of men. However, she had a hard time believing that the man she met in the woods was the hostile type. He seemed friendly, spoke English, and fled at the first sound of her sister's footsteps. Other than a hunting knife, he hadn't even been armed. Surely, after a week's passing, if something else were to have happened, it would have. No need to raise the men into a novel-worthy frenzy of protection.

She turned her face to the sky, wishing for the sun's warmth, but glad for the dim light which kept her headaches at bay. Her memory took her back underneath the sunny Carolina summer sky, to a happiness she would be able to remember even when she could no longer see her many freckles in the looking glass. Where her father held her hand, their toes curled in the sand together, darkness all around but for the crash of waves. A melody they would still hear because they could. It didn't take eyes to listen.

"Look, Miss Martha!" Aphid cried out from where she knelt. Another wave pushed foam around her knees and under her ankles. "I found another one!" She held up something round in her hand, wet sand oozing down her arm and into her dress sleeve.

Martha looked up from the skirt she held. Her needle paused within the fabric. "How wonderful, Aphid! You can add that rock to your collection." With a satisfied smile, the girl tucked her prize into her apron pocket and dug her fingers back into the sand.

"She'll be a mess," Sarah pointed out.

"We can toss her in the stream," Marie said. "At least she's happy. They never had this much fun in Charleston, and I'm apt to say we haven't had much goodwill since."

She smiled at Quint who was passed out on the quilt beside her, the shade from his mother's body keeping the sun from torching his delicate toddler skin. While Jonah had been called off to assist Levi with the building, the other three happily splashed in the surf under Alice Ann's orders to collect oysters, mussels, and shells. Of course, the little ones' finds were mostly rocks and only the prettiest ones at that. Then they would get distracted by a gull soaring off the coast or a wave carving the sand beneath their toes and nothing would be accomplished.

Coraline couldn't blame them for their frivolity. It was a gorgeous day. Part of her wanted to splash along with them, but despite living near the shore, she had never become an ample swimmer. Not like Alice Ann. Coraline was afraid that if she stepped too far into the waves, they would cover her up and pull her out to sea.

She would leave the seafaring to her sister. Right now, she had more important matters on her mind.

"Speaking of happiness and goodwill," she announced, "Marie has given me a fine idea for a celebration. We need some merriment before we die of exhaustion or wind up with fingers at each other's throats."

Sarah drew her needle high over the cloth. "My husband will be the first."

"The first one strangled or the one doing the strangling?" Martha asked.

"Either. Both. Surely, I am not the only one who has noticed his worrisome nature lately."

Marie paused in her stitching, her eyes seeking Sarah's from beneath lowered lids. "We all noticed."

"Which is why we need a celebration," Coraline said.

Sarah shook her head. "Tobias thinks church services and family suppers are enough. We don't have the resources for more. Maybe when others join our town—"

"When do ya suppose that will be?" Marie asked. "We haven't seen another soul pass by since we've been here."

"The next time they go into Astoria—"

Martha's hand landed gently on her friend's arm. "There wasn't any luck to be had the last time they went. I've placed my faith in Tobias too, but I fear he's wrong this time."

"He's my husband. I have to believe he'll lead us through this." Sarah drew her next stitch up with such force the line snapped. Two frayed threads poked up through the fabric like stalks of prairie grass in the sunlight.

"This is exactly what I mean," Coraline told them. "We're arguing like the men. I know this isn't what we thought it was going to be, but we can't use our disappointment as punishment. We need to remember the friendship we have."

And I need something to keep my mind off everything I can't control.

Like her eyes, their supplies, Jamison's affections, and her sister's rebellious nature. The wind and rain through the cracks in their cabin walls, how more seeds had failed to sprout than pushed skyward through the soil... For days, she could list examples, until she fell into a pit of despair so deep, she had little reason to go on.

"Well, I like the idea," Marie said. She set her mending in her lap and leaned forward. "Levi can play his fiddle so we's can dance and eat more than we ought—Aphid, come away from that water. Only up to your knees now, ya hear?" She flapped her arm at the little girl who obediently splashed upshore from the waist-high water she had waded into. Both hands were clenched tight around fistfuls of shells. Unfortunately, Marie's call also woke Quint who flopped himself over onto his mother's lap and narrowly avoided impalement by the needle between her fingers.

Sticking the needle back into the cushion, she hefted him into her arms and immediately wrinkled her nose. "Smells like ya need a changing, my biscuit." She pushed herself up from the quilt, a talent considering the toddler squirming in her arms. With his movements came the ripe odor of soiled drawers. "Keep on planning," she told them. "I'll return soon."

"Coraline's right," Martha said after Marie had trudged away. "A holiday would be splendid. Sarah, you could share with us all those beautiful dresses Tobias made for you." She elbowed her friend in the side with a teasing wink.

Last year, when Tobias retained his Gift, not only had he been a fine carpenter, but he had also crafted many other items, including garments. When Sarah and Martha arrived on the trail with little to their name, he stitched them each several new dresses, but Sarah's were by far the more stunning.

"I'm not sure how fine my finery is anymore," she argued. "Not after the paces we put it through on the trail and now here."

"We'll take some time to darn the tears and make it worthy," Martha said. "We need time to harvest the garden and hunt good game for our feast. Let's not skimp like we usually do."

"Do you think we could have everything prepared by Independence Day? It's only a month away."

Martha's nose scrunched as though calculating, then her face relaxed into a smile. "I think we could. Perhaps the rain will have settled by then too. Otherwise, we'll have to celebrate in the stable."

"Oh, please, no!" Sarah grimaced. "The stable smells like horses and the things horses leave behind."

"Better than our cabin," Martha said. "It smells like the wet fish clothes Alice Ann leaves behind." All the women had a good laugh at that.

Coraline listened to them chatter on with contentment. It was good to have something to look forward to again. She drew her threaded needle through the patchwork and then into the edge of the tear on Cade's trousers. The unpatterned fabric made it easy to follow the lines and cast each stitch parallel to the one before. Her eyes found it more difficult to keep in line when they competed with a hundred tiny flowers. She crossed the same pattern lengthwise down the patch then back up the other side until she had rounded the entire section. She hoped the men would appreciate the suggestion of a celebration as much as they appreciated the women darning their shirts and trousers.

"Coraline!"

Alice Ann trudged up the beach toward them, each hand carrying a tin bucket. A fishing rod was tucked under her arm, its wooden buoy bobbling on the line behind her head. Her sea-soaked skirt and blouse clung to her curves in a most scandalizing fashion. Coraline certainly hoped this wasn't how she appeared when Cade joined her at the water. Unfortunately, even without asking, she was certain she already knew the answer.

At the edge of the quilt, Alice Ann dropped her rod and settled the buckets into the sand at her feet. More fish stared out at her, unable to swim as they bobbed for air.

Coraline scooted away. There were apparently some things she wouldn't miss seeing when she went blind.

Alice Ann rolled her eyes. "You're such a worm, Cora. They're only fish. Also, your beau is here." She pointed toward the ridge.

Jamison shuffled his way down the slope, one boot heel sinking into the sand then the next. He carried a tin bowl and a good amount of grime across his person.

As soon as he reached the edge of the quilt, Alice Ann swung a splash of salt water at him from the fish buckets. He leaped back as droplets peppered the sand and also splattered across the quilt and Sarah's lap. She glared up at the younger girl.

"Oh, honestly," Alice Ann laughed. "We're already caked in filth. You could use a bath as much as the rest of us."

"No one needs a bath as much as you do." Sarah side-glanced at Jamison. "Except maybe you. Have you finished the outbuilding?"

"Not yet, but fair progress was made. Try telling Tobias that, though. He's liable to rip your head off."

Exactly why they needed a holiday. The defeated expression on Sarah's face alone was enough to insist on it, even without Coraline's personal problems muddying the waters. The greatest of which stood right in front of her.

Jamison's expression was difficult to understand, however. They hadn't spoken since he walked her home the night she cut her arm. The wound was nearly healed now, although it still twitched from time to time and the scar remained a deep pink. She didn't know what to make of that. Shouldn't it have healed completely by now? Did that mean he wasn't Gifted or that his Gift was failing?

"I brought you some poultices for your eyes," he explained. He squatted in front of Coraline and set the bowl on her lap atop her mending. It contained several strips of torn fabric coated in a brown paste. He peeled two fabric strips apart and held them up. A glob dripped off the end back into the bowl. "You place these over your eyes and let them rest. They contain a mixture of herbs and a tincture of my own design. They'll remove the irritation and provide some ease."

Alice Ann snorted and Coraline glared at her. She was making fishy kiss faces behind Jamison's back. Had she been closer, Coraline would have pricked her with her sewing needle. Meddlesome child.

"Could we apply them somewhere else?" she asked. When he visibly drew back, she quickly amended. "Just up to the bench outside my house? Away from the possibility of having sand and salt flung into the ointment?"

With so many eyes watching, it would be impossible to approach him with the next step of her plan. Especially with Alice Ann interjecting every five seconds. If Jamison was ever going to trust her enough to marry her, she needed to establish a connection between them. One that didn't involve knives and medical attention. She wouldn't yet expect him to take her under his wing as man and wife, but each private encounter was another step in that direction.

For the slightest second, she feared he would say no. Then his shoulders relaxed and he smiled. "Certainly."

10

"I'm glad you suggested we part from the others," Jamison said as they walked even stride for even stride toward Coraline's cabin. "I'd like to check your arm and see how that wound has healed."

In truth, it was only one of several reasons. Primarily, he disliked being surrounded by women who could shift innocent friendships into June bride bluebells in a matter of moments. All it took was one look, one word from his mouth to their ears, and it would be turned around for something it wasn't.

Especially with Alice Ann there to pour another bucket of cow pies on the fire. Both literally and figuratively. He had prayed they were through with those noxious things once they left the trail. Yet at least once a week, they were tipping another mound of them into the cookstove.

Otherwise, the day's atmosphere was perfect, the bench outside Coraline's cabin like a seat inside a museum gallery, revealing a broad watercolor for their consideration. The mountains rose behind the multitude of spruce trees, some of their trunks so large he couldn't wrap his arms a quarter way around. Up close they stood like great organic smokestacks made not of metal and coal soot, but bark and thickening branches, deep enough to swallow a man should he wander too far. Above the forest's breadth, a rare blue sky emerged and the sun shimmered between cloud breaks. Rain or shine, he must admit to Washington's exquisite beauty, made all the lovelier by Coraline's presence. Yet, thinking of her in such terms was only bound to find him tumbling head over heels into trouble.

Seated side by side, he set the poultice bowl in his lap and extended a hand. "Your arm, please."

She began to unbutton the three black beads upon her wrist cuff. "I thought you had no concerns."

"Even so, I wouldn't be an educated doctor if I didn't follow up with my patients. In order to avoid possible infection."

Cradling her arm in his left hand, he gently unwound the bandage one fold at a time until the layers pooled upon the bench between them. Left behind was an ugly red line upon her skin, scabbed over and healing far slower than it should. He ran the pad of his thumb over the raised crust, considering. "Does this cause pain?" he asked.

"A little, but it hardly troubles me much anymore."

"That's good. We've avoided infection which is what I wanted to avoid."

"That's hardly proper usage of the English language." Her lip curled upward in amusement. An adorable gesture if he hadn't been so consumed with consideration over her wound.

Usually, his Gift assured that a patient's skin retained only a faint line within a few days after injury. After that, nothing, not even a scar. The only people he knew who had scars were those he hadn't been able to help, and every single one of them were his brothers.

Tobias's words came back to him. *There were six other men on that ship, Jamison. Despite what Father said, I believe their lines are still alive.*

"Is something the matter?" Coraline's eyes bored into him from behind spectacles flecked with salty sea droplets. He had paused too long in his ruminations.

"No, nothing. Everything's fine. I must have miscalculated the depth of the incision, and therefore the timing of recovery." Drawing a clean bandage from his vest pocket, he re-wrapped her arm in reverse procedure. "No need to worry. You should expect a full recovery within another week at most. I'm sure there won't be a scar."

"You said that when you stitched it."

"I still mean it."

Coraline couldn't be Gifted. He felt as ridiculous supposing it as he had thought Tobias to be when he believed Sarah to be Gifted. Sarah's "Gift" turned out to have a logical explanation, so, there must be an explanation for Coraline's wound, too. One which he suspected lay with him, not her.

After Tobias was shot, he lost his Gift. Not long before that, Garrett's Gift too had faltered when Gabriella vanished. Which meant it was only a matter of time before Jamison's Gift failed, and Cade's likely to follow. Perhaps, it was as Garrett surmised before he left for California: the brothers' Gifts were stronger together. Apart, they would eventually be as ordinary as Daniel.

Whoever is in Christ is a new creation; the old things have passed away; behold, new things have come.

It was a favorite verse, recited many—many—times throughout his youth when trying to make sense of life and why it unfolded such as it did. The Corinthian letter gave him comfort when considering the new life his mother would gain in heaven, that his family would have with his father gone, and that of them all as slave and freedmen joined together to form a new society. A literal passing away of the old and coming of the new. New life offered ordinary people greatness.

That wasn't such a bad thought. He could accept being ordinary if it fell in line with God's plan.

He buttoned Coraline's cuff and turned to the bowl of sticky poultices. "This part is much simpler. Please remove your spectacles." She complied. "I'm going to lay this fabric over your eyes. The herbs will help with inflammation and discomfort. I can't guarantee that last one, however, as I haven't yet had a patient with such an ailment."

"Until me."

"Yes."

One strip at a time, he laid them across her eyes, checking after each one to make sure she remained comfortable. "It's cool but bearable," was her only reply. With circular movement, he gently massaged the strips along her temple, then pressed lightly against each eye. Her contented sigh provided assurance that at least the poultices weren't harming her. That was a relief. He hadn't lost complete control of his abilities yet.

Without warning, her lips pivoted downward, a definitive tension rising beneath his fingertips where they pressed against her skull. He drew his hands away. "Am I hurting you?" he asked.

Her voice hitched. "No, but I've hurt you, haven't I?" She tripped over her next words. "I need to...to, well...to apologize. I should never have tested your abilities, especially not in such extreme fashion. It wasn't fair to you, nor was it wise. Bordering on insane, I suppose." She paused as though she expected him to verify her mental incompetence, but he knew enough about women to not affirm such a statement.

Eventually, she continued. "As you noted that evening, what if you hadn't been able to help me? I could have died. I didn't consider how that would affect Alice Ann. We've made a family here, and despite my sister's many flaws, that isn't something I should take for granted."

"Alice Ann isn't the only one who would be affected."

It was a personal opinion he hadn't intended to make so flagrantly, but now that it aired between them, he couldn't deny it. He too would be like rice crushed under heel if he were ever to lose her in such a way.

Yet, her response held none of the raw honesty his had. Rather, she changed the subject completely, slamming shut the door on anything else he might have said. A blessing in disguise? His disappointment said no, wisdom said yes.

"The ladies have decided to host an Independence Day party."

Both his eyebrows hiked, even though she couldn't see the motion. "Can we afford a party? It isn't as though our coffers are overflowing."

"Everything we need is found right here in nature. We can string berry garlands and create table centerpieces with evergreen boughs and shells. Such decor leans toward Christmas, but seeing as we didn't have a proper Christmas either, I think everyone will make an exception. The men can hunt for our feast and we can spare a little flour for pie." She smiled, her upper lip dipping into the poultice strip above. "Small slices though."

"Where would you intend to hold such an occasion?"

"In the supply outbuilding. I hope the weather will appease, however, and we can gather in the yard. We'd be stifled all inside there together."

"We would, yes." He liked the idea. They needed something to keep their wits—and defeatist attitudes—at bay. It was either festivity or fisticuffs and he did not see himself coming out on top if fists were raised.

"Cora, I think it's a delightful notion." He lowered his voice and hoped she heard the mischief in it. "Don't tell your sister, but I might even aim to take a bath."

"I promise I'll keep it a surprise."

"Good. I'm going to take the poultices off now." As each strip left her skin, she blinked against the glow and no doubt, his foggy impression. He handed her a cloth to wipe her face then her glasses which settled upon her nose. Her usual smattering of freckles had faded some in the dingy Washington weather and he had to admit, he missed the tan spots upon her cheeks.

She dropped the washrag back into the bowl. "Forgive me if it is too forward, but would you escort me to the party?"

With those words, his thoughts marched right back round to every forbidden place they shouldn't go.

"What exactly do you imply by that? What would I need to do?" He knew of course—he wasn't socially stupid—but another thing he had learned about ladies was to never assume you knew how their minds worked. You would nearly always be wrong.

"We attend together. As one Southern gentleman would entertain a lady he admires."

"I never wanted a Southern lady, even when I was a Southerner."

She smiled. "Of course. Forgive me for forgetting. You wanted to be a priest."

"Yes. I mean no, that wasn't the reason. I wasn't interested in having a part in my father's life. None of us brothers were, except for maybe Daniel. We despised our father's arrogant affairs."

Her smile remained, but it was now tinged with sadness. "Once upon a time, I thought I might become a Southern lady. Have a debutante party and all. Unfortunately, hard times meant fewer extravagances. I spent more time in a library or on a boat than in a ballroom."

"I wish I could have been so lucky. To avoid my father's parties, I cloistered myself away at church."

"I thought you loved God. It seems you would want to be there."

"I do, and the Mass has a beauty I dearly miss out here, but there on the water, I imagine it might be easier to hear Him. In the place He calmed the storms."

"'Yes, as everyone knows, meditation and water are wedded forever.'"

Her words sounded familiar, but he couldn't place them. "I don't recall that verse. Is that the Book of Job?"

"It isn't Biblical. It's from *Moby Dick*. Herman Melville, published only two years past. You must remember, Jamison, not all wisdom comes from the mouth of God."

"Perhaps not," he replied, "but all wisdom should be inspired by Him."

11

Their days at the shore were short-lived. All too soon, **charcoal** foam again covered the sky, each day filled with drizzle that never seemed to dissipate. They finally told Cade to stop providing weather updates, since it was always the same, and he certainly suffered for it. Headaches plagued him every day for a week, at least for a few hours if not the entire day.

All Coraline could look forward to was next week's Independence Day party and the thrill that Jamison had agreed to escort her. Everything was falling together perfectly; she couldn't have asked for a better plan. Despite her blunder with the *Moby Dick* quote, he had still been drawn in with little effort. A day of dancing and merriment was certain to place his affections squarely in range of a proposal.

Today's dreary rain brought cool temperatures, necessitating an ever-tended cabin fire as well as both lanterns lit for extra light. Coraline and Martha moved the table and chairs closer to the window, shawls tied around their shoulders and the newly cut dress fabric laid between them. Alice Ann, having been forbidden from fishing due to the high-crested waves, sulked instead. She sprawled on her stomach across the bed, bare feet dangling off its edge while she read *The Posthumous Papers of the Pickwick Club* opened flat upon the quilt. She had already read that one—and most of their collection—several times since leaving Charleston and low would she let Coraline forget it.

As their days in Larksong passed, Alice Ann seemed to care less and less about her sister's eyesight or her lost librarian dreams.

Coraline was torn between gratitude that Alice Ann's own vision hadn't been afflicted and grief over a friend who could truly understand.

Rain pattered against the cabin's outer walls, the crackle of the fire laughing merrily while their needles slid back and forth between the fabric. Thankfully, the purchased material was all of solid colors, making the task easier on her eyes. The dresses wouldn't be as attractive as those in Charleston, but they would be infinitely more functional. Two sizeable pockets would lay against either hip with moss padding and cedar wood stays sewn directly into the bodice. For the first time, there would be no need for laborious corsets. Theirs were near to ruin anyway.

Martha smoothed flat the cut of the bodice she worked on, its center now hemmed and ready for the sleeves' attachments. As usual, her stitches were cast as if with one of Howe's newly patented sewing machines. How quickly they would have been able to finish if they had one of those!

"Martha?"

"Hmmm?" her friend murmured, but didn't glance up from her stitching.

"Was your mother a good seamstress?" All Coraline knew of Martha's mother was that the woman had been a field hand when Martha and her siblings were sold as children.

"I didn't learn to sew from my mother. My sister and I were pretty enough that we were assigned to the house. We learned to sew from the head house slave, Tipta."

Coraline watched the gentle movements of her friend's needle without so much as a shake to her fingers. Like they were speaking of any other day and any other woman except Martha's mother. Coraline wanted to ask what happened to her, but found she didn't have the stomach for any possible response. "I'm sorry," she said. "Sorry you were parted from them."

Martha's eyes didn't so much as raise. "Odds are they're all dead now anyway. Slaves, as you know, don't live too long when they aren't with good masters. I was one of the lucky ones."

"Where did you live before Sarah's?" Alice Ann asked. She had her thumb stuck between the book's pages and the cover closed.

"I don't know the name of the place. Was in Carolina, that's all I know."

"I wonder if we knew the family from before. We used to have a little money before Papa became ill. What was their family name?"

Martha was spared answering when a resounding thunderclap startled them all. Alice Ann's book slapped closed as a torrent opened upon the roof, sending a sudden spray of moisture through the open window.

Coraline grabbed for the tanned skin shade. "Quick! Draw the hides and keep everything away from the walls." From the sudden whistle of the wind and vigorous rain, what chinking that remained was being brutally molested. Water trails slipped through and swerved down toward the floor. All they could do was rip rags and stuff the pieces into the holes, praying the scraps held until the storm ended.

Another thunderclap covered the grind of table legs as Martha dragged it away from the window while simultaneously attempting to carry their fabric load under her arm. She dropped the pile atop the bed and turned back for a clean washrag to dry the tabletop.

"That's rather the storm." She pushed damp tendrils off her forehead. "We haven't had one like this yet."

"Think it could be a hurricane?" Coraline asked Alice Ann. Her sister stood near the opposite window, tacking down the last of the animal hides. They would likely be ruined after this. Another hunting trip would be in due order.

Alice Ann wiped her damp hands on her skirt and trudged back to the bed. She bent for her book. "Nah. It'd have to grow a lot worse to be a hurricane. Cade's the weather expert though. I'll ask him."

"Wait!" Coraline called, but her sister was out the door in a flash as quick as the lightning which followed.

Martha slammed the door closed before Coraline could run out into the rain like a fool equal to her sister. "She'll return in a few minutes. It's not night and she'll be right next door."

Sure enough, Alice Ann returned ten minutes later with Cade on her heels, the both of them drenched and she looking like she either wanted to murder someone or perhaps had just done so.

"Cade, your brothers are incompetent, insolent, ignorant..." Alice Ann paused in her huff to ring her hair out right there on what served as the kitchen floor. She flung the wet tangles, now scarlet in color, behind her shoulder. "They're a lot of other words that start with "I" and a few that don't."

Cade tried to take her arm, but she yanked it away. She dropped onto the bed and folded her arms, almost certainly leaving their good quilt soaked. A final comment of "they're insulting" punctuated her argument.

Coraline looked to Cade whose jacket and trouser hems dripped rainwater all over the floor. His dark curls stuck flat along his jaw. "What in high heaven is going on?" she asked. "I thought you were going to tell her the weather."

"Oh, he did," Alice Ann snapped. "He said it looked like we were in for one of our worst storms yet. Called it a squall, like it's some screaming babe in need of its mama."

"A squall?" Martha asked. "Is that worse than a thunderstorm?"

Cade nodded. "My feelings say yes. I heard some of the men talking about them the last time we were in Astoria. They said they can be terrifying here, not like the coastal storms back in Charleston. Except for hurricanes, of course, but that's an entirely different business."

"But now that we know what it is," said Alice Ann. "Cade's Gift can guide me through it. I told his dolt brother that we could get to the shore, fish, and get back under roof before the worst of it hits. Jamison said that's not how Gifts work and I was unreasonable."

"You are unreasonable," Coraline admonished. "You know how the ocean waves can change. Papa had friends who went out and never came home."

"I only wanted to set some lines! Maybe dig up a couple of oysters. How am I supposed to have a business if an entire day goes to waste?"

"It isn't a business," Cade muttered and Coraline wondered if her sister was ready to complete that murder now. Alice Ann leaped to her feet and stalked to where he stood.

"Pardon?"

Cade tilted back, his sights set somewhere toward the window flap threatening to loosen and flood them all. "My *brothers* don't think it's a business," he amended. "There's no one in Larksong to sell to and Tobias doesn't want us trading with the natives. None of the Astorians will come up here either. We have no commerce, no roads, nothing to entice them. Plus, they've made it real clear how they feel about former slaves. I don't mean to offend you, Martha, but they have the exclusion laws for a reason. They don't like living with colored folks."

"Perhaps that's just as well," Martha began, but Alice Ann spoke over her as she did with everyone.

"Is that how you see it, Cade?" She flung out a hand, her mess of hair swinging with the motion. "I thought we were to run our business together."

"If I thought there was a chance for success..."

"There's better than a chance. You'll see how wrong you are, believe you me." Without even a shawl against the wind, her hand lifted the door latch. The storm poured in, a sweep of cold air that extinguished the lanterns and threatened to douse the fire.

"Alice!" Cade grabbed her arm, the sharp rain pelting against his face. His dark hair slapped around his cheek and stayed there. "You can't."

The nearest animal skin broke free from the window and flapped mercilessly, a dull thump against the logs. Rain splashed upon the floor and Martha's front when she ran to tack it down again.

"It's going to get worse," Cade shouted over the sound of her hammering. "It's going to be like nothing we've yet seen. Do you remember the tornado in the Nebraska prairie? It could be like that."

Alice Ann's expression darkened. "Of course, I remember." She took a step out the door and Coraline lurched toward her. Rain hit her glasses and blurred what was left of her visible world.

"Alice Ann Owens, didn't you hear Cade? You can't go out there!"

Her sister's voice warbled before her. "I'm tired of being cooped up in this house, forced to follow absurd rules because you all think I'm ignorant and fragile."

She disappeared into the storm, chased after by Cade, but Coraline knew she couldn't follow. She remained frozen in the doorway, rainwater striking her from every direction, unable to see past the tip of her nose. She wanted to go after them, but if she did, she would never see to make it back.

She closed the door, her heart racing. With the windows secured again, the worst of the storm was contained, although the floor remained waterlogged and everything else damp. Blessedly, the fire still sparked in its hearth.

"They'll make it back," she told Martha. "Relight the lanterns then put some water on the fire. We'll have tea while we wait."

Martha didn't argue. She turned for the water bucket and poured what remained into the kettle while Coraline mopped up the floor.

After securing the lanterns, Martha hung up her damp apron and sat near the fire with Oliver's Bible. They had been working their way through The Book of Jeremiah together, each of the women taking a turn reading aloud. Coraline always made certain to temper her voice into reverent tones when really, she was avoiding any suspicion over her inability to believe the words. Having people read to her wasn't her favorite, especially the Bible, but she would have to get used to it.

"'*Thus says the Lord*,'" Martha began. "*If you disobey me, not living according to the law I placed before you and not listening to the words of my servants and prophets, whom I send you constantly though you do not obey them, I will treat this house like Shiloh, and make this the city which all the nations of the earth shall refer to when cursing another.*'"

Ten minutes passed. Fifteen.

"'*For I know well the plans I have in mind for you, says the Lord, plans for your welfare, not for woe! Plans to give you a future full of hope. When you call me, when you go to pray to me, I will listen to you. When you look for me, you will find me. Yes, when you seek me with all your heart, you will find me with you.*'"

Twenty-five. Thirty.

"'*How long will you continue to stray, rebellious daughter?*'"

A knock sounded at the door, loud and banging.

"Oh, thank goodness," Coraline gasped. She didn't know how many more religious accusations she could take.

She stumbled to the door and threw it open, but it was not who she expected. Rain poured over the half-naked Indian man from the stream, Alice Ann's unconscious form nestled in his arms. Her chest rose and fell with life, but a substantial gash ran across the right side of her skull, and her cheek was wet with blood. The lower half of her right shin crooked at an unnatural angle. Coraline barely registered her shock before the man shouldered his way inside.

"Who are you?" Martha screamed. She brandished the hot iron kettle like a club. "What did you do to her?"

The Indian said nothing. He stared at Coraline with those dark eyes, shadowed between swaths of dark hair that hung limp against his shoulders. She ran to the double bed and pulled back the sheets, then gestured with wild motions for him to lay Alice Ann atop the straw-packed mattress. Her wet and sand-dusted clothes and hair immediately soiled the sheet beneath her.

Coraline gestured to Martha. "He won't hurt me. Go get Jamison! Quickly!" Her friend immediately ran from the cabin, still carrying the kettle.

The Indian stepped away from the bed as Coraline moved closer. She pressed a hand to her sister's chilled skin. "Alice Ann? What happened?" she asked him.

"She fell off the cliff rocks into the sea. I dove in after her."

Oh, Alice Ann. How foolish you can be, my sister.

Coraline met his gaze over her shoulder. "Where is the man who was with her?"

"Left on the cliff. He saw me pull her from the water."

Then, for now, Cade was safe. Hopefully, he would return soon.

"If you saved her, the Indians are peaceful then?"

He hesitated. "Not all of them. Quea'Quim is peaceful."

"Who is Quea'Quim?"

He raised his hand, placing his palm flat upon the center of his bare chest. "I am." Then he turned and struck out the door into the rain.

"Wait!"

She ran to the doorway and peered through the storm, but either her vision was incapable of the distance or, like the day at the stream, the squall too had swallowed him up.

12

"Where is she?"

Coraline looked up from her bedside vigil as Jamison flew through the door, thankfully, with both Cade and Martha on his heels. He shed his drenched coat and tossed it over the bed's footboard as he knelt beside her. She still held Alice Ann's hand between hers, gently rubbing her sister's fingers, praying to bring some warmth back into them.

Cade rounded to the bed's opposite side, crawling up to kneel on the mattress beside Alice Ann. He pressed a hand to her cheek. "Alice Ann," he choked. "Wake up. Wake up."

Coraline didn't expect the order to do much as she had been attempting it for the past few minutes, but amazingly, her sister stirred. She shifted under the quilt and winced with the movement. A slight groan parted her salt-chapped lips, although her eyes did not open.

Jamison took her wrist from Coraline's grip and pressed two fingers against the tender pulse point. "Is this the first movement she's made?" he asked. Coraline nodded. He counted the heartbeats for a moment more before returning the wrist into Coraline's care.

"Alice Ann," Cade said again, louder this time. "Come back." He nudged her shoulder with his free hand and Jamison shoved him away.

"Stop. You're going to make it worse. Now, Coraline, tell me what happened."

While Jamison tended to Alice Ann's head wound, gently cleaning the cut and examining her eyes, Coraline explained how the evening's events unfolded. How Cade and Alice Ann argued, how her sister ran out into the storm and Cade followed, but it was Quea'Quim who brought her back.

"He knows English, Jamison. I spoke with him once before, about a month ago at the stream. His diction is perfect; it's rather incredible. I wonder where he learned it."

"He must be in contact with other settlers who taught him. That means there are others nearby who could possibly help us. And other natives too. We need to tell Tobias and Levi about this and find out if they mean us harm."

"Don't," Coraline said. "Please don't. Quea'Quim had plenty of opportunities to hurt us but instead, he saved Alice Ann's life. Tell Levi if you must, but Tobias will only get worked into a frenzy."

"Why didn't you tell us the first time you saw him?" Martha asked. Her fingers clenched within her apron folds "We could have, at least, been on awares."

"I don't know," and she honestly didn't. "There was something that made me trust him. In Tobias's current state, I don't believe he would have even considered it. If I hadn't trusted him, Alice Ann would be dead now, and that's enough for me."

Jamison looked to Martha. "I don't know what the answer should be, but we all know Tobias is more nervous than we'd like."

"Very well," she agreed. "For now, we'll keep this between us."

Jamison motioned to his patient. "Cora, Cade, help me hold Alice Ann still so I can set her leg. She'll likely stir and I can't have her flailing against me. Martha, once the leg is set, I'll need your help to bind it."

After stripping the quilt off Alice Ann, Cade and Coraline positioned themselves on either side while Jamison examined the break. Eyes closed, his palms slid over her shin, feeling the bones and muscles beneath the skin. Thankfully, the bone had not broken through which he claimed made it easier to tend to.

With two deep breaths and a whispered prayer, he seized the leg and, in a jolt, he shifted the bones back to where they should be. With a cry, Alice Ann's eyes flew open, darting about at the faces above her, before closing once again.

"Alice Ann!" Coraline cried. Cade's voice joined hers. "Alice!" They froze, listening. There was no more sound other than her soft breathing.

Jamison wrapped Alice Ann's leg in swaths of bandages, tattered from overuse and overwashing. They still hadn't been to Astoria to purchase or barter for more, but such travel required money and goods they couldn't spare. Cora resolved to repurpose her new dress material into better bandages the first chance she had.

"Will she be all right?" she asked.

"Yes. She will recover without even a scar." The wrapping wound around and around, smooth and sure, yet his voice was not. He didn't believe himself and Coraline wasn't sure she did either. The long scar on her arm was evidence enough.

Once the wrapping was complete, Coraline and Martha maneuvered Alice Ann out of the rest of her wet things, clothing her in a simple house dress that would conceal more than a nightdress. Jamison and Cade remained on the opposite side of the cabin with eyes averted, save for the one moment when Alice Ann assumed a measure of consciousness.

They laid her back down on the dry side of the bed and covered her with the quilt when her eyes fluttered open. "Cora?" she said. Coraline was beside her in an instant, but she had already fallen back into slumber.

In due course, Martha retired to her bed and Cade fell asleep sitting against the headboard beside Alice Ann. He cradled her hand between his and Coraline smiled sadly at his devotion. She hated that her first thought was how Alice Ann didn't deserve a kind man like him and that Cade didn't deserve the treatment her sister served him. She hated how her second thought was whether Alice Ann would have a chance to ever mend her ways.

"You should rest too," Jamison told her. They sat at the kitchen table across from one another, nursing two teacups while rain continued to splatter against the wooden walls and tacked down animal hides. He appeared as weary as Alice Ann looked and Coraline felt. The sun had long since set and they hadn't even prepared supper.

She hadn't thought to make it, nor would she have been able to eat if she had.

"I'll stay awake," he told her. "I'll keep watch in case Quea'Quim returns."

Coraline glanced at the book trunks they had braced in front of the door. "We've barricaded the only way in. I don't think he'll be back tonight, especially not in that storm."

"He was already out in it. I wonder why he's been following us?"

She lifted her teacup before remembering she had drained it long ago. "He told me not all the natives are peaceful. Maybe he's trying to protect us."

"Hmm, maybe. You should get to sleep," he repeated.

"I don't know how I can. What if Alice Ann wakes up?"

"I'll wake you. You won't be at your best to care for her if you're unrested. Worry drains a person. You need to do what you can to preserve your strength."

"Will you..." She paused, uncertain if she should pose the question. Her proposition wasn't at all like her and would likely give the wrong impression, but her overwhelming emotions couldn't bear being alone right now. At least her parents were not there to hear her ask.

"Will you sit beside me? Until I fall asleep?"

Her cheeks flushed clear to her ears, but Jamison only smiled. Kind and inviting, sympathetic, and she felt its warmth down to her toes. "Have no fear of being scandalized," he said. "I'm the closest to a priest we have here. That should settle your conscience."

The closest to a priest... Well, that way of thinking would never do. She needed him to view her as a potential life partner, who could support him in all the things he most held dear...rather than the reality that for most of their days, he would be supporting her. As he was doing now.

Scooting her chair closer, she settled herself into his side and his arm drew around her, those long fingers gently pressing her head to his shoulder. Soft heat filtered between them with the comfort of a gently flickering fire on a cool summer evening. He still smelled of the workday, the crisp bite of cedar logs and spruce resin. Mud splattered his trouser legs and covered his leather boots. A smear of Alice Anne's blood had dried where his bare forearm rested upon the table. His exterior was one element where he never tried to hide his true nature and she always appreciated that.

"Tell me about your family," he asked. "What was it like growing up in the Owens household?"

Coraline swallowed a sob. Alice Ann lay so still, save for the rise and fall of her breath indicating life beneath her closed lids. "She wasn't always so crass, my sister. That came as Papa's eyesight grew worse. It fell to her to manage the fishing boat until he decided to sell it. She became rather sullen when we left for the west. She never wanted me for a parent and I never wanted to be one."

"You don't want children?"

The question—and the deep-seated sadness behind it—forced her to stifle another sob. She pushed the feeling deep. "Of course, I want children. Several. What I didn't want was to be a mother to my sister. We both knew I wasn't as capable as the one we already had."

"It seems you are doing your best. Alice Ann doesn't come with a sympathetic nature toward your efforts, nor does motherhood come with a manual."

"Mercy would have done better. She's the eldest and could take Alice Ann in hand. I never did well with managing multiple worries at once." She glanced at Alice Ann again. "Do you truly believe she will recover?" She knew she had asked it too many times since Quea'Quim laid her in the bed. All Jamison could provide was the same response.

Except for this time, he didn't.

"'The prayer of faith will save the sick and the Lord will raise him up,' he quoted. "We are good people, Coraline. We have to believe God will not take another of our family."

What did being *good* have to do with God's favor? She had been a good person her entire life and look what it wrought her. Likewise, Mercy and their mother were near saints for the struggles they accepted in nursing their father. What blessings had they received? Her father too had been kind and generous and also went blind as swiftly as a man without a conscience. Oliver drew his last breath as a good man in the company of good men. He had dedicated his life to healing others, but he himself had not been healed. Therefore, she could say with certainty—*goodness* was of little impact when it came to life's inequities.

"I don't believe in God."

When his entire form tensed beside her, she knew she had committed a grave error by speaking the words aloud.

Lips slightly parted, he stared down at her with a pale countenance, which thankfully, she could not fully view in the darkened room. The firelight flickered slightly as the embers dimmed, leaving only a shadow of the shock which must be reeling inside. To him, her admission likely felt as though she had thrown him into the baptismal font and it was full of ice.

What had she done?

"You don't believe in God?" he sputtered. "But you attended Mass back in Charleston. You pray every day. I've heard you at meals and at our services. You lied?"

"I believe He exists. What I meant to say is I don't trust Him."

That wasn't a lie, at least she didn't think so. She thought she still believed in God's existence—she assumed someone had to have made the world and everything in it—but she found it impossible to trust a God who remained so silent and aloof.

Jamison's arm slipped from around her and in desperation, she snatched his hand up before he could move away. He stared at their entwined fingers but didn't try to part them. "I know your faith is strong," she told him. "It is one of the many reasons I hold your friendship dear. That you believe does bring me much comfort. But my family was prayed for many times, and it never changed our situation. No doctor could fix my father's eyesight, no prayer kept our money and saved us from losing our place in society. Why did God bring me west if only to steal my husband and leave Alice Ann and me at the mercy of strangers?"

"Is that all I am?" he asked. "A stranger?"

Before them, the fire sputtered, the last wisps of flame extinguishing into glowing embers within the hearth. With the window flaps drawn, the room pitched into darkness, the staccato nature of their breaths the only sound—and warmth—between them. A rumble of thunder sounded somewhere to the west, a telltale sign the storm was far from over.

His fingers squeezed against hers, the outline of his leg firm against her outer thigh. It was far too intimate a position, even out in the open with Cade and Martha so near. In their slumber, they may as well have not been there at all. She should draw away, count her steps back to her sister's side and take her hand instead. Except being in Jamison's presence was the only soothing darkness she had ever experienced. The thought of being blind, blackness everywhere, always...it terrified her. She knew Jamison couldn't cure an ailment like hers, although he still wasn't aware of exactly what ailed her. Her blindness wasn't natural; it was so very unnatural. Like his Gift, she supposed, but not at all the same.

When he shifted closer, she realized she had never answered his question. He spoke before she could.

"Cora, how can you trust anyone else if you cannot trust God?" Hurt marred his tone, a deep despondency she could only imagine was synonymous with pity in his mind. It raised her guard and her irritation. Her disbelief did not deserve such a somber reception and it caused her to speak out of defense.

"That is a reasonable question, which has no answer you wish to hear. I am not as pious as you, Jamison, but that does not mean I have no worth."

His voice lowered, soft as lamb's wool against her cheek. "It is the opposite, Cora. To Christ, you have every worth, and who am I to defy the thoughts of God? I am no one."

Then there in the darkness, under the umbrella of a mighty storm and dying crimson embers, surrounded by her injured sister and his brother's slumber and their friend—at her most undeserving of moments—it was then that he leaned forward and kissed her.

13

What had started as an act of obligation was becoming very real, at **least** to Jamison.

He didn't know what to do with his feelings, made only more complicated by kissing Coraline. He couldn't make a declaration like that and not place a commitment behind it, or at the least a dedicated announcement of his affections. But he hadn't and neither had she. She had fallen asleep against his shoulder and he had remained more awake than ever in his life.

He shouldn't have kissed her. It went against everything in his nature and everything that was expected of him. He was her friend and spiritual council, her physician. Even without Oliver standing between them, she still wasn't the type of woman he ever pictured himself with, not with the way spiritual disbelief fell so easily from her lips.

Gently, he removed her glasses and laid them on the tabletop lest they bend in her sleep. He brushed a stray hair from her lips and forced his fingers not to linger. How peaceful she was in slumber, not an ounce of tension upon that beautiful face. He would heal every ailment and fix every trouble if he could, but there were so many problems his Gift couldn't fix. He couldn't force her to share the faith he had. He couldn't stitch God's truth into her heart. She didn't trust the Lord just as she didn't trust him and he had no tincture or bandage to bind that wound.

Perhaps that was why he had kissed her. He wanted to heal her heart, her mind, and most importantly her soul. He couldn't understand how a person could travel through life without anything to believe in or trust except themselves. If he was braced solely on his own understanding, he would not survive. Without Christ to lean on, he would have fallen long ago.

She was the answer to his prayers, but not the one he had asked for.

I wanted you to take these feelings from me, Lord, and you only made them stronger. How can a man of faith love a woman with none? My heart feels like it's dying.

The answer came quickly. *Mine knows how that feels.*

When Coraline awoke, she found herself in the bed beside Alice Ann and atop the quilt rather than on the still-soiled sheets. Jamison, Cade, and Martha were missing, but someone had placed a pillow under her head and draped her shawl across her. Her spectacles sat upon the book trunk, now pushed against the bed at her side. She replaced them on her nose and the room returned from its quiet blur. Vestiges of light outlined the animal hide flaps, and the storm appeared to have settled, leaving only dampness along the wall's missing chinking.

The last she remembered was falling asleep against Jamison's side, his arm resting around her shoulder right after he kissed her.

Jamison Lark *kissed* her.

She had never been kissed like that in her life.

Her lips lifted into a girlish smile, although they quickly lost their levity. Jamison had offered to steer her fragile heart through the storm, but he was using the wrong map and his compass was broken. All she had to do was tell him the truth. All she needed to do was step away from the wheel and let him steer. If only she could pry her fingers from it.

She rose, taking the shawl to drape her shoulders. Stretching her stiff muscles, she moved to lay a gentle hand on Alice Ann's brow. Cool yet clammy to the touch. At least, her breath rose in a steady cadence. If she awoke during the night, Coraline had been unaware and Jamison hadn't decided to rouse her. She couldn't sit here simply waiting, doing nothing. She would go to Sarah's in search of coffee and then gather water to make her sister a warm soup.

Dropping a kiss to Alice Ann's brow, she donned her boots and grabbed the water bucket, moving to the door on silent feet. Voices on the other side, however, stopped her direction and instead led her to the window. She pried the hide's corner back just enough to allow the voices entrance.

"All night?" Sarah was saying.

Martha's voice carried the reply. "Yes, the both of them. Nothing shameful. My presence saw to that."

"Cade's attachment to that girl worries me, but Jamison...he deserves some happiness. He and Coraline both, especially after last night."

"Do you reckon he'll propose?" Martha asked.

"He might. He's always wanted to save people's souls. Why not save them while they're still on this earth? Marrying would provide them both with a more solid foundation, and the Lord knows they could use one."

"But does he love her?"

"I hardly think that matters. Oliver Shay didn't love her either."

"He didn't?"

"She didn't tell me until long after he died, but he placed an advertisement in the paper. 'In want of a wife for the west.' He made it clear that it wasn't a romantic situation and she was amicable to that. Still, Coraline's a fine woman and Jamison's a faithful man. It seems like they'd be the answer to each other's prayers."

Not prayers, Coraline thought. *Manipulation.*

Sarah believed Jamison might be willing to propose. His kiss certainly seemed to imply a similar assumption. But between the scar on her arm and her lack of faith, Coraline feared she may have all but ruined his intentions.

This disparaging thought proved little concern, however, compared to the sight which met her when she entered the courtyard ten minutes later, water bucket in hand. The squall had done its damage. Their carefully planted garden was ravaged, and all the newly planted crops overturned. Dirt splattered the exterior walls of every cabin save for one.

She sucked in a breath. The bucket fell from her fingers and into the mud beneath her feet.

Jamison and Cade's cabin was completely destroyed.

14

Everything Jamison owned was gone. Either demolished, ripped away by the wind, or ruined by water, and all equally unusable. They had so little as it was and now there would be even less.

He and Cade climbed through the remains of their cabin, now a mass of splintered wood and twisted rubble. The structure hadn't been much to begin with, but it had been theirs. The first true home they had made for themselves without the benefit of their father's money or his persuasion. Jamison watched as Levi and Clinton dug out a punctured straw mattress and then the fractured bedposts to match. At least he would have somewhere to rest, if he ever had time to rest again.

Even if he did, where would he sleep? Certainly not with Coraline, much as his heart sped over the thought. Not with the Harpers whose cabin was full to tipping with children, and not with Tobias and Sarah who were still newlyweds and suffering their own troubles. It was the moist earth of the outdoors or the stable stink for him and Cade. At least the stable was dry.

Reason told him they would make it through this; with God's assistance, he knew they could overcome anything. But there in that moment, looking at the pieces of his life in...well, pieces, it was impossible to visualize, so difficult to understand how more could be taken from them now. As he wiped a layer of mud from his wooden crucifix, he could only thank God for sending Alice Ann out into that storm. Without her injuries, he and Cade would have been in their cabin when the roof collapsed. Without her irrational behavior, they would now be dead.

"We'll rebuild. It'll take all of us, but we'll manage." Tobias stood at the house's weak foundation, arms folded upon his chest, eyes narrowed as he surveyed the damage. This turn of events wouldn't help his mind from its tenuous state. Jamison wished he knew what to do to make everything right. Short of suggesting they abandon their claims and head back east—which would only make his elder brother more depressed—he was at a loss.

He stumbled over the remains of the north wall and pitched the bottom of a crumpled brass lamp into a quickly growing pile of unsalvageable debris. He placed the crucifix into the smaller pile to clean and keep. "We don't have the time or resources to rebuild right now," he told Tobias. "We still haven't fully finished the interior of the outbuilding and the ice box isn't even started. We *need* that come winter. What about crops? The government will take our land if we can't prove we've farmed it."

"These forests are full of fruits and nuts we can collect once you teach everyone which ones aren't poisonous." Tobias's brow rose as he stared cross-eyed at his brother. "Your Gift should be able to tell us that right?"

"It can, but what about meat? We're going to survive all winter on nuts and preserves? Do we even have any empty jars left for canning?"

"We can hunt. We'll dry what we can."

"And let the rest spoil?"

A crash pulled both their attention back to the cabin. Cade sprawled on his back between soaked wood planks, struggling to lift himself out of the wedge he fell into.

"Here, lets me help ya." Levi shoved a log away to offer Cade a hand out. He wiped his palms on his trousers. "Jamison has a point, Tobias," he said. "I know I can't claim myself, and the only way I get to stay is if you have land to give me."

Jamison nodded. "We lose the land and Martha and the Harpers are no better off than slaves again. We should have stayed in Carolina then."

"We're not going back to Charleston," Tobias growled. He slapped both hands to the stone fireplace mantel, the only part of the house still upright. "We're not going back," he repeated. "We've worked too hard for this to return to Father's way of life. I won't stand for it." His chin dipped, sights focused on Levi over his shoulder. "I won't fail you and Marie."

"You only fail us if you abandon your heart. You lose faith and the rest of us won't be far behind."

Tobias's only response was a heavy exhale and a palm swiped down his face. "I suppose we should get to work then. My arm's bum for nothing, but what can I do to help?"

"Cows!" came the nonsensical response. Through the muddy courtyard, Jonah Harper half-sprinted, half-slid his way toward them, shouting his head off. Behind him, Marilee and Aphid scrambled up the ridge, their skirts clutched high to keep from snagging on beachgrass.

Jonah stumbled to a halt in front of his father. He clutched his side with labored breaths. "There'sa...cows...in the...surf." With his opposite hand, he pointed back the way he came. "Saw them runnin'...northa here."

Levi clasped his son's shoulders. "Whatta mean there are cows in the surf?"

"Just what I said. There are cows runnin' up and down the sand. They was eatin' grass and I almost got close, then they ran when they saw the girls comin'." He glared at his sisters who giggled between themselves.

"I like cows!" Aphid declared. "Pretty!"

"Can we keep one, Pa?" Marilee asked. "For our own? Mr. Reed keeps 'em all at his place and it ain't fair."

All eyes swiveled to Clinton. Tension stormed its way into their circle, its static a prediction of squalls of a different nature. Clinton rubbed his bearded jaw. "Ah, yes, I suppose I should explain. The pasture fence broke again in the storm. I was headed here to tell you when I saw the house. Plumb forgot after that."

"You *plumb forgot*?" Tobias yelled. "All the cattle—nearly our only source of ensured trade and possibly food—are running wild and you *forgot* to tell us?

Clinton shrugged. "They aren't all gone. 'Bout half stuck around. I mended the fence as best I could before I left them."

Tobias stepped forward, his fingers curling. "What good are you, Reed? Your fences are always breaking and you never pull your weight."

"Tobias." Jamison gripped his brother's arm before he leaped at the other man. "Clint didn't send the squall. He made a mistake, but he fixed the fence. Now, we need to retrieve the cattle."

"If they ran down the surf, the natives could pick them up and we won't retrieve them."

"Do you think our mysterious friend is part of that party?" Cade asked, which was precisely the very thing Jamison should have warned his brother not to say. He had promised Coraline that he wouldn't tell Tobias about Quea'Quim but failed to ensure that Cade had been paying attention.

Tobias's jaw clenched and Jamison gripped his arm tighter. "Tobias, I don't think we need to worry about the Indians."

His elder brother clearly didn't agree. He stepped out from Jamison's reach, maneuvered over the next rubble pile, and squared up to Cade who backed himself into another rubble hole.

Tobias didn't offer him a hand up. "What mysterious friend are you referring to?

"Last night, Alice Ann went out in the storm. She was hurt real bad and this Indian saved her. He brought her back to the cabin, then left."

"*What?*"

"He didn't hurt anyone. Coraline knew him, she had seen him before at the stream. She said he even spoke English."

"This is good news," Levi said. "If he knows English, then he must know other settlers."

"Well, what are we waiting for? Let's go find them and get my cattle back," Clinton said.

"No." Tobias's tone dropped to an eerie register. "We need to barricade the doors."

Jamison couldn't believe his ears. Coraline had proposed that knowledge of Quea'Quim would send Tobias spiraling, but he hadn't fully believed it. "What happened to trusting first? This is supposed to be a town where all are welcome. These natives have done nothing to harm us. The one we have seen has only helped us. Perhaps the rest of his tribe doesn't even know he's been here."

"Or perhaps he's alone because he was banished from the tribe. Who knows what he could have done?"

"Then why save Alice Ann? Why not let her drown? Why didn't he kill Coraline when he saw her alone at the stream?"

"I don't know, but we cannot take the risk. I have an obligation to keep what's left of this town together."

Jamison tripped closer, kicked a broken table leg in the process, and sent it flying. He snagged hold of Cade's hand and helped him up. "No, Tobias, you have an obligation to keep this family together. We all do. We did not leave Charleston so we could fall apart."

"Look around you, Jamison, our family has fallen apart. We don't have Daniel, and we don't have Garrett. Josiah was like family and he's gone too. We carefully curated every person in our wagon train and now you are proposing that we accept the natives without any indication of their intent. It seems to me that you are the one trying to ruin our family, not the other way around."

"You don't mean that." Cade took Tobias's upper arm, completing the brotherly triangle. There should be five of them, but there weren't. There never would be again. They had to make the most of who they had left. To insinuate that Jamison, who had given up everything so Tobias could chase his dreams—who had rejected both the priesthood and the comfort of plantation life—was now trying to sabotage them...well, the insinuation drove deep.

"Mama and Pa say it's bad to fight," Marilee scolded into the silence.

"Yeah," Jonah said. "In the fields, if ya fought, ya got whipped. That's how Poniper died."

That stopped the conversation, the argument, everything midstream. Simply froze and turned all eyes toward the nine-year-old. It hadn't been that long since they were on the plantation, keeping their heads down and noses clean lest Alonzo Lark discover their misdeeds. When it came to physical punishments, he treated his sons hardly better than the servants. Poniper's offense had come on one of Alonzo's most unpleasant days and the result had killed him.

After two years away, seeing Levi and Marie's children laughing and playing daily, it was easy to forget that plantation life affected them too. Their youth hadn't protected them from slavery's violence; it had only made it more difficult for them to understand. No child should witness another beaten to death or fear that the same could come for them.

"Jonah's right," Jamison said. "We wanted to make life better, and we can't if we're at odds. We have to figure this out for the sake of our families and our town."

Tobias shook his head. He shoved his hair back and stared heavenward. Thick clouds sped across steel-grey skies. "I know you're right, James, but I...I can't right now." Then he stalked to his own cabin and slammed the door behind him.

A metallic clang punctuated the sound, drawing attention across the courtyard. Jamison met Coraline's eyes where she stood in disbelief, her lips parted as she took in the squall's destruction. His home gone. Hers the structure that had been his savior. Climbing over the rubble, he made to move toward her, but with his approach, she fled.

He saw her tears fall all the way back to her door.

15

oraline swiped away the remainder of her tears as she halted before her front door.

Why hadn't Jamison followed her? Didn't he care at all?

Of course, he does, she reprimanded, *but his house is gone. He has more important things to worry about than your troubled heart.*

First, Alice Ann almost died and now Jamison... If he had been in his cabin last night, he would have been killed. She would have lost him.

She hadn't realized *she* cared so much.

So, so much.

A sob escaped her lips, and she buried it beneath her palm before its fellow could join it. She couldn't go back into the cabin like this. If Alice Ann awoke, Coraline's emotion would compound her discomfort. If Martha returned, she would assume something terrible about Alice Ann's condition. She needed a moment. Just a moment.

With a twist of her heel, she raced into the forest, pushing through tree branches and letting them snap back behind her. Spruce sap slicked her fingers, sticky upon everything she touched. She wiped her hands on her apron, only to add tan lint to her finger pads. She cut right toward the ocean, her boots stomping a pattern across the evergreen needle and conifer cone strewn floor. Through a gap in the tree trunks, waves appeared, their color a deep charcoal to reflect the sky. She missed the blue waters under the Carolina summer sun, despite the mosquitoes and interminable humidity which clung beneath her skirts. Here it was the rain which would not let go, like tears that never stopped falling.

As her own wouldn't.

She braced a hand against the nearest tree and refused to move from beneath its shelter. The waves crashed in a steady roll, so similar to those outside her Carolina bedroom window. The sound should have calmed her, yet didn't.

An unexpected hand turned her arm, its twin lighting upon her waist to draw her into Jamison's embrace. Willingly, she fell into his arms. When his lips asked for a kiss, she granted his request like she had done so forever.

"Your house is gone," she said when he gave her leave. His arms still held her close, her fingertips sticky against his shirt.

He nodded.

"Where will you live? With Tobias?"

"I think the stable will be best for now."

"Oh. Of course." What had she been expecting? That he would chase her through the woods, passionately kiss her, and declare marriage to be all he wanted? They had shared only two kisses. Such did not account for an automatic betrothal. Maybe in Charleston, but not on the frontier.

Unwinding herself from the circle of his arms, she tried to wipe the sap from her fingers, and again, failed.

Another pause commenced with only bird song and wave claps to cover its awkwardness. When it grew too long, she finally turned to face the sea. "Did you intend for last night to happen? After we kissed, you didn't say a word. Then morning dawns, your house is destroyed, and you return to make a second motion, yet still without declaration. I fear you believe the entire situation a grave mistake."

"I didn't plan it," he replied, "but I cannot say I have not imagined it." Needles crunched underfoot as he shifted closer. "I'm still trying to reconcile what I should do with what's best." The intensity in his tone didn't sound like he was trying to reconcile anything. It seemed he had already made a decision and was simply at war with whether to fight it.

"Cora, we all sacrificed so much to be here, to build our own town. I want it to mean something that we left everything else behind.

I...I've cared for you since the day Oliver introduced us and have only come to love you more since then. I always wondered why God would give me a woman I couldn't have, and in truth, the only way we are having this conversation is through Oliver—through *me* being unable to save him."

She forced herself not to show the joy she experienced at his words. Joy and confusion. He said he loved her. Despite their conversations, despite her blunders, he actually loved her.

"It wasn't your fault," she said, her tone even. "Oliver should have told you about the snake."

"He didn't know he could. He didn't know there was more to me than what I told him. It wasn't my fault, but how can I not blame myself? I'm not worthy to be with you even now. I don't expect you to accept my offer when I know I don't deserve it."

This time when he sought her attention, he didn't touch her, didn't turn her into him or convince her with his kiss. He stepped around so his broad shoulders filled her vision and hid the sea. Her periphery sported the dark shadows of the trees, but the way forward held only him.

He claimed her hand again, sticky fingers and all, and pressed it to his heart. "Ever since Oliver died, I've wanted to be with you. Before that even, though propriety kept those wants at bay. Oliver was my business partner and my friend. I would never have interfered, no matter my feelings. I had hoped they would fade with time. I suppose God had other plans."

"Do you truly believe that was God's plan?" she asked. Everything felt as hazy as the Washington air.

"For us to be together?"

"No. For Oliver to die. Is that something God would do to rid him from interfering in our divinely-ordained relationship?"

"No." The response was too quick, too certain, and his shoulders sagged a bit with each subsequent statement. "I mean to say, I don't know. I've struggled with the question myself. Would I give you up to bring Oliver back? I think I would. It would be better than the guilt which sits stone-cold in my stomach. Does God have a plan? Yes, but He does not deny us the choice. I chose not to tell Oliver about my

Gift and he chose not to tell me about his injury. The choices we made said more about our lack of trust in each other than our lack of trust in God."

Did it truly matter so much if it was God's plan or her own? This was what she wanted. She had planned for this day, done everything to capture him and his proposal. Now he was nearly there. She should be happy. Thrilled. Women leaped for joy and wetted handkerchiefs clear through when they found a man who loved them. Then why were her eyes now dry as trail dust?

She blinked up at him. "I know you couldn't save Oliver, but you did save my sister, and that means everything to me."

"It was Quea'Quim who saved her. I only patched her up. But last night's storm and subsequently this morning's aftermath showed me that I don't want to spend another moment without you as my wife. Had Alice Ann not been injured, had the squall come for your home rather than mine...any small difference could have changed it all. I don't want there to be any more loss. Please, Coraline..."

Taking her hands, he dropped to one knee upon the spruce needles. Water-logged earth soaked moisture through his pant leg. Spattered with mud and muck, his fingers hardly clean and hers so sticky. It almost made her want to laugh.

If this were Charleston, he would have likely proposed in her parents' parlor or under the Spanish moss of his plantation gardens, dressed tip-top in a freshly pressed suit jacket and polished shoes. The golden band he presented would sport a gemstone, a pearl perhaps or a sapphire. His hair sheared short brushed the sides of his neck rather than wayward curls against his shoulders. Her brunette waves, meanwhile, were expertly pinned, and her gown the best Sunday style she could afford. It would be a dignified proposal, one any lady would be happy to accept. Eight years ago, she would have been happy to accept it.

But now, all the traits she had grown to love about Jamison were those the other Southern gentlemen were not. She adored his oft-ragged appearance, the one that stated hard work and honest intention with every step. He didn't fit the pastor's standard for a priest or a preacher, nor did he mind. Coraline knew his heart and his heart was kind. He did not deserve a deceitful wife nor a marriage formed upon it. If she were honest, she loved him too much to destroy his world.

Yet, fear...how powerful a motivator it was.

"Yes," she whispered. "I love you, Jamison, and I would love to be your bride." She squeezed his fingers, although the motion was more to ground herself than assure him. Even so, joy lit his expression. His hands wrapped her waist and drew her down beside him for a gentle kiss.

Taking her hands again, he guided them both to their feet and slapped the dirt from his trousers. Their fingers seemed to entwine of their own accord. "We'll travel to Point Ellice for the wedding," he told her. "There's a Catholic mission near there and, unlike in Astoria, they're not likely to question Martha or the Harpers' presence should they decide to attend. After the wedding, I'll move into your cabin until we build one of our own, and Alice Ann and Martha may stay with us. I would never set them out on our account."

His words fell so quickly she had trouble keeping up. The syllables tumbled into one another and then jumbled up inside her like two kittens wrestling over a knitting string. He was thrilled and she was numb and what more was there to say, except the truth which she could not.

By their own admission, they loved each other, which was more than she and Oliver ever had. More than many married couples could admit to. Perhaps together, they could overcome the darkness. Or perhaps, as she suspected, it would only stifle the affection they now shared. Either way, Jamison's faith did not allow for divorce. She had him exactly where she needed him, easily and without much effort.

In a few weeks, she would be Mrs. Jamison Lark.

When Coraline and Jamison returned to the cabin, Alice Ann was finally awake. Coraline ran to embrace her, careful to avoid her sister's injured leg and bandaged scalp. "Thank goodness!" she cried. "I've been so worried."

Alice Ann offered a lopsided grin. "Not too worried if you left me alone." When Coraline sputtered an apology, Alice Ann patted her sister's hand. "Don't fret. I was fine without you. Now, Jamison, tell me when I can get out of this bed."

Upon a quick, but thorough, examination, he pronounced she would be out of the woods soon enough.

She rolled her eyes. "We live in the forest, Jamison. I'll never be out of the woods."

He smiled. "Metaphorically speaking. You are going to be just fine. Wait a week before you attempt to place weight on that leg. My Gift may be a quick healer, but it isn't instantaneous."

"Thank you, Jamison. Truly."

"Yes," Coraline said. "Thank you for everything."

"You're welcome," he said, but his smile said there was much more to be grateful for than her sister's recovery.

The door had barely closed when Alice Ann lifted herself on an elbow and smirked. "Tell me, Cora, for I would love to know. Does Jamison kiss well?"

It took everything in Coraline to keep her voice steady even as her face heated like a sunburn. She turned for the water bucket and poured herself a glass. "Why would you think he's kissed me?"

"Oh, please, I heard you last night. I thought I was dreaming at first, then everything grew quiet and when I opened my eyes, you were kissing him and he was kissing you and—"

Coraline drained the glass. It didn't help the surge of embarrassment scorching her from collar to ear. "Well then, little busybody, you also saw that a kiss was as far as it went. We didn't do or say anything after that and eventually, I fell asleep."

"That's all?"

"Well..." Coraline flushed, thinking of Jamison's knee in the mud, his fingers caressing hers. His voice had tender whispers floating over every inch of her skin...

She abandoned the glass and turned. "He asked me to marry him."

"Squeeee!" Alice Ann's squeal could have brought down birds. She bounced only once upon the mattress before her eyes tightened and she pressed a hand to her head. "What a terrible decision that was.

Never fall off a cliff, Cora. It's never a good idea."

"Is it serious? Should I call Jamison back?"

Alice Ann continued to rub her scalp but opened her eyes. "I'll live."

Sensing a chance to escape her sister's prods, Coraline reached for her cape, only recently discarded. "You should rest. I'll help Sarah get supper started."

"Not on your life, you will not! My head doesn't hurt that badly. Now you sit down and tell me everything." She patted the empty quilt beside her. "I knew you fancied Jamison. Didn't I say it too?"

Coraline sighed. "You did." She hung her cape back on the hook and settled herself upon the foot of the bed. Tugging her boots off, she folded her legs beneath her. "Why would you condone a relationship with him? You don't like him."

"I never said I didn't like him. I said I was angry with him. He's as nice as they come, but he's also selfish and a liar."

"That makes absolutely no sense."

"Yes, it does. He's polite and caring, yet ignorant. He does stupid things without realizing that they're stupid, which is worse than if he knew they were. If it wasn't for his brothers and their secrets, we could have a claim with Oliver. A house with lots of land and my business all planned out. The least Jamison can do is marry you."

Was his proposal merely an obligation? It didn't feel like it. Jamison certainly didn't kiss her like it was. "Maybe you should blame me instead. Father sent us here so I could see the world. Otherwise, you would still be at home fishing. We wouldn't be such a burden to one another."

"By that logic, I should blame Father."

Her sister wasn't wrong. If Father hadn't gone blind, then passed on the affliction to Coraline... If their mother never found Oliver's advertisement in the newspaper... If they hadn't insisted Alice Ann have an adventure too... If, if, if...there was nothing gained by circling blame. It was what it was.

"We're going to figure out your fishing business, Alice Ann. I'll help you with whatever time I have and you'll become a grand...what's the word for a woman fisherman? A fisheress?"

She laughed. "I think it's supposed to be 'fisherwoman', but really, I always preferred 'fisherman'. I'm proud to have the same occupation as our father." A pause followed where she ran a split thread from the quilt between her fingers. "I'm glad you're marrying Jamison. He loves you, I can tell." Another pause, even longer than the first. The thread snapped and she tossed it away. "Have you told him?"

There was no need for clarification. The thought of Jamison finding out had stolen Coraline's thoughts more than any other. "No, I haven't. I know I should, but—"

Alice Ann's raised palm stopped her scramble for excuses. "It's your decision, Cora. Tell him if you wish or don't." She sniffed. "You don't need to explain your excuses to me."

Her next words were unspoken, yet still so loud Coraline heard them cut clear through her.

Place your care in his hands, Cora, so you can take it out of mine.

16

As soon as Alice Ann was well enough to leap from bed and run to the shore without a hobble, the wedding plans began. To avoid the natives, they would wind around the most heavily populated tribal lands, then approach Stella Maris Mission from the east rather than via the more direct northern route. It was the only way Tobias agreed to let them make the trip at all.

Originally, he demanded their entire group travel the thirty-mile journey, but Levi pointed out the logistics of trekking five children through the wilderness for such an occasion. Surprising to everyone, Mr. Reed stood at his back on that decision. He noted that it was foolhardy to leave their town unattended for something as "feminine as a wedding." He would not allow the rest of his cattle—or their supply cache—to be set upon by thieves in his absence. Tobias reluctantly noted the wisdom in his words and it was decided: Mr. Reed and the Harpers would guard the town while the remaining members bore witness to Coraline and Jamison's nuptials.

First, however, Sarah, in all her romantic southern hospitality, insisted they retain their plans for Independence Day and turn it into an engagement social. Traditionally, such parties involved a multitude of food and frills, both of which they didn't have, but she maintained they could still create merriment even in simplicity.

The women readied themselves most of the morning, and once Martha finished arranging Sarah's blonde curls, she went outside to help Marie set up the luncheon. Meanwhile, Sarah attacked Coraline's brunette tangles with vigor. Seated at her cabin table, Coraline ran her fingers over the dulled yellow fabric of her borrowed dress and tried to focus on anything except the afternoon and subsequent trip to Point Ellice.

"Hold still, Cora," Sarah reprimanded. "I'm nearly finished." She tweaked Coraline's hair so it pulled against her scalp and stopped her nervous jitters.

"I'm sorry. This is different from my first wedding. Oliver and I were so...well, business minded. There was comfort in the necessity. There's certainly necessity with Jamison, but there's also..."

"Love?" Sarah smiled. "It makes all the difference."

Jamison did love her, didn't he? She had to believe she loved him too. She had since even before the trail began, although her marriage to Oliver hadn't allowed her to define her feelings as such. Now she could choose to love Jamison differently, and it was something she wanted very much.

But was it right? He didn't know what trials her future held. She had experienced first-hand what it took to help her father learn to live a different way. He hadn't been able to maintain employment and the burden fell to the rest of the family. Mercy never again accepted an offer of courtship, taking up the role of financial caretaker through her laundry business with their mother. If Coraline didn't marry, she ruined Alice Ann's prospects too. She would have no choice but to remain by her sister's side. Either way, Coraline stole the happiness of someone she loved. Pain pressed behind her eyes, making the darkness at the edges deepen momentarily.

She inhaled deeply. *Relax*, she told herself. *Everything is fine.*

"I just hope that it's enough for him," she replied.

Sarah slid one last pin in place then patted Coraline's crown in a final affirmation of a job well done. She shifted her chair sideways so the two women sat face to face. "You are a vision. You will be more than enough for him."

As quickly as she had arrived, Sarah scooted the chair back and went to fetch their gloves and capes from the bed. It was a pleasant enough day—according to Cade, no indication of storms—but a morning mist had risen off the sea, summoning cool breezes along with it.

Sarah handed over Coraline's things, then shimmied into her beige gloves one lithe finger at a time. "It's a difficult enough thing," she said, "living in the shadows of a dead husband, but an even harder thing to live in the shadow of a talent you can never possess. I will never be Gifted and I fear, neither again will Tobias. As he continues to build his life, he will always be one step behind his brothers. It's rather lonely for him, feeling he can never measure up. As his wife, I want to help him create his dreams, but he won't let me in."

Coraline wrapped her arm around her friend's shoulders and offered her a sympathetic smile. She had known Tobias was having difficulty with losing his Gift and that his frustration took a toll, but she hadn't thought how it could affect his marriage. Not being in a loving marriage before, there were many things Coraline hadn't thought about. "Oh, Sarah, I had no idea you were hurting so. I've been a terrible friend. What can I do?"

Sarah shook her head and with a smile, grabbed their bonnets from the hooks by the door. They had been specially made from scraps for the occasion, with enough room to highlight their delicate curls while still providing appropriate coverage.

"You can be happy with Jamison. And you can be happy for me that in a few months, I will give Tobias the very legacy to restore his joy." She bit back a giggle that quickly erupted into a laugh, then a radiant smile. Leaving her bonnet strings where they dangled, she pressed both hands to her middle. "I'm having a baby!"

"Oh, Sarah," Coraline said again, but this time, her inflection was of a very different sort. Her friend was having a baby. That was a blessing, no matter what the circumstances. It was time God had handed a blessing their way.

"Does Tobias know?" she asked.

"Not yet, but soon. Just as soon as I know nothing is wrong. Now come, we must get you to your party."

One glance at the central courtyard, and it was clear Sarah had outdone herself. The space had radically transformed. Three kitchen tables sat all in a row, covered with quilts for tablecloths, and twine-tied evergreen boughs attached to the back of each chair. Every ounce of their mismatched and chipped china was laid out like a garden party. Instead of floral centerpieces lay arrangements of bark, evergreen boughs, and seashells. One of their friends or family members stood behind each chair, everyone dressed in the best they owned, each bathed and pampered as they hadn't been perhaps since Charleston. Even Alice Ann had exchanged her fisherman attire for her Sunday dress of pale green, her red locks braided down her back with a black ribbon. At the foot of the table stood Jamison, smiling at Coraline the way she had always dreamed.

She pressed a gloved hand to her lips. "Oh," she breathed. "This is beautiful."

Martha spoke up first, her smile radiant. "It was Sarah's idea, but we all helped. We wanted everything to be perfect for you."

"Oh, it is. It truly is. Thank you."

How grateful she was to marry now, while her eyes could still see her friends and family gathered around. Her husband-to-be led her to her seat with such gentleness, his own eyes taking her in with the devotion of a man in love.

Luncheon rushed by in a blur and before she knew it, he was reaching for her hand again and leading her from the table.

"Shall we dance?" he asked. At the same time, Levi raised his fiddle to strike the first notes of a country ballad. Martha and Sarah pushed them forward and laughter rang as she felt Jamison's arms come around her. Everyone was so happy. How could she ruin this? It was exactly what she wanted, too.

They swung around and around, Coraline's skirts flying across the dirt, uncaring of the quickly soiled hemline. She would clean it before she returned it to Sarah, but for today, neither muss nor fuss mattered. Everyone else coupled off, dancing and singing, all exchanging partners except for her. Jamison wouldn't let her go even when the others began a group dance which traded partners on every fourth rotation.

He ducked his head, peering straight into her eyes. "I never thought I deserved this," he said low. "But I'm starting to think I might."

Her mother's words came back to her. "*No one deserves this life, Cora bean. We make the best with what we've got.*"

A flash of light shot across her vision. For a second, her right eye went cloudy then refocused, leaving a grey lightning bolt flickering in its wake.

She had experienced these sensations before, when she was married to Oliver. He always told her there was nothing to fret over. The problem always righted itself. But what if this time it didn't? Eventually, it wouldn't. She couldn't go blind right here, right now, in front of everyone. Could she?

Was this it? The moment when she lost it?

She forced her muscles to relax lest Jamison suspect her tension. But her chest only tightened in response. This was her engagement celebration; she couldn't swoon like a literary damsel at her own party. Jamison would think her hysterical and no one wanted to marry a hysterical woman, especially not once he found out she was also a liar.

"Mind if I cut in?" Cade asked. He appeared beside them, hand outstretched.

Jamison turned her out of his brother's reach. "No, sir, she's all mine."

"Aww, come on. Just one dance. You've had her all day and I'm growing tired of Alice Ann stepping on my toes."

Jamison glanced down at his brother whose expression appeared the bit of a penitent beggar. He shook his head, barely managing to hide a grin. "Very well, I'll save you, but after I teach Alice Ann how to dance, I'm stealing my fiancée back."

"Understood." With a kiss to Coraline's cheek, Jamison headed off to swing Alice Ann into the next song, loudly counting the steps while she argued that she didn't need lessons.

The jagged stripe in Coraline's vision continued to flicker, but she allowed herself to be tugged into Cade's lead.

He turned her so his back was to everyone else. His voice came in barely a whisper. "I experience them too."

"Experience what?" She watched the grey lightning bolt move over his face. His dark eyes were heavy with worry, lined with something she couldn't understand.

"What you're feeling right now," he explained. "Tight chest, sharp breaths, the feeling like you're going to faint. This overwhelming intense panic you try to hide from everyone...and succeed, I might add. Anyone who hasn't experienced it, wouldn't have any idea. But I have. I know what to look for."

She had never had a moment like *this* before, where her vision troubles were complicated by such an utter need for escape. This was worse than even the first time it had happened with Oliver. She remained silent, but Cade's acknowledgment eased some of the pressure inside.

"I've had them for a long time," he told her. "Since I was young, probably since... Anyway, I've always managed to keep the worst ones from my brothers' knowledge. I suppose if I asked Jamison, he could tell me what they're called, but I don't want him or Tobias to think I'm not up to task. If I guessed, it's why you're not telling him either."

With each soft word, her breath began to slow. She had never had an intimate conversation with him before; he was always so wrapped up in Alice Ann or off secluded somewhere. She knew he wasn't courageous—wasn't the leader type—but she hadn't suspected his fears to manifest in such an erratic manner. Nor that they would have such in common.

"Coraline, can I ask you something?"

Finally, her eye refocused. The lightning bolt was gone as quickly as it had appeared. She lifted herself back from the haze she had descended into and nodded.

Cade looked around, and noting that everyone was engaged in their own frivolity, turned her in a circle which led them behind the Harpers' cabin. Once they were alone, he let go of her and backed away.

Fiddle music wafted around the wooden structure, laughter its accompaniment. It wasn't acceptable for them to be alone, not when she was engaged to Jamison. Yet, how much more acceptable would it have been had she and Jamison been discovered kissing in the woods? She still struggled to understand which rules were allowed to be broken and which to hold tight in her heart.

"We shouldn't be alone—" but he spoke before she could finish her rebuttal.

"I'll only need a moment." He looped his thumbs through his suspenders and with chin to chest, stared at the ground. "I would like to request your blessing on a marriage to Alice Ann."

What?! Panic tumbled around her belly once more, threatening to explode out through her throat. She pressed a hand to her chest and willed the feeling to subside. She must look at this logically. Cade cared for her sister. He likely even loved her, as best he knew what love meant. There weren't many women to be heard of in these parts and it made sense that Cade would look to eventually start a family. He was perhaps, even now, being pressured by his brothers to do so, in order to expand the town. Jamison had mentioned nothing, but that didn't mean he hadn't discussed it with Tobias and Cade. If she kept secrets from him, surely, he had his own.

But Alice Ann? She was feckless, reckless, consumed by her own wanderings, and unconcerned with those things that did not support her goals. Coraline had questioned time and time again why her sister bothered herself with Cade when clearly, she did not fully reciprocate his affections. Cade's sensitive soul deserved devotion, not tepid enthusiasm.

"I know it isn't appropriate timing," he continued. "I don't want to overshadow your wedding, but priests are scarce and so are women." Finally, he met Coraline's eyes. The trouble in his irises had been replaced with determination. "I love Alice Ann and that's the truth."

"But does she love you?"

"I hope so."

"She hasn't said?"

"No, but that doesn't matter. You weren't there when she fell from that cliff. I watched her hit the water and I knew she was dead. Even after Quea'Quim dove in after her, I thought for sure it was over. I had my chance and I lost it. But then...she survived and God gave me another. I'm usually such a coward. I've been that way about everything since I was young. I have to prove I can be brave."

"It was bravery to tell me that."

His eyes flicked to the ground and back up again. "Does that mean I have your blessing to ask her or do I need to write to your father?"

He had proved his determination. She had no doubt that—at least in his mind—he would do all he could to protect Alice Ann and give her everything she wanted. Could marriage tame her sister? Could it give her a vital sense of purpose and hopefully, compassion? Or would she string Cade up and discard him like the fish she drew from the water?

It wasn't Coraline's decision to make. Ultimately, it must be Cade and Alice Ann's. They had reached the age of maturity and in the West, it seemed traditional parlor room rules did not apply. She understood that now. Like Cade, she needed to be brave, too.

That awful pressure returned, now lodged tight in her throat. She swallowed...hard.

"Cade, I grant you my blessing."

With a smile as delighted as children chasing fireflies, he grabbed her hand and rushed them back to the party.

17

Alice Ann, of course, provided a resounding and immediate "yes" when Cade asked to be her husband. She made sure everyone knew she was the luckiest woman alive and that she had a better catch than Coraline. The only pity, in her opinion, was their lack of a Southern ceremony, a splendid party, and new dresses. Cade used to be a plantation man. If they had been married back home, they would have, no doubt, planned an extravagant occasion with all the practical trimmings and many impractical ones too.

For a girl who had wished half her life to go to sea and wear trousers, the sentiment was rather unexpected in Coraline's eyes. Unexpected, yet also pleasant. Alice Ann knew her own mind enough to reject Cade's proposal if she believed marriage would tamp down her dreams. Despite Coraline's—and everyone else's—doubts, she must harbor real affection for her future husband.

Although Stella Maris Mission was not far in distance, the trip took over five days due to the extended route. As planned, they avoided all the local tribes and encountered no trouble on their way. The distance provided an opportunity to plan any bartering they wished to pursue and to write letters back home. With a new post office in nearby Chenookville, they hoped to persuade Father Lionnet to deliver the post on his travels to visit the local tribes.

By the time they arrived, they had written a stack of letters tied with twine: one each to Garrett and Josiah, Ned and Octavia Owens, Mercy Owens, Sarah's parents Redmond and Elda Walcott, and lastly to Mr. Reed's cousin which he provided before they left the claim.

Coraline suggested posting one to Daniel as well, at least to inform him of the weddings and that all was well. Jamison agreed, with some reluctance. The wound between the brothers still cut deep and while they rarely spoke of it, Coraline could guess he would have preferred for all his brothers to be beside him on his wedding day.

Stella Maris's spruce log chapel substituted for a church, a wooden crucifix upon the rectangular cabin's door the only indication that reverence lay within. Coraline's periwinkle dress exclaimed the beauty of a bride as did the green and gold calico which adorned Alice Ann. Purple foxglove and mountain daisy bouquets provided the perfect compliment. Coraline could almost imagine she wore her grandmother's dress as planned and prepared to walk down the aisle with its petticoats swishing about her.

She gripped her sister's hand and then reached for Martha's, who in turn clasped Sarah's fingers. Martha was not blood, but she had grown most of her years as Sarah's sister which in a few brief minutes would make both of them Coraline and Alice Ann's sisters as well. In Charleston, the law would have forbidden such interaction between white and colored. How blessed they were to have no such restrictions here.

Even so, she missed her parents and Mercy terribly. They had witnessed her first wedding to Oliver, but they would not see this one to a man she actually loved. Someday, when enough time passed, she would likely forget the sounds of their voices and details would grow hazy. One day, the darkness behind her eyelids would hold only that—darkness—and not even a clear memory anymore. In moments like this, she wondered why her father was so insistent to have her go.

Sarah retrieved both bouquets and handed one to Coraline. "Are you ready?"

Coraline pressed a thin smile. "Were you this nervous on your wedding day?" she asked.

Sarah stared. "Tobias was the first of eight men to survive a wedding night with me. Nervous is hardly an apt word to describe what I felt."

"How about distressed?" Alice Ann suggested. "Apprehensive? Uneasy, tormented, tortured? What about terrified?"

Sarah practically flung the other bouquet at Alice Ann who caught it against her chest. Several petals scattered to the dirt. "Yes, clever girl, those would all be appropriate terms."

How stupidly insensitive they had been. Sarah's first husband, Linden, had died of cholera then her next six husbands were murdered by Linden's father. Coraline's unease over keeping secrets from Jamison was nothing compared to the terror her friend—and soon-to-be sister-in-law—must have felt with every wedding.

Alice Ann's lips broke into a smile as though her remarks were on nothing more than the weather, which as usual was rather cloudy with the threat of rain. Having acquiesced to Cade's request that she wear shoes for one day, she bounced upon her boot heels, causing her twin crimson braids to sway. Lifting her flowers to the sky, she declared, "Come, ladies! Our lovers await!"

"We're about to enter a church," Sarah scolded. "Must you be so profane?"

A grin was her only response as she pushed open the chapel door.

A musty breath exhaled from the dark interior, lit only by several tin lanterns and a damp fire in a blackened stone hearth. Wooden benches lined the central aisle to a wooden altar covered in cream cloth. The usual aspects of the Eucharistic celebration topped the altar—a chalice and paten, carved from wood rather than the usual gold or silver. Even Father Lionnet's vestments were woven from simple cloth with no adornments other than a gold-trimmed stole across his shoulders. Extravagances seemed wasteful for a mission and only spoke of finery the Indians were not accustomed to and held no regard for. Trying to impose unfamiliar practices too soon would never sway them to a Christian lifestyle.

Coraline wondered if Quea'Quim's people ever visited Stella Maris and if so, if they were drawn to its religion, even in the slightest. She had lived twenty-four years under the mantle of Christianity and found little sanctuary in its regard. How likely was it truly for any of the natives to accept beliefs a world apart from their own?

She quickly discovered the answer when her eyes fell upon a small contingent of natives seated directly behind Sarah, Tobias, and Martha. Three women and two men turned to watch the sisters, revealing appearances so unusual in nature as to shock her sensibilities. Unlike Quea'Quim, they wore clothing similar to the settlers' usual attire: the women in plain white blouses with flowered skirts and the men dressed in tan trousers, flannel shirts, and suspenders. If not for their long black hair and copper skin, they could almost pass for any other traveler along the western trails. Almost, if not for one other surprising feature: their foreheads. Each was completely flattened, providing a semi-conical shape to the skull. Only one retained its natural shape—a young woman with a tight braid and a bracelet made from cobalt blue glass beads and white cylindrical shells. A young boy, likely no more than four, stood beside her. His similar coloring and skull shape suggested him to be her son.

What had happened to these people? Had they suffered a horrible accident to cause such disfiguration? On the trail, there were regular tales of Indians who bashed others' skulls in with clubs. Was there another implement which could create this sort of damage? Why had the boy and his mother been spared? And why was she the only one who didn't seem at peace?

"Have no fear, daughter," Father Lionnet called. As he spoke, Coraline realized her procession had stalled a quarter way down the aisle, yet Alice Ann now stood at the front. The priest extended his arms to encompass the strangers. "These are recent converts to the faith, although they retain some physical signs of their people. They still struggle with our language, but are anxious to embrace our beliefs. Every Mass holds mystery for them."

"As it should for us all," Jamison said softly. Even from a distance, his voice carried. She felt that familiar tickle of dread feather her neck until he met her eyes and let her see his smile. Like the rest of them, he wore his Sunday best, the same tan trousers, jacket, and charcoal vest he always preached in, his grandfather's pocket watch chain visible within his open jacket. Even with his overzealous piety, she loved all the beauty of him as he was. She wished she felt so confident that he would continue to love her just as well once he knew her hidden pieces.

She continued forward, took his hands, blinked, and before she knew it, the ceremony was over. As Alice Ann accepted Cade's arm and Jamison offered Coraline his, she glanced at the altar and tried to recall if she had truly stood there. She remembered saying the vows. Jamison said his. Cade too and Alice Ann...although, Coraline believed her sister shouted more than spoke as a lady should. What happened after that? Had she smiled? Laughed? Her cheeks felt damp. Goodness be praised, had she been crying? Her fingers still clung to her wildflower bouquet; otherwise, she would wipe her tears away.

Jamison whirled her outside into the midst of cheers and embraces. He snatched her up in his arms and twirled her around and around, his laughter reaching for the heavens. With a chaste kiss, he set her down and turned to the priest. "Father Lionnet, thank you for providing us with the sacrament. I hope we can convince you to come north from time to time to offer Mass in our town."

The priest smiled. "It would be an honor, if I might convince you to return to the mission on occasion. You see there is so much work to do..."

With only a gentle tug to her arm, Coraline was swept away from the conversation and into a copper-armed embrace. It belonged to the young Indian woman with the blue and white bracelet and the unflattened brow. Her soft whisper fluttered across Coraline's ear. "Come to the chapel at midnight. Quea'Quim wishes to speak to you. Alone."

With a sharp glance of deep brown eyes, she let go and hurried her son away down the mission road.

Jamison's arm came around her. "Who was that?"

Who indeed? "One of the converts. She didn't give her name. She wanted to wish us well." Another lie. How many did that make now?

He smiled down at her. "How kind. Perhaps tonight I can grant my wife some wishes of her own."

Coraline willed herself to smile back. A typical bride should understand her wedding night expectations. Hers, on the other hand, was neither typical nor did she understand.

18

Separate bedrolls under a wagon wasn't Coraline's ideal wedding night; nevertheless, that was the wedding night she had. It induced memories of her fitful dreams back on the trail, waiting for sunrise so she didn't dream of snake bites or Oliver anymore. She didn't want to think about him tonight either. She was a bride and she wanted to be made to feel like one. Such an act, however, would prove embarrassing with so many family members close by.

"Why don't we wait?" she said when Jamison suggested they go down to the shore or the forest floor or into the ocean. Anywhere would be acceptable for him. If it had only been the two of them on a proper wedding trip, she would have consented, but not here when their family knew the circumstances. Certainly not for her first time.

After her refusal, Jamison fell into a stupor quicker than she expected. A half-moon lay silent above the forest, its glow only mildly visible through the prickly evergreen canopy. As the campfire burnt to embers and her eyes adjusted—albeit poorly—moonlight illuminated the mysterious Indian woman's return to the chapel. Another native, presumably Quea'Quim, strode at her heels, both of their footsteps light as a breeze. The young boy from earlier was not with them.

After a single glance in either direction, they slipped inside the chapel and left the door ajar.

Without hesitation, Coraline slipped from her bedroll, lit a lantern, and followed. Slipping inside the chapel, she pulled the door closed behind her.

Quea'Quim sat in the first pew while the woman lit the two altar candles. She genuflected before the crucifix and crossed herself before rising to turn Coraline's way.

"I'm glad you came, Mrs. Lark. Please, sit."

The twin altar flames burned like dragon eyes as Coraline took the pew opposite Quea'Quim. He glanced in her direction, raising one brow, then the other, then both. He was clothed in his usual native attire—bare chest with animal skin leggings—but no string of fish this time. Candlelight flickered off his worried features, reminding her of the night he barged his way into her house with Alice Ann's near-lifeless body.

Coraline wanted answers for why he always appeared wherever she was. Had he followed her again or was this mission his home? Was he a convert like the others? He didn't wear their clothes, and he hadn't attended the wedding Mass. How then did he know this woman?

"Why are your heads round?" she blurted, which was not at all what she most wanted to know and probably came across as quite rude. The two natives exchanged a look of understanding before the woman met her eyes again.

"Why is *your* head round?" she asked.

"I was born like this."

"Then there, you have your answer."

"But the other natives are different. Their heads are...what happened to them?"

"Like many of the northern tribes, the Chinook believe in flattening the head from birth. Two pieces of wood are fitted upon the infant's skull and tightened. By the end of twelve moons, the shape is in place for life."

"How terrible!" Coraline gasped.

"It is not. It does not harm the infant and they are as intelligent as any other. Some would say they possess even greater capacity than your people."

"If it is such a gift, why do neither of you have it?"

The woman glanced again at Quea'Quim. "We are different from the rest of our tribe."

"Because you are Christian?" Coraline asked and jolted when

Quea'Quim leaped from his seat.

"I am no Christian!" He stomped halfway down the aisle and turned. "That priest has filled Anwillik's head with lies, turned her away from her own people and her own religion. It is not the way our family taught us."

"They are only part of our family, brother," Anwillik said, her voice soft. "I needed to know the other part."

"Your brother?" Coraline stuttered. "Was one of your parents a Christian? Is that why you do not have a flattened brow?" Now that she looked closely, even in the dim candlelight, there was some resemblance between the two. A distinct shape to their faces that matched, among other small indications. The difference in their clothing had been what concealed the connection.

Quea'Quim returned to his seat and his sister moved to sit beside Coraline. "In a manner, yes," she said. "We are Chinook, but long ago, our ancestor was a Boston man. Quea'Quim lives at his own pace, neither with the tribe nor completely alone. I live here at the mission with my four-year-old son, Tleyuk, whose father went to heaven three years past. He is young, but will soon be man enough to take his spirit quest. He will have a choice to make, to return to the tribe or remain here with me."

"Tleyuk will choose the tribe," Quea'Quim said. "He will take the quest and earn his place and you will return to see him fulfill it."

"Whether I return to the tribe or not will not change what I believe."

A silence punctuated her statement. Coraline could not fault Quea'Quim for his disbelief in the Christian God when hers was so skeptical. She understood his desire to have his sister back within the tribe. However, she also understood Anwillik's decision to choose her own path and find the roots she had never known.

"That is why our family is forbidden from flattening our children's heads," Anwillik said finally. "Our ancestor's blood will never be forgiven."

"Anwillik!" Quea'Quim snapped. "This is not the reason we asked her here. Our ancestor's story is of no importance."

A shadow covered Anwillik's expression. "Our ancestors are always important."

She fingered her blue and white shell bracelet, her lips turned into a sad smile. "His name was Thompson. He came with his ship of Boston men for temporary refuge. The sea had been rough. They said they were merchants, but they had need of everything. They stayed on for a week and at the end, the man pledged his heart to a young Chinook daughter, Spaärk. He had made a promise to his men, but once that promise was fulfilled, he pledged to return for her.

"Shortly after, there was a violent storm. The waves crashed, then the mountains trembled and sent their fury upon the land. A great flood followed, a sea serpent who devoured the shore and all who did not run into the forest to escape. Spaärk survived but discovered she carried a son. Some of the tribe declared it to be the serpent's, foul and evil. They wanted to throw her and the child from the cliffs and return the serpent to the sea. Spaärk swore of her romance with the white man and begged to be spared. If he did not return, she would take the child away, though she knew not where they would go.

"When the child was born and no sign came of the man's return, she was convinced he must have died. Surprisingly, rather than banishment, the tribe showed mercy, but neither her son nor his future generations would obtain the flattened brow. It is a sign of honor for our people, and to not have it is to be a foreigner or a slave."

This was a turn of events Coraline had not foreseen. "The Chinook own slaves? But Washington is a free territory."

"We do not keep slaves like yours. Ours do not wallow or writhe in their situation. They have their families and will remain until they either die or are offered in a treaty. The Chinook battle rarely, so few of our slaves are acquired in that way. It is more common to earn them through trade. We do not use the coin of the white man, but we have other ways to pay. Like these." Anwillik removed her bracelet, holding it out to Coraline. "The howqua shell is our most important currency; used for trade and for its beauty, it is both worn and offered as payment."

Coraline spun one of the cylindrical shells on its cord. "But aren't these shells scattered up and down the coast?"

"Yes. They are easy to come by, but our true wealth does not lie in money. It is a proverb Father Lionnet says is espoused by your Jesus too."

"He also says that He came to set us free," Coraline countered. "I imagine Jesus would be appalled by how we treat each other in this world."

"Yes," Anwillik said. "I imagine He would be."

A hush fell with her words, as though the entire chapel held its breath. Not even the candles flickered, nor did the wind press through the wall cracks. Coraline clenched her fingers together in her lap and let her gaze fall from the native's. Anwillik had just placed a mountain of information upon her and asked her to understand. But understand what exactly? She had been invited here, but still she couldn't say for what purpose. Certainly, it wasn't so she could counter them on their beliefs. Not when she held tight to so few herself.

Her eyes flicked to Quea'Quim across the aisle. "Why have you been following me?"

Intensity met her gaze with a chill that his full lips could not soften. When he rose, his soft-soled slippers padded silently upon the floor. Coraline stood before he could reach their pew, so that she might meet him eye-to-eye rather than toe-to-toe.

"I have followed your people since long before you knew me. There are other settlers whom our tribe calls allies, but none are so strange as yours. You mix colors in your midst. You treat the black man the same as white. You did not run when you saw me at the stream and when I entered your house, you did not cower." He tilted his chin. "How strange you speak our language."

"I think it stranger that you speak mine."

His next words were for his sister, still rooted to her seat, but her attention fixed solidly on him. "She could be the one we have sought from the spirits."

"That remains to be determined. You and I have rather different opinions over which Spirit guides us."

So, there *was* a reason he had been following her. Something had convinced him she was someone special, someone he had been waiting to find. But that couldn't be her. She was a poor, soon-to-besightless widow from Charleston, who didn't know anything about the Chinook people or their customs.

"Who do you think I am?" she asked. "I can't be who you believe me to be."

Before an answer could be given, the creak of hinges and lumber announced the presence of another to the chapel. In the doorway, Jamison stood in silhouette, darkness at his back and candlelight upon his astonished expression. He stepped forward. "I heard voices. I knew it couldn't be you, and figured I should check before running a search party into the woods. But it *was* you. Holding a conversation with them in *their* language."

Coraline looked from Anwillik to Quea'Quim who both appeared as confused as she. She shook her head. "You must have still been asleep. They were speaking English the same as when Quea'Quim brought Alice Ann home. The same as at the stream."

Jamison quickened his pace until he stood beside her. His stare held a million questions. "No, they're not. I don't know what they're speaking—and what you're speaking—but it isn't English."

Was he in cahoots with the natives to drive away what little sanity she had left? "The only language I *know* is English. I've never even heard another language. Go ahead and say something to them if you don't believe me. They'll understand you too."

Jamison looked to Quea'Quim this time. "Why are you so interested in my wife? She doesn't belong to you and if you intend her harm, I will not hesitate to protect her."

"Jamison!" Coraline's fingers flew to her lips. When her eyes met Quea'Quim's to extend her apologies, the blank confusion reflected back stilled her voice. His expression said he wasn't sure if he should be insulted and if so, how offended he should be. He hadn't understood a word.

"Say something, Quea'Quim," she whispered. "This time in your own language."

"I've been speaking in my own language since the day we met. It's the only language I know."

She was too afraid to ask the question. A glance at Jamison's expression told her enough.

She tumbled backward into the pew, before she crumpled in a heap on the chapel floor.

Anwillik took her hand. "You understand them both?"

Coraline nodded. They had spoken two different languages and she heard every word as though they were one and the same. How could that be?

Unless her ancestor also sailed through the *Oblique*'s storm, the same as every other person's ancestor in this room.

19

How can you be Gifted?" Tobias asked for the third time. "Women can't be Gifted."

Jamison wanted to reach over the pew and smack his brother, then beg the Lord's forgiveness for defiling His house with violence. Tobias wasn't a backward thinker. He had believed in females being Gifted longer and louder than any of them. Yet now, when one actually revealed herself, he refused to accept reality. Losing his Gift had done more than shatter his self-esteem. It had made him question everything about them.

An hour ago, after the initial shock fog cleared, Jamison ran to rouse his family and drag them back to the chapel. Tobias and Sarah now sat in the second pew behind Coraline, Jamison on her left and Martha on her right, with Alice Ann stretched out on her back in the pew across the aisle. Cade, meanwhile, paced the chapel's darkened perimeter. His eyes never seemed to stray too far from Quea'Quim and Anwillik who sat side by side in the front pew which Quea'Quim had previously occupied alone. One of the back pews had been positioned as a barricade against the door, ensuring no one entered without their knowledge, not even Father Lionnet.

Jamison supposed Tobias's incredulity was logical, especially after the trials of the past year. He, himself, still reeled from the news. The beliefs his father slammed across his ribs with that fire poker were gone, and every assumption he ever knew turned on end. Only the memory remained seared upon his side, like it had happened yesterday.

"If they say it's true," Coraline said to Tobias, "then it's true. I told you, I don't hear a difference."

"Say something to them again."

She released another string of Chinook and translated the natives' response in English. Jamison knew she was tired of repeating herself and answering questions she couldn't explain. She didn't know how to activate her Gift or how to turn it off. It appeared she couldn't. She claimed everything she said and heard sounded like English, and to her, it probably did. But it was still bizarre for the rest of them to hear those strange words from her lips. It took everything in him not to stare slack jawed, like a boy seeing ocean dolphins for the first time.

"What about other languages?" Martha asked. "Or can you only speak Chinook?

"I don't know. As far back as I remember, I've never heard anyone speak in another language. I realize now how ridiculous that sounds when we were on the trail and surrounded by all sorts of nationalities. I suppose that means I can understand every language." She paused in the resulting silence, her face ashen. Her eyes widened with a sort of awestruck fear. "I can understand every language." A wondrous revelation from his wife of all of ten hours. What a strange way to start a life together.

He cupped her hand within his own. "I love you," he whispered. Her eyelashes lifted with uncertainty. "I think this is wonderful."

"You do?"

"Of course. Your Gift is incredibly useful in an area we aren't familiar with. It will make trade negotiations easier and should I need to minister to a foreigner, you can help ease their worries. Father Lionnet asked if I would return to the mission to help spread the Gospel. We could come here together."

"Oh." She shifted on the bench, peering over his shoulder where Cade continued to pace. "You've sorted everything out rather quickly."

"I think it's a wonderful idea," Sarah chimed in. "Anwllik has already come to the faith, as have other natives. Think how much stronger their message will be when heard in their own tongue." She smiled at the Indian woman who returned a nervous smile. She didn't ask Coraline to translate and Coraline didn't offer.

Martha reached for her friend's opposite hand. "Think how excited Levi and Marie and Mr. Reed will be when we tell them."

"Woah, hold up a minute." Tobias rose from the pew and turned to face them head on. His folded arms matched the scowl dragging his lips into the wood planks beneath him. "We haven't agreed to anything yet. Alice Ann," he called to the empty space where the girl's body lay hidden behind the pew. Her head popped up with a frown. Across the room, Cade froze within the flickering firelight.

"Are you Gifted too?" he asked.

Alice Ann snorted and laid back again. Her boot heels pounded down upon the wooden bench, knees up beneath her skirts in a most unladylike fashion. If she were Jamison's daughter, she would receive the talking-to of her life. But he wasn't her father and he couldn't control her. Even if her father was here, she was a married woman now. If anyone was to bestow a reprimand, it should be Cade, but he would never.

"Were your ancestors sailors?" Tobias tried again. "Maybe they were on the shipwreck which gave us our Gifts. The *Oblique*."

He had asked Alice Ann, but after a minute of silence, it was Coraline who answered. "Our father came from a line of seamen. He manned his own boat out of Charleston Harbor. I can't say I recall how far back or the names of the ships they sailed on. For me to do what I can, they must have been on the *Oblique*."

"For pity's sake, grease and gizzards, Cora." Alice Ann swung her legs back off the bench and sat up, her skirt tangled around her knees. "They could have been on a sloop too. We don't know and I don't care. I'm not a freak of nature like you all. My gift is life on the sea and you can all thank me when you have supper on the table and you don't starve."

At this, Anwillik spoke up, a long string of unintelligible words of which Jamison could only understand one—*Oblique*. English or Chinook, that word everyone seemed to understand.

"What did she say?" he asked Coraline.

"She recognizes the ship from legends of her ancestor." Quickly, his wife relayed the rest of the story she had been told before Jamison entered the chapel.

The legend was bold and similar to many Indian tales he had heard since leaving Charleston. But sea spirits and serpents impregnating women? Monsters destroying the sea and devouring villagers? It was too fanciful for serious consideration.

Yet, he supposed his own beliefs likely seemed far-fetched to the Chinook as well. It was no wonder Father Lionnet had trouble enticing them to Christ. Especially when the source of the Larks' unusual Gifts was still unknown. All they knew was the ship's name and now the assumption that its loss was due to a storm. Beyond that, nothing.

"Ask them about their spirit quests," Tobias asked. "What type of Gifts did they receive?"

"They didn't," Coraline said, translating Quea'Quim's words. "No one in their family ever showed signs of unnatural ability past the usual skills inherited on the spirit quests of their people. Quea'Quim's quest wasn't even successful by Chinook standards. He didn't receive any messages from the spirit world, even after several attempts. Now he is too old to try again."

Tobias's brow crinkled, his glare sliding from Quea'Quim's soft slippers to his black hair. "He told you this?"

"Yes. They were very open with their intentions."

"What exactly *are* their intentions?"

"If you would stop questioning her credibility, perhaps we could find out." Alice Ann said. "Coraline isn't a liar. She's too boring for that."

"She's right," Cade interjected. For the first time, he stepped from the shadows, walked the aisle, and stood beside his wife. He placed a hand upon her shoulder which at a closer distance, Jamison could see was taken with trembling. "We've heard the proof with our own ears, Tobias. There's obviously something at work here greater than ourselves. Just because we don't know all the details, that doesn't make what she can do any less real."

It was like the Pharisees, Jamison thought. When they saw and heard Jesus's words and miracles right before them, but they would not believe it. They let pride stand in their way, refusing to acknowledge their human weakness and their lack. Indeed, blessed were those who had not seen and believed.

"We need to get to the heart of the matter," he said. "What Coraline can do is as amazing as what any of us can do—"

"Used to be able to do," Tobias muttered. Jamison ignored him.

"Coraline's Gift can be a great asset. We have the advantage of being able to speak with anyone we encounter. This could be our opportunity to bring those of other nationalities into Larksong."

"But how can we follow a singular system of government if we have no way to explain its rules? Does Coraline plan to translate every word to everyone forever?"

"Of course not. We will find ample interpreters among those we recruit. They will help the new citizens learn our language and we can learn theirs."

Quea'Quim spewed off a string of words, spitting them with force. He gestured to Tobias and back to Coraline, then threw up his arms.

Coraline flushed. "He says you talk too much." The blush of her cheeks admitted that he said a bit more than that and not appropriate for translation. "He says he has a solution, if you will listen. I have been shown favor with their spirits by a Gift far greater than their people are granted on their quests. He says I have been chosen to prepare the path."

"What does that mean?"

"It means," Quea'Quim continued through Coraline's translation, "that your people and ours are meant to live as one. I have followed you and tested you and this one—" He nodded to Coraline. "—has passed the test. We have other Boston allies on the bay, good men, but they are not the ones meant to return our village to us."

"What village is that?" Tobias asked.

"The village in the north, at the edge of the Mouse River. Many years ago, there was a chief, beloved by his people, who died suddenly. Fearing the spirits' rebuke, his home was burned and the village abandoned by the rest of the tribe. In this age, they live on the bay with the rest of our people for they cannot return out of fear."

"Fear of what?" Alice Ann leaned forward, hands on her knees and a bright fire of excitement within her eyes. Macabre stories of death and evil spirits intrigued her? Perhaps that girl was searching for more excitement—and in more trouble—than any of them realized.

Quea'Quim's hushed tone relayed his trepidation even before Coraline translated the words. "Fear of the dead. The village is a haunted place. If the Chinook go there now, the bad spirits will come and take our lives."

"Quea'Quim," Anwillik reprimanded. "You are frightening them."

"Not all of them." His gaze landed on Alice Ann who sat so far forward she teetered on the edge of the bench. Cade had stepped away, his countenance paler than the ghosts Quea'Quim spoke of. What a pair those two were, Jamison thought, and now they were bonded for life. If ever a mistake was made... He couldn't think about that now. He must focus.

"How can we return your village to you?" Jamison asked. "If you need to drive away evil spirits, you would be better served to ask Father Lionnet."

Disgust marred Quea'Quim's smooth features. It drove hard lines across his chiseled forehead and sucked in the sides of his almond eyes until they drew to mere slits. "I do not need the help of your *father*." He spat the word. "I am ill enough to stand in this place you kneel before in worship. This place that steals my sister from her people."

Jamison found his insides at war. The spirits Quea'Quim spoke of were not the One the Lark brothers were raised to believe in. There was one God, one Spirit, and He did not possess the air or the trees or the rocks. Christ did not haunt burnt-out homes and He certainly did not flee before white men, nor attack the indigenous peoples. Such beliefs seemed to stem from a darker place than the one Jamison knew.

"I am afraid I must defend my brother." Anwillik's soft words told of a woman with much love. "He does not understand why I choose to serve your God. I do not understand how he continues to fear spirits I no longer believe exist. Yet, I see the importance in his mission. His people believe the village spirits will flee before the white man and Coraline can build the bridge between your people and his. If she inhabits the village, Quea'Quim's tribe may also return in safety. They have promised to work alongside you, teaching you how to fish, plant, and gather in exchange for a fair share. There are cedar plank lodges already made, enough for every member of your families. My brother would regain the respect our ancestors lost. His son, should he have one, would be allowed a flattened head once more."

It wasn't the Christian way for everything to have a spirit, but Jamison would have to be blind not to see the importance Quea'Quim's faith played in his decisions. For over one hundred and fifty years, this native's family had been all but rejected by their tribe. Not allowed to partake in their most important traditions. Not even special enough for the Gifted legacy the *Oblique* had offered others. Abandoned by his sister to what he viewed as a "white man's God." Now, he had a chance to earn all of that back. To be loved in the eyes of his people and create a legacy worth passing on to his future generations. Jamison could not condemn him for such a desire. He, too, wanted a better legacy than the one Alonzo Lark left behind. He wanted to set his eyes on Heaven and know that one day, he would be there.

Minutes passed where the chapel remained silent. One of the altar candles snuffed out at the end of its wick, sending the pungent aroma of sulfur through the air. The remaining one teased the same outcome, but remained lit. The steady crackle of the fireplace continued as Cade moved to drop another log upon its reaching fingers.

Coraline finally spoke. "I think the answer is obvious."

"It is," Tobias said. "Our answer is obviously no."

A chorus of voices chimed their confusion together.

"But, but why?" Sarah spluttered. "What they're offering is exactly what our town needs." She pushed herself to standing and gripped her husband's arm. "Tobias, they're offering us help. We won't survive much longer without it."

Instead of answering her, he looked at Coraline. "Tell them we need to stand on our own."

"Yet your claims stand on *our* land," Quea'Quim spat again. He took a step closer, the fire in his tone hotter than the new sparks of the hearthstone. "You have taken our land without discussion, Boston man, but we offer this place freely. Will you not take it in the name of peace?"

"You do not need us to reclaim your village. By your admission, your ancestor is of European descent. If a white man is all that frightens your spirits, you can scare them yourself."

"It is not enough. I would not dare pass among them without a white man at my face." Coraline gasped as she translated his next words. "Do not make the natives your enemy. This is a war you are not prepared to fight."

Tobias stepped closer still, only barely restrained by Sarah's hand on his arm. "Are you threatening us?"

Quea'Quim moved to meet him toe-to-toe. "No. The Chinook are peaceful, but the Boston people want to take more than our brothers and sisters wish to give. Other tribes will not be as forgiving as we, and if driven to it, we will defend what is ours as well."

At that, Tobias at last retreated. He sank back to the pew, pulling his wife down beside him. He ran his fingers through his already mussed hair and with a sigh, seemed to depart his gaze toward heaven. "It's too soon. We walked two thousand miles. We have our own claims. How can we simply abandon them?"

"Because your beloved claims are dying!" Alice Ann shouted. Hiking up her skirt, she stomped up on the bench in direct violation of every common church courtesy ever established. She let her skirts fall back to her ankles, but propped a hand on either hip instead. "We're supposed to prove to Uncle Sam that we did something with it in two years' time. But one year is almost gone and we haven't a stinking penny to show for it. You failed us, Tobias."

"Alice Ann!" Sarah cried and, as usual, was ignored.

"You aren't the only one allowed to make plans, Tobias Lark. Stop passing edicts like we're part of your claim. I don't take orders from anyone."

"You're married now," he countered. "You had better get used to taking orders."

Crimson shot through her cheeks and she jumped down from the bench. Her boots smacked the floor as she stomped toward her brother-in-law. Her index finger poked right in his chest. "I. Take.

Orders. From. No. One."

Tobias's brows hiked higher than his hair. "Cade?" he called, but Cade said nothing. He slid so far into the corner, he disappeared like mist in a shadow.

Pull yourself together! Jamison wanted to yell at him. *Is this how you let your marriage start? Your wife fighting in a church?*

Oh, good gravy and hot biscuits, they were *all* fighting in a church. How much confession would he need tomorrow?

"You think you make all the rules, don'tcha, Tobias?" Alice Ann continued yelling. "That you can decide when something's worthwhile and when it isn't? Like my scant fishing business? Well, I can make life-altering decisions without your approval too." She opened her mouth again, clenched her fists, and Cade's hand slapped over her open lips with such force, he pulled her back against his chest.

Jamison looked around. Hadn't his brother been standing in the corner? Where had he come from?

"Alice, don't!" Cade pleaded as he held his wife's wriggling body against him. "You said we wouldn't. Not yet."

She shook her head vehemently and muffled incoherent shouts until, with a defeated sigh, her husband finally released her. She shoved him out of the way and wiped her mouth with the back of her hand. "Cade, you're such a milksop. We deserve our moment in the sun, what precious little of it there is to be found."

"This isn't the time."

"With you, it never would be."

"Alice, please," he begged. "Don't."

"You tell them then."

He looked around, his complexion going paler with every family member's face. "Well," she snipped, "go ahead. Unless you think we made a mistake."

"No, I..." He looked at them all once more. Sweat peppered his yellowed skin like one of the storms that made him sick to his stomach. "I...we...Alice Ann..." He wiped his palms on his trouser leg. "We're having a baby, probably in January, please forgive me. Let's go, Alice."

Alice Ann gave a sheepish grin. "Sorry, Cora."

He ran down the aisle, pulling his new wife behind him. Together, they shoved away the pew blocking the door, and leaving the rest of them floored at all they had witnessed.

20

Coraline understood now why Cade had been so insistent on marrying her sister. He did love Alice Ann, but the urgency had been because of her pregnancy rather than love itself.

She blamed herself for not recognizing the steep cliff the couple was headed toward. As the elder sister, she should have intervened before Alice Ann pushed Cade off of it. Instead, she had given her blessing. While a baby deserved two married parents, Cade was now trapped with his wife's irresponsible immaturity for the rest of his life. His only hope was that marriage and motherhood would create a change in her.

On the other hand, Coraline debated inwardly, how could she speak to the matter when she also trapped Jamison into marriage? Yes, they found love in the process, but her original intentions were perhaps the same as her sister's. At least Alice Ann had been honest about her pregnancy, while Coraline still harbored her blindness to herself. It felt hypocritical to reprimand her sister for choices she also made.

Which was why she said nothing contrary the morning after the devastating reveal. She expressed joy at gaining a new brother and soon, a little niece or nephew. After returning from the mission, Jamison moved in with Coraline and Martha, while Alice Ann moved into the stable with Cade. She didn't seem to mind. In fact, she acted like she enjoyed its rough nature. Even so, a new house was erected for them within the month. Smaller than Jamison and Cade's first home, but large enough for the couple and their forthcoming baby to have some privacy.

Cora was secretly glad for the arrangement. It allowed her to remain someplace familiar for when her eyesight disappeared completely. She already knew the layout of the cabin, the number of steps to each piece of furniture, and the distance from the door to every important location in town. She had told herself that once she and Jamison married, she would share her secret, except that their town's status hadn't improved. They couldn't afford to lose another member, even if she was Gifted.

In Coraline's eyes, being Gifted hadn't changed anything. Her vision continued to deteriorate, except that now that wasn't the strangest thing about her. She still didn't understand how she knew foreign words and couldn't even acknowledge when they were. Everyone in Larksong spoke English, making her Gift essentially unnecessary. As the days passed by, every one like the last, she felt less and less useful.

At night, she often lay awake thinking about Anwillik, her soft words, and the faith which separated her from her brother. It would be so easy for her to leave the mission, return to her tribe, and restore her relationship with Quea'Quim. Coraline could tell the siblings cared deeply for one another. It pained both their hearts to be divided on such an important issue. What would they do when her son, Tleyuk, chose his path? What if he chose differently than his mother? Would she stay with the mission then?

There was no more discussion about moving into the abandoned village. Tobias had decided and that was that. For the rest of them, being together was more important than being separated. If they left Tobias and Sarah on their own, the couple would never make it. With the baby coming, it would have been a cruel punishment.

Instead, Jamison rode down to the mission twice a month as had been requested by Father Lionnet. He spent a week among the converts, claiming to learn as much from them as they learned from him. Their English being rudimentary, he was forced to keep the lessons simple, and it frustrated him not to dive into the complexities of Church history, Biblical accounts, or Catholic doctrine. Coraline's Gift could have easily cleared those barriers, not only for the current converts but those yet unfamiliar to the faith. Still, she couldn't bring herself to join him. It felt too close to another lie, telling the natives to believe in a loving God while her heart held so much emptiness.

She was glad for Martha during those lonely days without her husband, especially as the sun shortened and her vision grew worse in the winter light. They spent their days sewing or cleaning, drying meat or canning preserves. By September, the ice box was finally installed in the stream and well stocked for the coming months. In the evenings, Martha continued to read aloud from the Bible—now, from the Gospel of Luke—and Coraline would listen as she readied herself for bed. Most nights, she insisted on turning in early to spare herself the embarrassment of tripping over a table leg or risk collision with Martha as she moved about. Daytime was still manageable, but evening was only the prelude to a long, dark night.

The last week in November, Coraline hefted a basket of wet laundry across the cabin to join Martha at the line strung from wall to wall. With the mucky weather, hanging laundry on the outside line proved counterproductive. The moist air and intermittent rain kept the clothes as wet as in the wash bucket.

When a knock sounded at the door, both women paused in their pinning to exchange a glance. Although Jamison had been at the mission for nearly a week, they didn't expect him back until tomorrow. And, besides, why would he knock on his own door?

Perhaps it was Quea'Quim?

Being closest to the door, Martha wiped her hands on her apron and lifted the latch. Coraline managed to contain her disappointment when it was not Quea'Quim after all. Instead, Clinton Reed stood with hat in hands, appearing damp but not too worse for wear. He must have caught a lucky spot between showers. Never before had he visited their cabin unannounced.

"Mr. Reed," Martha said. "What can we do for you?"

"Had a break in my chores and I know Jamison's down at the mission again. Thought Mrs. Lark might be in need of some assistance."

Martha's voice rose. "Just Mrs. Lark?"

"Well, the both of ya." It wasn't a secret that in the past, Mr. Reed had maintained some racial grievances, but they had hoped those views were behind them now. He had never made trouble with Martha or the Harpers while in Larksong, but Martha didn't appear convinced.

"Cora's got me to help her."

"I know that. But I also know there's use in having a man about the house. My Gabriella used to tell me as such." His eyes met Coraline's from across the room. "Jamison's away half the time and the other half he's tending to the chores, helping his brothers, or I imagine, writing up those sermons he delivers on Sundays. You've got to be lonely for him and frankly, Mrs. Lark, I'm lonely too. I miss my wife and I could use someone to talk to."

He took a step inward, but Martha's hand against the doorframe barred him entrance. She started to close the door atop him. "It isn't appropriate. If you're lonely, go find one of the men."

"They have wives of their own!" he called through the last sliver before the door closed. "They don't understand me like you do. Oliver died like my Gabriella. You know how it feels."

Her palm against the closed door, Martha looked to Coraline for a response. She felt badly for Mr. Reed, she truly did. They both knew what it was like to lose a spouse, although Gabriella had only disappeared. No one could confirm her dead; they could only assume. After almost two years, however, it made sense that he would hope to move on.

She waved her free hand. "Let him in. There's no harm in a friendly chat. He probably is lonely."

With a sigh of clear disapproval, Martha opened the door and waved Mr. Reed inside, first insisting he remove his muddy boots. He yanked them off and stacked them side-by-side against the wall. When he turned, he revealed woolen socks, the left with a hole atop the fourth toe.

"Would you like me to darn that?" Coraline asked. She pointed to the sock.

"Nah, I'm used to holes here and there. Never been good with a needle."

"Then all the more reason why I should do it. Hand it over please. Martha, could you set some tea on?"

With a "hmph," Martha went for the kettle, still partly full from that morning's tea. She placed it back over the fire and returned to her laundry pins.

"This is sure kind of you," Mr. Reed said as he took a seat at the table and rolled his sock down. He handed it over to Coraline who pretended not to notice the stench of male sweat wriggling off it like worms in a rainstorm. It took her four tries to finally thread her needle and tie off the end.

"How are your eyes?" he asked. "I assume Jamison's ministrations haven't been working?"

She kept her attention on the needle as it slid in and out of the wool. "I am sorry to say, they have not been."

"I thought he was Gifted."

"Giftedness only goes so far."

"I see." Several minutes of silence followed where the only motions were Coraline's needle and the click of laundry pins as Martha draped another skirt over the line. Then the kettle boiled and she hurried to relieve it from the fire. Tossing in an extra leaf, she placed a steaming cup before Mr. Reed and walked away. The *click-clack* of laundry pins continued.

He tapped his thumb on the rim of the cup as he waited for the steam to dissipate. "I hear tell that people have gone to the Willamette Valley for the fresh air and healing properties. It ain't far. I could take you."

Coraline's fingers stilled on the sock threads. Still, she didn't look up. She didn't believe the air in Oregon could heal her eyesight any better than the air in Washington. Hers wasn't a natural condition. It wasn't brought on by sickness or poison or a childhood infirmity. If it had been, Jamison's Gift could have found a way around it.

Mr. Reed, however, took her hesitation for another matter. "I don't mean anything sinister. I want to help and pull my weight around here. All y'all have a history together, family in one way or the other.

But me, I'm just the last of the wagon train who stuck around. I know I have to earn my place by earning your trust."

She let herself continue with the needle, now nearing the end of the tear. "It isn't trust. It's that it wouldn't do any good. I've prayed for a miracle for years, but there's still the same awkward silence every time I bow my head. From now on, I've decided to simply move forward."

"Not a believer then?"

"Not certain what I am."

She tied off the end of the thread and jammed the needle into the pin cushion, handing him back his sock. He took it, smiled, and slipped it back up his foot, followed by his boot. He dropped his pant leg and reached for his tea. "God aside, the Bible is a historical record. Surely, you're a believer in history."

"Of course."

"Have you heard of the Pool of Bethesda?"

"Yes. Jesus is to have cured a cripple in its waters."

"Not only Jesus, but many people are said to have been cured there. It is known throughout the ages as a healing place."

Martha sniffed. "You want to take Coraline to Israel? How do you plan to accomplish that?" She had a hand on her hip and the opposite upon a pin on the line. Her expression indicated a substantial desire to roll her eyes. It all did seem a fairly spectacular notion.

"I doubt that I can," Mr. Reed admitted. "Which is why I suggest trying the Willamette Valley first. Or perhaps Soda Springs. We passed right by it along the trail and never thought to stop. The settlers in Astoria claimed it has healed many. Even your Indian friends might know where to start."

He took a sip of tea as he peered across the table with curious attention. "All I'm sayin' is there are chances worth taking. Giftedness isn't the only way to salvation."

"Jamison would say there's only one way to salvation." She didn't like how intently Mr. Reed watched her or the small sad smile on his lips. It set her uneasy and made a part of her wish for her husband. She had never spoken to Mr. Reed much before now and already feared she had said too much.

"Ya know, my Gabriella was a church-going lady."

"Oh?" she said, thankful to move the conversation along. Martha's eyes met hers over every fresh clothes pin. "Is that how you met?"

"Heck, no. I worked on her Pa's farm. That's how I came about my cattle. They were his."

"What happened to him?"

His lips pressed thin. "Murdered. Him and her Ma both. Right there on the farm. I was thankful to have Gabriella spared. After that, there was really nothing for us there. I heard about the Larks' wagon party and it seemed the best way to go."

Murdered? Coraline sat back in her chair, stunned. She had never considered...perhaps that was why Gabriella had been near-mute and self-confined to her wagon. It was no secret that the weathered trail did not agree with her.

"Do you think that's what happened to your wife? That she was...well, that she suffered the same as her parents?"

"I reckon it must have been. Garrett's Gift wasn't able to find her and there's not a living soul he can't locate. It's the answer I have to accept, at least enough for me to move on to my next task."

"And what task is that?" Martha asked at the same moment the door swung open.

Jamison strode across the threshold, his pack over one shoulder and every inch of him soaked to the bone. His hair hung in tangled lumps against the tips of his shoulders, but his expression lit when he saw Coraline. With that smile, she felt something in her loosen. A tension she hadn't fully appreciated until it was gone.

Then his eyes landed on Clinton occupying the chair he usually filled, having tea with his wife, and his expression considerably sobered.

"What's going on here?" he asked.

Coraline leaped from her seat and ran to greet him with a kiss. She stepped back, her palms moist against his coat sleeves. "Mr. Reed stopped by to see how Martha and I were. He thought I might need help without you here."

Jamison's frown only deepened. "I'm certain you were fine. Martha was here."

"That's what I told him."

He swallowed. "Still, I appreciate his concern. It's good to know you are cared for when we're apart."

Mr. Reed stood and pushed in his chair, stepping a little closer to Coraline. "She was a true delight." He nodded to Martha. "They both were. I'm sorry if I offended. I'll leave you to the Missus."

He was halfway out the door when Jamison called for him to wait. He reached into his pack and withdrew a muddied envelope still closed with a black wax seal. "A letter arrived for you."

"Mighty thanks." Clinton took it, but left the seal unopened. "I'm sure I'll have a reply for you to take back with ya." With a tip of his hat, he closed the door behind him.

It seemed as though the room performed a mutual exhale with his departure. There had been nothing untoward about his visit, no words exchanged that one could take offense to. But there was still an air in his presence that made Coraline feel ill at ease. Something about it felt unsure.

Martha dropped the empty laundry basket at the foot of the bed with a thunk. The room now resembled the Owens' house back in Charleston on most days. There were never enough outside strings to keep up with their customers, making it necessary to string inside, too. White sheets and aprons and colorful skirts and pantaloons made for a maze that Martha danced through on her way to get her cape from the hook.

"I'm going to check in on the Harpers," she said. "No doubt Marie has her hands full. Sarah hasn't been able to help much lately." With a smile and a squeeze to Coraline's elbow, she slipped out the door. She was always so intuitive, knowing when her friend wanted her to stay and when it was best not to.

Coraline expected Jamison to reach for her, but instead he drew another envelope from his bag. This one was already open. "We received a letter from Garrett, too. Nothing from your parents or Daniel though. It's bound to be another six months at least before anything arrives. If it ever does."

As much as she longed for news of home, she wasn't naïve enough to believe a letter would actually come. Not from a country apart.

"What does Garrett say?" she asked.

He opened the letter and began to read.

"Tobias, Jamison, Cade,

I would have written before, but I didn't know how to get you mail. Now that I have an address, I'll write more often.

Life in San Francisco is a different world than anywhere we've been. I can't begin to describe it. You'll just have to trust me. Or come visit. Actually, don't come visit. You might not return to your wives alive. Kidding...sort of. I was surprised to hear about Jamison and Coraline's wedding, more so to hear of Cade and Alice Ann.

—Wait until he receives the next letter I sent about the Tobias and Cade's babies," Jamison chuckled. "He'll be shocked."

"Do you think anything can shock him after two years in San Francisco?" Coraline asked. "Don't they have every sordid thing there?"

"I'm sure there's one or two he hasn't seen yet. For his sake." He continued reading:

"My search for gold has only been semi-profitable. I haven't hit it rich yet, but my luck is coming, I can feel it. Josiah and I are rooming above a saloon. The walls are like rice paper and we can hear all sorts of despicable goings on at night. I suggest not reading this to your wives."

Coraline shrugged. "It is California, after all."

"'I wish I could say when I might return, but I know my work here isn't done. I'll write when I know more. Garrett.

P.S. James, I always said you'd never become a priest. Glad to know as usual, I was right."

"I'm glad too," Coraline smiled.

Jamison immediately pulled her toward him, still clothed in his wet shirt, vest, jacket, trousers and all. His rough hands caressed her face as he kissed her breathless and there was no shortage of reciprocation on her part. It was like this every time he returned. When she was finally back in his arms, she realized how much she missed him.

Thirty minutes later, they lay before the fire, their thirst for one another fully satiated. With a kiss to her brow, Jamison pushed himself up and wove between the fluttering laundry to retrieve his only clean outfit from the clothing trunk. Coraline gathered the scattered pieces of his wet clothing, laying them out near the fire to dry, then turned to her own garments tossed in a heap.

She tugged on her chemise and pantaloons then stepped into her dress and tugged up the sleeves. Dressing was simply an act of propriety at this point. While she and Jamison were unlikely to leave this cabin until morning, at some point, Martha would return. There was no sense to scandalize her friend in her own home.

"How was your trip?" she asked.

"Positive. I think I might be reaching a few potential converts."

She smiled. "That's wonderful."

"Mmm." He ducked between two flowered skirts and she turned her open back to him. She could feel his fingers slip each button back into the loops he had so easily released before. She turned to face him, but his expression had fallen. He fumbled with his shirt buttons and gently, she shifted his fingers to button them herself. One by one up to the top. "Anwillik gave me some more of those shells you like," he told her. "She said we could use them to trade with Quea'Quim."

"If he ever shows himself again."

"She thinks he will. We attended Mass together every day while I was there. You have no idea the freedom that fills my soul in those few hours..." His hands covered hers and held them. "I want it to be important to you too. How can I convince you of God's goodness?"

She tensed beneath his touch as she always did when he brought up her skepticism. Nothing he ever said convinced her of anything except what she already knew. There was a God and He was silent. End of story. There were plenty of couples who never spoke of religion. Why couldn't he let the subject rest?

"I love you, Cora, and I want you to go to the mission with me. You can speak to the natives in a way I never can. I've been trying to learn the Jargon while I'm there, but it isn't the same as speaking it as you do. They will listen to you."

"Jamison..." She tried to shift away, but his grip moved to her waist.

"Anwillik misses you. Her brother hasn't visited Stella Maris since we fought in the chapel."

"That's my fault, I suppose."

"No, it's Quea'Quim's fault. He makes his own decisions. But if you went, it might convince him to visit too."

The plea in his voice, in his eyes, and the grip of his hands was unbearable. She loved him. She wanted to give him what he wanted. She just couldn't give him what he wanted in the way he wanted it. She feared a hundred years would pass and she never could. But she could give him a piece of what he asked.

"I offer a compromise. After Sarah and Alice Ann have their babies, we will go. They'll want to have them baptized."

"Do you promise?"

"I promise." With the smile that lit up his face, she would have thought she had just promised him the world.

21

December blew in soft and breezy rainstorms most every day. Hard waves crashed against the shore and left foam upon every cliff face. Based on Jamison's estimates, it was early for him to attend to the birth of Sarah's baby, nevertheless, he or she was on its way. Pinning a conception date was difficult in the best circumstances, and especially so living out here. She could be farther along than expected.

Likewise, Alice Ann's rotund belly indicated that his other niece or nephew wouldn't be far behind. Perhaps only a month or so. Which meant that, upon additional calculations, Alice Ann had been nearly three months along when she and Cade married. Not what he would have expected from his timid brother or from a family raised within their mother's virtue.

He didn't know who to reprimand more, his brother or his brother's wife. At least Geraldine Lark was no longer living to see this mess; however, he suspected if she was, Cade wouldn't have found himself in such a predicament to begin with. Certainly not with such an inhospitable woman.

Delivering his brothers' babies was hopefully as awkward a situation as he would find himself in with their wives. He little relished seeing Sarah or Alice Ann in such a delicate condition, and while a midwife would be a better fit, none were available. He was the only one in Larksong with medical knowledge enhanced by extraordinary skill. Having successfully delivered a few other babies on the trail, he trusted this time would be the same. He would simply need to overcome the awkwardness of femininity only a husband should ever see.

He snapped his black medical bag closed and reached for Coraline's hand. Together, they made their way across the damp earth to Sarah and Tobias's. Tonight, their town would finally start to grow.

When they entered the cabin, they found Sarah beside the bed, still on her feet but supported by Martha and Marie as she huffed through a birthing pain. Each woman held her by an elbow while Sarah's hands splayed upon her swollen abdomen. The skin visibly taut under her white nightgown, it left little to the imagination.

Flushed with embarrassment, not lessened any by the fire's warmth, Jamison moved farther into the room and toward his patient, only to be cut off a few steps in the door. Tobias jumped from his seat by the fire. Sweat pebbled his brow.

"I'm glad you're here, James. I've been so worried."

Jamison gripped his brother's elbow. "She's going to be fine."

"You're certain?"

A sharp cry echoed from Sarah's lips as her pain lessened and Marie and Martha eased her back to sit on the bed. Coraline went for the water dish on the bedside table, dabbing Sarah's brow and cheeks with gentle movements. The mother-to-be already looked spent and she had barely even begun to labor. Jamison worried that she might not have enough strength if the delivery carried into tomorrow. She had told him once how her mother suffered many miscarriages, eventually resulting in their purchase of Martha as a type of sister substitute. Stillbirths tended to carry in families. If Sarah had inherited the trait, there was little he could do to stop it.

He turned his attention back to his brother. "I'm certain. Now, this is no place for a father. Why don't you find something else to occupy your time? Levi's helping the children with their lessons, but Cade and Alice Ann planned to fit the cradles together today. They could use some help."

The suggestion was met with Tobias's usual grumbles. "Building isn't what it was without my Gift."

"But you still have hands and a brain to move them. Would you rather have lost your Gift or lost your hands?"

"I guess I see your point." He glanced at his wife, her own hands pressed to her knees. "If there's any change, find me immediately."

"I will."

With a tender kiss to Sarah's cheek, a squeeze to her hand, and an "I love you," Tobias grabbed his hat and exited the cabin.

After that, time seemed to lengthen. Afternoon turned to evening which in turn became darkest night. The sun rose then set once more and still Sarah labored. Marie left the first evening to care for her children and only returned with each meal she delivered. Since Sarah's cabin contained the only stove in town, family meals were cooked on a campfire in the yard. They were sustenance enough to provide Jamison, Coraline, and Martha energy to tend their patient. Sarah, meanwhile, couldn't keep even a morsel down. The one biscuit she chewed came up immediately and the birthing pain which followed sent her to weeping.

He thought about his own sisters, all three, who were stillborn. The Lark brothers always believed their father had been the death of those babies, but what if it had been natural? Jamison wasn't magical and he wasn't God. Others had died under his watch. Even with his Gift, it was entirely possible something could happen beyond his control.

Eventually, he had to remove himself from the cabin to escape the horrid thoughts swirling in his sleep-deprived brain. He claimed to need the necessary and strode calmly from the cabin.

The second he closed the door, however, he was set upon by Cade, Alice Ann, and of course, Tobias who appeared crazed in the light from Cade's hand lantern. His sleeping hours had been as minimal as the rest of them. "How is she, James? How are they both?"

"Fine as far as I can tell. It is taking longer than I would have expected, but since she's never birthed before, it could be the right amount of time for her. Every mother is different."

"Shouldn't *you* know, though?"

"I have extraordinary medical skill, Tobias, not omniscience. I'm sure she will turn up right as rain. Besides, 'it is better to take refuge in the Lord than to put one's trust in man.'"

"Yes, but also 'the Lord giveth and the Lord taketh away.' Babies and mothers die in childbirth all the time."

"They also live all the time, too. Have faith, Tobias. When was the last time you ate? A meal would help your nerves."

His brother stopped his pacing. "You might be right. I'm going to go hunting. Cade, would you care to join me?"

As usual, it was Alice Ann who spoke first. Her arms folded upon her bulbous stomach. "Should you be handling firearms in your current state? I'd like to live to see this baby born."

"You're probably right," Tobias agreed. "How about we walk down to the shore instead? Can you find me a couple oysters? Tell me about your business?"

She appeared startled by his interest. "Oh, certainly. I think we're going to have a banner year." Accepting Cade's offered arm, they started down the path.

Tobias shot his other brother a look as he moved to follow. "Take care of her, James."

Jamison waved him off with a smile. "She's going to be fine."

Those words repeated in his head as he watched his brothers and sister-in-law approach the ridge and then disappear down the opposite side. Waves rolled in the darkness, each crash like the Four Horsemen's thunderous hoofbeats chasing them down.

He felt Coraline's hand on his elbow. Her tired eyes met his. "We think it's finally time."

Either way, they would soon find out.

Coraline had guessed correctly. Within fifteen minutes, Sarah delivered a squalling son, then to their great amazement, another child began to crown. Jamison handed the boy off to Martha who set about wiping him clean while he instructed Sarah to ready herself a second time.

"There's another?" she gasped.

Coraline gripped her friend's hand and smiled. "Yes, you're to be a mother twice over."

Sarah released a lopsided giggle, a mix between a laugh and a cry.

"Tobias will faint."

"No," Coraline whispered. "Tobias will be overjoyed."

"Indeed," Martha said as she ran a wet rag over the newest Lark boy. "Babies are blessings, even unexpected ones. And what an adventure these ones will have."

What adventures indeed. Not long ago, Coraline doubted her vision would last to see any of her nieces or nephews and now, she was aunt to two and Alice's Ann's would make a third. Granted, the dim firelight was hardly helping her eyes relish the details, but she would hold fast to even the palest sights.

Sarah's face pinkened, her jaw clenched tight as she bore down once more, then again, and again. "Last one!" Jamison shouted. "Give me everything you have!"

Oh, Jamison, Coraline secretly smiled. *You're delivering a baby, not a sermon.*

Sarah's fingers squeezed Coraline's as she managed one final heave and collapsed back against the pillows. Her breath came in shallow gasps. "How...how...does he...look?"

Jamison paused and, in that pause, Coraline's excitement died. Her husband silently stared at the tiny human nestled between his palms.

"Jamison?" she said, but he didn't look at her. He didn't look at anyone but the baby.

"Here's your youngin'," Martha declared. She laid the still squawking boy upon his mother's chest and eased her nightdress open so the infant could suckle his first meal. He latched on immediately, his lips moving full vigor. "Looks like he's strong and healthy," she laughed. "What will you name him?"

But Sarah craned her neck around her friend, nearly oblivious to the child at her breast. "Cora," she cried. "Can you see the other one? Is it a boy?"

"A girl," Jamison said.

"Will you bring her to me?"

He shook his head and Sarah's cry raised an octave. She sat up and her son slid down her stomach, tiny arms flailing as he settled into the ridge between her legs. Martha snatched him up before he fell to the floor. "Jamison!" Sarah shrieked. Her arms shot outward. "Give her to me!"

"I'll do it." Cora ran to the end of the bed. She extended her arms for the child and in the same instant felt them fall to her sides. In Jamison's hands lay a porcelain figure, half the size of her brother with blue skin, semi-translucent in the candlelight.

The infant's beautiful eyelashes didn't flutter open. Her chest remained still as stone.

22

On the bench outside Sarah and Tobias's cabin, Coraline sat with folded hands, fingers curved around her glasses. A lantern flickered from the ground beside her, but even so, without her lenses, the night left her nearly blind. For once, she was glad. She hadn't wanted to see Jamison's face when he delivered that baby girl so still and fragile. She hadn't wanted to see Sarah's when everything inside her friend shattered. The joy of a healthy boy could not overcome the grief over a dead daughter.

They had all suffered death before, but not like this. None of them would ever be the same.

Tobias, Cade, and Alice Ann hadn't gone far when Sarah's mournful wails drew them back. Tobias tore up the ridge like a man chased by the devil's whip and threw open the door without a word of greeting. Initially, he saw his son in Martha's arms and his smile tore Coraline's heart to ribbons. Despair made her flee outside, right past her sister and Cade, amid all their happy laughter and the baby's slight squawking.

Only to be followed by the overwrought devastation of a father grieving his loss.

Her entire body winced at the sound. She flattened her palms over her ears, but couldn't block out the noise. Tobias's wails, his curses, language she had never heard uttered by any of the Lark men. Curses she would never forget.

"Father told us this would happen!" he shouted. "He told us women can't be Gifted, that any female children of the Gifted wouldn't survive. Our sisters didn't and neither did this one. We thought Father killed them, Jamison, but what if he was right?" His tone turned torturous, as though the mere words were like fire to his soul.

Jamison's, rather, were much softer. "He wasn't right, Tobias. Sometimes things happen."

"You're Gifted, Jamison! You should have saved her."

The breath chilled in Coraline's lungs. Her poor husband, being pressed from every angle. Guilt weighing like stones on the chest of the convicted. He wasn't to blame for this or for Oliver's death or anyone else's. She had been there as he delivered the babe. There was nothing he could have done.

Jamison released a cough before he spoke again. "She was stillborn, Tobias. She couldn't be saved. It happens sometimes with twins where only one survives."

"You're blaming this on my son then."

"He's a baby!" Sarah cried. "He would never do this intentionally."

"No," Jamison agreed. "He would have loved his sister. Just like we would have loved ours."

The door opened and he stepped from the house with the weary tread of a man thrice his age. Coraline settled her glasses back upon her nose, the thin light from the lantern enough to silhouette his movements. Without acknowledging her, he butted against the closed door and sagged his chin to his chest. Then he pressed a hand to his eyes and let a shudder pass through him. Running his palm down his face, he looked up and saw her watching him.

"You heard." Not a question. He knew she had.

She nodded. He sighed. "I don't want my father to be right."

"He isn't."

"He could be."

"He can't." She pushed up from the bench, counting her steps until she could clasp his arm. Her opposite hand threaded behind his neck as she lifted on toe to kiss him. "You've forgotten about me, Jamison. I'm Gifted and I'm still here."

It was the first time she had truly acknowledged herself as being like them, but there was no other reasonable explanation for what she could do. Normal polyglots needed to learn their languages, and they heard every language for what it was. What she did was something else entirely.

"I'm here, Jamison, and I don't plan on going anywhere. Alice Ann may not be Gifted, but she's an Owens woman, too, and she's alive. So is our sister, Mercy. You are not responsible for what has happened tonight. Neither is Tobias."

"Coraline...I just...I don't know anymore."

"How can you believe in God, yet not believe what I say is true? Isn't this far easier to understand than a faceless being?"

"I don't like when you talk about God that way."

"Maybe what you don't like is that I'm right."

She wished she could see his expression better. From what she could make out, apprehension lined every shadowed feature of his gaze upon her, eyes so filled with love and also a fear yet undefined. Once again, he wouldn't address the great Alexandrian Library that stood between them, his faith versus her logic. She might as well count herself back to the house. Heaven knew her exhaustion was greater than her need to convince him.

She refrained from laughing at her own poor jest. Heaven knew so much and yet did nothing.

"I'll see myself to bed." Retrieving the lantern from the ground, she had only reached a count of two before rain poured down, another ill-timed treat from heaven. The lantern's fire doused with a sizzle, pitching everything into darkness, save the dim outline from Tobias and Sarah's cabin window. Cold water streamed beneath Coraline's collar and down her spine, spreading chills through her as she turned about in the darkness, now uncertain which way led back to their cabin. Jamison's form was only an expanse of darker shadow which moved without clear form.

She grasped until her fingers located the wet cloth of his sleeve. With both hands, she clung to him in an attempt to catch her breath from the suffocating darkness. For weeks, her night vision had been disintegrating. She never tempted fate by leaving the cabin after supper. Until tonight.

"Coraline?" Jamison's tone held uncertainty. He likely thought her distressed over their conversation of faith or from grief over Sarah and Tobias's loss. Perhaps overwhelmed from a hostile rain on top of all else which had occurred. He would never suspect the truth. Not unless she told him.

She needed to tell him. There was no more skirting the subject. No more pages of the story she could artfully remove to write a different truth. Tears moistened her eyes, and it felt cruel to still be able to cry from eyes that couldn't see.

"Take me home, Jamison," she begged. "Please, please, take me home."

23

Despite a distance of barely fifty paces, the walk back to their cabin seemed interminable. Jamison led the way, keeping hold of Coraline as she sniffled into his coat sleeve and every sodden step felt laced in iron boots. Desolation gripped him by the suspenders and tried to drag him into the depths, where he would find nothing worth mulling over and everything worth casting aside. But still, his body wanted to fall back and land there, at least for a little while.

There was nothing he could have done for his little niece, but to have brought her brother so perfectly into the world only to watch her wither...it left him utterly helpless. If only he could lay hands and heal like Christ's apostles were commissioned. They went from town to town curing ailments, calling out demons, and saving lives, but Jamison was chosen for a Gift that only allowed for medical knowledge, but not ways to use it. Limitations to a legacy which his father held in such high regard. Limitations for a life that Alonzo Lark sacrificed everything for, including his own wife and children. Including his faith.

Thunder rumbled across the sky as Jamison peeled Coraline's wet hands away to lift the latch on the cabin door. He took a step inside, halted only when she grabbed the waistband of his trousers. When he glanced back, she was staring past him. "Don't leave me," she begged. "I can't see anything."

"I'm not leaving you. I'm going to light the lamp."

He moved farther into the room, expecting that she would release him, but her grip only tightened. He tried to make out her expression, but it was too dark to see what she was playing at. This seemed an inappropriate time to engage in intimacies.

"Stay here while I light the lamp." He moved to unlace her fingers, but her other hand seized upon him, her nails scratching through his shirtsleeve as they fumbled to find their grip. Both her arms came around him, and her cheek pressed against his back, sharp breaths punctuating his spine. She was practically gasping, fear palpable with every inhale.

His hands covered hers upon his chest. "Cora. We're going to get through this."

"Are we?"

He turned within her grasp, wrapping his arms around her so she folded into his embrace. Slowly, he ran his palm along her spine with soft shushes until her breathing slowed. He was a physician. He couldn't handle everything, but he could handle this. "Cora, everything will be fine."

She shook her head. "It won't. I should have told you before, but I'm going blind, and there's no cure."

"What do you mean? You told me you only worried over not having proper spectacles."

She continued to speak into his chest. "I have a disease in my blood. Passed from my father's family. Thankfully, Alice Ann and Mercy were spared. Every day, my vision grows worse until one day, it will disappear altogether. I've known since I was seventeen."

His throat plummeted into his stomach. What was she saying? She was going blind? This couldn't happen to them, not after everything else. They deserved fewer trials not more. "But the poultices. You said they helped."

"I lied. They did nothing. You told me yourself, your Gift can't fix what is meant to happen. This was ingrained in me when I was born. Some things are what they are. Like what happened to Sarah's baby."

Not for the first time, or the five hundredth, did he wonder what purpose their Gifts had. At one time, it seemed like they might be increasing in aptitude until Garrett left, Tobias lost his Gift, and Jamison failed to save another life. What good were these Gifts if they couldn't change the natural order of things? Coraline walked her life for twenty-five years with no knowledge that she even possessed a Gift. Now that she did, it rewarded her by stealing her sight?

She was right. Sometimes Giftedness could only go so far. Right now, it felt like it wasn't getting them anywhere.

"Why didn't you tell me?" he asked.

"How do you think it feels to have pity every second, others doing tasks that you're perfectly capable of yourself? Or worse, resenting you for not carrying your own weight? I worried if your family knew, they would make me leave."

"Do you honestly believe us to be so callous?"

"I couldn't take the chance. Marriage was my best option, and I knew you didn't believe in divorce."

"So, you trusted that I, the almost priest, would honor my vows." How was he supposed to feel about this? She had lied to him since the day they met, then tricked him into marrying her. She had hidden a monumental medical diagnosis from him, and he was a *doctor*! He was the very person she should have told first.

"You never needed to trick me, Cora. If you had asked, I would have married you a thousand times over."

"I suppose I realize that now."

"Did Oliver know about your ailment?"

"Yes."

"Before you married him?"

"Yes."

So, she told Oliver, but she hadn't told him. An emotional boulder slammed into him like a real one had been thrown. He huffed out a breath, her proximity far too close for comfort. He wanted to move to the other side of the room because that's how much space felt like was between them right now. But he would never thrust her into that darkness and make her stand on her own. No matter how much she may have hurt him.

"See?" she whispered. "Your hesitation reads volumes. I'll be a burden to you. I've ruined your life."

"My life isn't ruined."

"It is. You just don't understand yet. One day you'll realize it and you'll resent me. You'll wish you went in a different direction."

"Cora, how can you say that? I admit this will take some dealing with, but I'll do it for you. I love you." For her, he would swallow his hurt and his pride and tackle this challenge like he had every other.

"You say that now, but are you truly prepared for the road that lies ahead? You didn't live with my Papa's blindness like I did. You don't understand how it wore my mother down and stole Mercy's prospects of ever having a family of her own. It is a challenging life."

"Why are you even telling me this? Do you want me to send you away?" He drew her closer, despite being suffocated by today's pains. He wanted his wife closer than anything, so close he couldn't separate her being from his. "My niece died today. I don't want to lose anyone else."

"I'm sorry," she whispered. "I'm being selfish."

"No, you're afraid and fear steals our common sense. You don't know how many times I've wondered if I should have stayed in Charleston or gone anywhere else except for here. None of those things you said matter, though. I love you, not your eyes, not your limitations. I questioned myself all those months when Oliver was alive because my affection for you never diminished, not for a moment. Since coming to Larksong, it has only grown stronger." Gently, he kissed the darkness of her brow. "You are not a burden. I want to spend my life taking care of you."

"It could be a long life," she said.

"I pray it is."

"What about children?"

"I would like them."

"It will be difficult for me to help you raise them. How can I care for a child when I can't even find them? They could fall and hurt themselves, be on the floor bleeding, and I wouldn't know. I could be standing right next to them and I wouldn't know!" When her breaths quickened again, he let his palm again stroke upon her spine. Again, he kissed her brow.

"It would be difficult, Cora, but not impossible. We will find a way, if that's what you want too."

"I do...I just..." She inhaled on a shudder. "I'll hear our children laugh, but never see them smile. Hear them cry, but never dry their tears. You will basically live life alone, caring for all of us without anyone to care for you."

"I learned how to care for myself long ago. All us brothers did. Now you need someone to care for you." He withdrew his arms from around her and she immediately reached for him. "Don't be afraid; I'm not leaving you." He moved his hands to either side of her face and held them there. His palms cupped her cheeks while his fingers feathered around the back of her neck. Eyes closed, his thumbs reached up to circle her temples.

Some days he wished his ancestor never stepped foot on the *Oblique*. Sometimes he wished he wasn't here. It didn't matter how he felt. Feelings betrayed people all the time. He was Coraline's husband and that required strength. For now, he would cling to the only truth he had left and pray that the rest would reveal itself in time.

He pressed a kiss to her forehead then leaned in, nestling another upon either eyelid. Releasing one hand from its hold, he tilted her chin and let his lips brush over hers as his thumbs swiped the tears from her cheeks. When he edged away, her eyes were closed, but her breathing finally steadied.

"God brought us together," he told her. "And I don't question God's judgment. That belief is all I have to find the reason in it all. Loving someone doesn't mean you never doubt or question. It means that when you do, you know you're not alone."

Tonight, his brother lost a baby. His wife was going blind. Their town was only months away from the edge of starvation. They were drowning in adversity. *Drowning.* If they didn't allow someone to draw them from the sea, they would all be lost.

Sometimes God performed miracles, but sometimes He sent angels instead.

He took her hand and threaded it through his arm. "Hold onto me and don't let go." Then he led her out the front door and closed it behind them.

"Where are we going?" she asked through the pouring rain. She shivered against his side.

"To the beach. **My brother may be too proud to ask for help, but**

I'm not. Will you translate for me?"

The crashing waves swept high as Jamison stopped atop the ridge. "Quea'Quim," he shouted. "I know you're out there. Please, we need your help."

24

After accepting Quea'Quim's offer, the first act in their new town should have been where to plant the crop fields. Instead, it was where to bury Mary Grace. Chinook customs forbade burial too near the village, so Quea'Quim suggested a tradition of raising the body in a canoe supported by wooden poles. Over time, the flesh would decay and once reduced to bones, the remains would be buried. Such a tradition, however, was in firm contradiction to Sarah and Tobias's Christian beliefs. Ever mindful, Anwillik directed them to a peaceful cedar grove at an acceptable distance from the village. There they buried her, the first gravestone in Larksong's new cemetery.

Shamefully, the day of her niece's burial was one Coraline couldn't describe. Not because she had gone blind, but because she refused to pay attention. She remembered enough from Mary Grace's tragic birth; she didn't want to remember anything from her death.

Instead, during the funeral, she pictured the beautiful book alcove Jamison promised to build her in their new home. She would spend every moment she could there, gulping the stories instead of savoring them like she used to. There were so many books she hadn't yet read and the thought of missing out was torture. It paled, however, in comparison to the agony on Tobias and Sarah's expressions as they lowered their infant daughter into the ground.

As soon as Jamison finished his prayer, Coraline didn't wait to be escorted back. There was light enough to see on her own. She tumbled her way through the brush until she reached the nearest cedar lodge, then leaned against it to catch her breath. The new Larksong had already rent her emotions, and its restoration had barely begun.

Upon arrival, the village had proved to be a disaster, a mess of tangled overgrowth across cedar plank lodges, each the length of five Larksong cabins and as wide as two across. Despite their neglect, the abandoned homes were surprisingly sturdy, built far stronger than the Larks' ill-developed cabins. In three separate areas of each roof, round holes revealed the open sky, the largest being at the center, and on the ground beneath each lay a shallow pit for a fire. About five feet below the ceiling ran crossed cedar beams "used for preserving salmon," Quea'Quim explained. Those beams would serve the same purpose now but also provide space for dried herbs and laundry lines. Outset wall ledges, once used for sleeping, made an ideal area for storage and food preparation above the damp dirt floor.

At the village's center, the largest lodge lay in nothing more than charred ruins. Per Quea'Quim's instruction, it would not be reconstructed nor removed out of respect for the chief who died there. While having the Boston men nearby supposedly warded off evil spirits, he would not risk angering them further.

Of course, not all the Chinook had transplanted to Larksong, especially when presented with its no-slavery rule. Slavery remained central to Chinook culture, and while no disrespect was intended, the Larks agreed that their moral code stood upon freedom for all. Any type of slavery went against that ideal. Quea'Quim was none too pleased at this result; however, he remained along with around forty others including Anwillik, her son Tleyuk, and every one of the Stella Maris converts. They designated one lodge as the town chapel, including daily prayer services and monthly Mass during Father Lionnet's visits.

Quea'Quim explained that in Chinook tradition, many generations lived in one dwelling and often several families as well. The Larks, however, held that while Southern hospitality was fruitful, good walls and privacy made for better neighbors. Therefore, Quea'Quim selected those lodges on the western side, and at long last, was welcomed back with his tribe, exactly as he wanted. The rest of them divided the eastern lodges, two families per lodge separated by a newly constructed central wall. Coraline and Jamison beside Cade and Alice Ann. Sarah, Tobias, and baby Philip with Levi, Marie, and their children. Martha agreed to share with Anwillik, Tleyuk, and the converts, but of course, assured Coraline she would be by every day to help her. As the odd man out, Clinton Reed erected an area within the lodge-converted-stable beside his fenced-in cattle pasture.

By moving to a new claim site, they would lose their previous claims, but the reality was they likely would have lost them anyway. The United States government required progress of settlement and sustainability over two years, and they had barely accomplished the first and failed at the second. With the help of the Chinook, they would now be able to do both.

"Pardon me? Mrs. Lark?"

Coraline righted herself as Mr. Reed stepped from the shadows of the forest path, glancing back briefly as the rest of their family passed in silence. Jamison met Clinton's eyes and held them, his gaze hard until it moved to Coraline. Then it softened into a sad smile. "You won't be long?"

She nodded. "I'll come right after." As much as they enjoyed the promise of their new town, he still didn't like her off on her own, where anything could happen.

Once he left, Mr. Reed leaned against the lodge wall beside her, propping one black boot heel on the cedar. From beneath hooded lids, tender brown eyes met hers. He hooked either thumb within his waistband. "How are you, Mrs. Lark?"

She glanced away, through the overgrowth back to the cemetery of one. Angelic Mary Grace with fingernails no larger than ladybug wings and a halo golden with bright blonde fuzz. Her brother, Philip, squalled every night and whimpered more often than not during the day. He missed his twin. He was used to having Mary Grace snuggled beside him. What confusion that must cause to find her gone.

Biscuits, she scolded herself. It seemed she wasn't able to block out those emotions after all.

"I grieve for my friends, Mr. Reed," she told him honestly.

He nodded. "It's a natural thing to do. Have you given thought to what I asked ya before?"

She scoured her memory, but there were only bits and pieces jumbled together. A headache teased around her left eye and flirted with the promise of further pain. "I'm sorry. To what do you refer?"

"Seeking care for your eyes. Now would be a perfect time to go. Mary Grace is buried, the family has moved into their new homes, and the natives will protect and provide. Everyone is cared for. It's high and away time we cared for you."

Oh, yes, now she remembered. His offer to take her to the Willamette Valley...or anywhere she wished to go.

"I'm sorry, Mr. Reed, but I don't think it would be prudent. As you said, Mary Grace is barely buried. How could I leave—"

"Tell me, how is your vision?"

"I admit it's growing worse."

"And it will only continue to do so. Take the chance while you can, before you lose your sight altogether. I've been sending letters to my cousin. He says there's a man in California who might be able to help."

Her eyes shot back to his, hoping the suggestion was in jest. "California is no place for a Christian lady."

"Alone, no, but I'll be there."

He was serious, then? Garrett had sent multiple letters from California and not all were as tame as the first one. San Francisco was a hive of hornets and a den of foul and nasty coyotes. Every man for himself and no man for another. Women only worthwhile if they could provide pleasure to a man. No, she would not be going to California with Clinton Reed.

But what if? her brain pattered. What if he knows something you don't? If it meant a better life, would you go?

She pressed a hand to her head as pain built. *Don't do this to yourself, Coraline. There is no cure.*

For some reason, her lips said otherwise. "Jamison would need to accompany us."

Mr. Reed's stare darkened as though she had suggested something criminal. "Do you not think it better for him to remain here? His mission work is of such importance to him."

More important than me? she cared to retort, but that same annoying brain patter continued. *Was* she more important than his mission work? She wasn't even a believer in the strictest sense of the word.

"We could not travel unaccompanied. You are not even family."

Shifting closer, he reached for her hand and held it between his. He stood less than a foot away. "Do you not think proximity has made us such? I have no one else. No parents or siblings and my only cousin is far away. I know my merits have been questioned in the past, but the Larks have encouraged me to take a new lease on life. Helping my new family is of the first and utmost importance." He squeezed her fingers. "I'll prove it to you."

"Do that, Mr. Reed, and perhaps I will consider your offer." She released his hand and stepped away. "But only if Jamison joins us."

25

Coraline soon discovered that entertaining any idea of asking Jamison to leave with her would be a conversation spoiled. Barely a week later, on a beautiful January morning, Alice Ann flew into their cabin without a knock or advance announcement.

She supported her bulbous stomach with both hands as she waddled across the floor and lowered herself onto the bed. "It's time, Jamison," she declared. "You need to pull this baby out of me."

Coraline's jaw dropped, but her husband barely glanced up from his breakfast. "Always a pleasure to see you too, Alice Ann." He stabbed his fork into another slice of venison. "Where's Cade?"

"Still asleep."

"Why?"

Alice Ann pushed herself up on her elbows. "Why bother him with it? He wouldn't be any help. Oh, fish fiddles!" Every muscle in her belly and her face visibly scrunched as a birthing pain hit her, clear and powerful. She gripped the quilt beneath her and released an exhale along with a low groan. When it ended, she leaned back against the headboard and looked to her brother-in-law again. "Well? Come here and help me."

Jamison dabbed his lips with his napkin, folded it, and rinsed his plate in the wash tub before he so much as glanced in her direction again. When he did, he stood over her like a sentinel, arms folded across his chest and not a hint of amusement. He waited for her next pain to subside before he spoke. "I'll help you, Alice Ann—"

"Good."

"Don't interrupt me." Alice Ann snapped her lips closed. "I'll help you, but in your house with your husband conscious and aware of a need for the helping. I don't know why you insist on degrading him as you do, but Cade is my brother, and if you want my help, then you'll start respecting him."

Another pain struck with force and she bore down with a guttural cry. A slight whimper followed and Coraline rushed to her sister's side. "I'm here, Alice Ann."

"Tell your husband to help me!" she shouted.

"I gave you my price," Jamison told her. "You would owe far more than a polite continence if you hired a doctor back in Charleston."

"Papa would have paid my bill in Charleston!"

"You think your papa would be pleased with the way you behave?" he asked. "I think not." He turned his back then and, snatching his hat and coat from the hook, headed for the door. He paused before walking out. "I'm going to wake Cade. If you want my help, find a way back to your side of the lodge. Or perhaps Cora will take pity and help you there."

His final words were released in the rise of another birthing pain and Alice Ann's scream was the only reply as the door slid closed.

Coraline waited for her sister's pain to subside before she gripped her arm and tried to lift her from the bed. "Don't mind Jamison. He's merely frustrated. Of course, I'm afraid I cannot argue his point. You do treat Cade rather poorly."

Alice Ann glared at her. "You're my sister. You're supposed to—cripes and a pail of crawdads!" She fell back to the bed, her fingers clawing at her stomach. "Get it out, Cora! I don't want this thing in here anymore. Give it to Cade. He can have it!"

For a solid minute after, a string of curses tumbled from her lips, instigating a newfound consideration for her request to be a sailor.

Coraline shoved another pillow behind her sister's back and propped her against it, then requested she raise and grip her knees. She grabbed her coat. "Hold on, Alice, I'm getting Jamison. He'll help you."

At least, he had better. Her sister was in no shape to walk even if she had changed her mind. And Coraline refused to deliver this baby all alone. Jamison would see sense once he heard how close they were to the baby's arrival.

However, fifteen minutes into their discussion, Cade was the only one headed for Alice Ann's side. Jamison actually put a pot of tea on to boil rather than attend to his sister-in-law's delivery.

"Are you mad?" Coraline spat. "My sister is in labor and you refuse to help her."

"Your sister," Jamison said as he watched the fire, "needs a swift kick in the behind. She's a married woman and yet acts like she possesses no responsibilities. I'm frankly sorry she married Cade."

"You would rather their child be illegitimate?"

"Of course not, but I don't want him to have a shrew for a mother either."

"What if something happens like it did with Mary Grace?" Coraline touched his arm and he regarded her with compassion, rather than the anger his tone exuded.

"Then you don't hesitate, Cora. Come get me immediately."

She returned to her sister, every worry tumbling through her mind, but it was too late for any of them to reach fruition. Cade already sat beside his bride, one arm around her shoulders while they gazed upon the red and wrinkled infant on her chest. He ran to greet Coraline as she entered and grabbed her arm, dragging her to the bed. "Meet Julep!" he cried. Happy tears lined salt rivulets down his cheeks. "We have a daughter."

"What did you say?" Cora sank onto the bed beside him.

"A girl!" he repeated. "The Larks finally have a girl and she's ours."

A cool, yet pleasant breeze floated through the holes in the cedar ceiling, while bright daylight featured the infant's pink skin and healthy form. Alice Ann had indeed borne a living breathing daughter, a gorgeous girl with midnight black hair like her father and fairly little resemblance to her mother. As seemingly quiet and content as baby Philip was fussy. The arrival of a second child in the family should have been a joyous event, but a baby girl's survival after the recent death of Mary Grace was like salt in fresh wounds. Coraline already mourned for Sarah and Tobias once they learned their daughter's death was not due to her lack of Giftedness after all.

Still, she forced a smile. Cade was clearly overjoyed and for him, she was glad. Alice Ann may be a questionable wife and mother, but of Cade's devotion, she held no doubts.

"How many children do you and Jamison want?" he asked her.

Alice Ann reached over and slapped him. "That is a very personal question and highly inappropriate to ask." She then turned to her sister and grinned. "But it is also an answer I would be rather curious to hear. How many, my sister?"

When Coraline simply continued to stare at the baby, Cade leaned in and offered her the swaddled bundle. Julep slept on, happy as one of her mother's oysters in a seabed. Even so, Coraline rocked her gently, enjoying the warmth of the child in her arms. She was pleased as a peach to dote on her niece.

How she wished she could have this type of joy several times over. Especially with a daughter whose button nose held a smattering of freckles identical to her own. Nevertheless, a large family didn't seem like a dream she should waste time on.

Bending, she feathered a kiss to the child's crown. "If we have one, Cade, I do believe I'll find happiness."

That same afternoon, Coraline and Jamison strolled arm-in-arm along Mouse River, all the way to the ocean's shore. He drew her back against his chest and wrapped her in his arms, rubbing the gooseflesh rising even beneath her coat sleeves. Together, they watched the waves roll in, foam upon their boot toes, then slink back into the vast waters. The sea was a pale blue today like the skies above with no sign of clouds or rainstorms to spoil Julep's birthday.

"I'm sorry about this morning," he whispered. His breath warmed her neck opposite the wind's chill along her other side. "I suppose I should have helped Alice Ann even without her cooperation. I have a Gift and a Christian duty."

Coraline turned her chin to kiss his cheek. "Piety is not required every second. Alice Ann does not make it easy for one to love her."

"Even so, I should have been there for her."

"Cade was there and he is her husband. Perhaps that is more important in the end." She turned back to the sea as the wind gusted a spray of sea salt upon her glasses. She wondered if her father ever made it to the shore anymore. Without her or Alice Ann to guide his steps, Mama and Mercy likely wouldn't. There wasn't time for leisure in their lives. "I will miss this," she said softly. "It is too many steps to navigate from town to shore once my vision leaves, and I would never want to bother you daily."

"I have been considering that myself, and I believe I have a solution."

"Do you?"

"I do." Releasing her from his arms, he turned her shoulders so they both faced the path back to town. He extended a hand in gesture. "Did you not notice the addition to the trail?"

Peering back from where they came, she noticed wooden poles lining the path. About three feet high and six inches around. How had she not taken note of their existence before?

"What are those for?"

She didn't need to see his smile to understand his enthusiasm. It poured from his words and the way his fingers curved with excitement around her shoulders. He pressed a kiss to her neck then a second. "They're for you. Cade is helping me braid rope. When it's finished, we'll attach it along the poles to create a line from our front door down to the water. You can visit whenever you'd like."

Whenever she'd like... She wouldn't be limited to the town. She could still feel the ocean breeze and dip her toes in the water whenever she liked, even without help.

She wanted to thank him for this beautiful gift, but what words could express her gratitude? She had noticed the burns upon his fingertips this past week, but assumed it was from all the other work being done to build the town. She never suspected that after those long days of service, he would force his exhausted fingers to carry on, only for her.

She closed her eyes and reached for his hands, drawing them around her shoulders. Her fingers grazed the rough skin of each palm and every fingertip. "I hope my eyesight holds until it's finished," she whispered.

"If it doesn't, I'll walk you here myself. Every day."

In the darkness behind her lids, she listened to his even breaths mix with the hard thump of each wave as it beat upon the shore. The soft swoosh as it pulled back out to sea and began the cycle again.

Experience all the beauty of this world, her father had told her, *before you can no longer see it.*

Her eyes still closed, she rose on toe to kiss her husband. She felt those calloused hands slip from hers and draw her in like sea spray upon stone.

Perhaps some beauty would still remain, even after the darkness.

May 4, 1854
San Francisco, California

Jamison,

*You **were** no doubt shocked at my bundle of letters, rather than the usual one. After you sent the news about Mary Grace, it seemed best to write everyone their own. Things I needed to say that probably should be read alone. Sorry if the extra correspondence becomes a hardship.*

How is Tobias? Remember how he was when our sisters died? He is probably doting on Philip far too much. Tell him not to get too sentimental.

In other news, Cade is a father now? You about knocked me over when you told me he got married, but having a baby with that wild girl? She belongs better here in San Francisco than washing mess from some kid's bottom and pretending to be happy about it. You mark my words— and you know they're always right—Cade's not coming out of this intact.

No luck yet on my Gift's calling. Haven't found anything yet that makes sense. The gold mine Josiah and I were working came up a bust, but we've been hired on at another and are seeing a slight bit more profit. Not a chance we'll be home by the end of the year. Hopefully, next summer will bring success.

Speaking of success, what is this you wrote about joining some Indian tribe? I'm happy to hear that they've been good to you, but this Quea'Quim fellow seems rather off. He spied on Coraline for months without her knowing? Back in Charleston, that would be grounds for an arrest. I hope you know what you're doing.

I must end this letter, but since it seems other men are allowed privileges with Coraline, make sure to give her my love too. No, seriously, all night. Prove you're not a priest. Just jest, James! My attraction certainly doesn't lie with your wife. It lies other places, but such stories would only scandalize your puritanical sensibilities. Perhaps when you're older.

To be serious for a moment though, does she romance you in other languages when you're alone? Because that sounds pleasantly provocative. Still can't believe there's female Gifted. I wish Father was alive so I could shove it in his face.

Good luck with the summer planting.

Garrett

26

Coraline was blessed with another year before the darkness swallowed her days as well as her nights. One more birthday, one more Christmas and Easter and Independence Day. Their first wedding anniversary came and went; Coraline turned twenty-six and Jamison twenty-nine.

The once-abandoned village had now blossomed into vibrance. Trees cleared to make room for wheat, corn, and potato fields. Freshly turned gardens abundant with green beans, sweet peas, and blueberries. A cleared path along Mouse River revealed a landscape fertile with blackberry vines, wild gooseberry, nettles, and ferns. Wild rose briars were transplanted and trimmed into tidy bushes beside each lodge, providing a small Southern comfort on their homesick days.

Where the river met the sea, Chinook canoes regularly streamed outward in search of salmon. At forty-six feet in length, six feet in width, and carved from a single cedar tree, they possessed naval beauty beyond compare. Each canoe sliced through the water with awesome precision, the waves no match for the natives' solid muscles upon the oars.

Nearly every evening, Coraline awaited their return through a Pacific sunset, its orange and purple glow burning itself into her memory. At night, she wrapped herself in her husband's arms, every lantern and candle lit so she could embrace every detail washed in their flickering glow.

She and Jamison were together the night before her vision finally extinguished. Hours spent awash in the other's love, almost as though they could sense that it was the final time anything about their lives would be normal. By that point, she could barely see more than a pinprick in front of her, like staring down a long train tunnel and no amount of squinting could make out the locomotive coming.

Not until it hit her dead on.

She opened her eyes one morning in February and everything looked the same as in sleep. Her fingers flew to her eyelids, but they moved up and down as before. There was simply...nothing.

She couldn't help it—and felt foolish for having done it—but she screamed. Her heart exploded in a twelve-horse racetrack of thrashing hooves and dirt explosions, unable to know which way was forward. She clutched at the front of her nightdress and choked on air that tasted like rain. Her eyes swiveled and she felt them move, but nothing changed.

Nothing changed!

"Coraline!" Strong hands cradled her against a broad chest, her husband's chest. Curled in a ball upon his lap, she wept and wondered how she could feel so unprepared. She knew this was coming. She *knew*. Her parents had prepared her. Her doctors had prepared her. Oliver then Jamison. She saw what life was like for her father, but she hadn't realized it would be like this. This...this paralyzing fear. Anger. Grief and distraction. Longing. Terror.

Please, God, she cried. *Please! I will do anything to make this go away!*

As usual He remained silent. She hated Him, and she hated herself.

She wanted her father.

She *needed* her father.

Maybe she should have gone to California. What if Clinton Reed was right?

None of that mattered now. There was no going back.

She couldn't bear to sit in this bed surrounded by her despair and Jamison's compassion for another minute. Her heart was about to flee her chest. She would die if she stayed here.

Something familiar, that was what she needed. Books. She needed books.

Shoving away from her husband, she dropped her bare feet to the dirt and stumbled her way toward the beautiful reading alcove Jamison created for her. Two entire bookcases dedicated to her novels and a rocking chair to read them in. A side table and a lantern on top. How she loved that alcove, although it wasn't technically an alcove at all.

Twenty-two, twenty-three, twenty-four. She was almost there. Just a few more feet.

Her foot slammed into the swoop of the rocking chair leg. Pain shot up her ankle as she tumbled over the piece and onto the floor. Jamison's shout followed and then he was there, lifting her up and setting her in the rocker. When she tried to stand, he settled her back, his hands on her shoulders.

"No, Jamison!" she shouted. "I need to do this. I need my books!"

"Cora..."

"I'm all right, Jamison!" Although, he would have to be dense as mud to believe that. When his hands disappeared, she pushed out of the chair. "Please, point me toward the shelves." Her vocal control surprised even herself.

With his direction and her outstretched hands, she found her beloved books. Her fingers traveled their spines, trying to remember what they looked like and the placement of her favorite novels. She realized that she couldn't remember. All her careful planning had been moot. Opening a book at random, the scents of parchment and cloth, leather and ink drifted over her. Another brought the dank odor of the trunk it had been packed in, surrounded tight with hay. Her nails dug into the supple fabric cover. It was one of the thicker novels, perhaps *Jane Eyre* or her father's beloved Dickens, but otherwise indistinguishable.

Grief found her anew. The volume tumbled from her fingers as tears flowed. By the sound, the book landed face up, but she had no way to find it except for casing the floor.

"How can I help?" Jamison asked. She leaped back at his nearness, her hip colliding with the shelf behind her. She hadn't realized he was there.

"What if I read to you?" he suggested. "I know it isn't the same, but it's...well, it's..." She heard him move. His warmth leaned past her as he selected a book from the shelf. "*Swallow Barn*? Would you like that one?"

She nodded. He led her back to the bed where they curled up together under the quilt, Coraline nestled within his arms which right now, brought her little comfort.

"'Swallow Barn is an aristocratical old edifice, which sits, like a brooding hen, on the southern bank of the James River," he read. "It looks down upon a shady pocket or nook, formed by an indentation of the shore, from a gentle acclivity thinly sprinkled with oaks whose magnificent branches afford habitation to sundry friendly colonies of squirrels and woodpeckers.'"

With every word, tears trickled down her cheeks. Oh, her dear sweet husband. He deserved so much better than this.

27

The day Coraline went blind, Jamison knew he lost more than merely his patient's eyesight. Somehow, he also lost his wife.

Ever since her scream woke him from a dead sleep, he never recovered his good sense. He hadn't meant to shout her name with such panic. His entire body had tensed, his arms stiff as he closed her tighter into his hold. Heat seared inside, brighter than fire and twice as hot. He had prepared for this moment, when her eyesight would fail completely. He told himself how he should react and to face it with the compassion of a husband drawing on God's grace. Every day he had prayed. But he hadn't been prepared. Could he ever be?

This is your life, he scolded. *You cannot lose heart on only the first day.*

Except the first day quickly descended into many days then weeks and months. Coraline's words became fewer and she reached for him less often until one night in May she didn't reach for him at all. He kissed her goodnight and there was no reply.

Her silence contributed to his own until their house resembled a coffin. Full of ghosts of a marriage that once brought them such joy. He could have sat at the breakfast table with his wife or read aloud to an empty room and found no difference in the experience.

"Coraline," he said one morning as he spooned oatmeal into her bowl and nudged it against her hand. "Please speak to me. I know this is difficult for you, but it is also for me, not being able to help you, not knowing what you need... What can I do?"

Her blank stare traveled past him to the cedar wall. Her fingers tapped across the tabletop until she found her spoon then tapped the air until metal clanked against the bowl's wooden rim. She scooped the first bite into her mouth without reply.

He swallowed a lump of raw sorrow, thankful she couldn't see the grief laid bare on his expression. Her tears kept him awake at night when she thought he couldn't hear. She didn't need to hear his now.

He picked up his spoon then set it back down. His fingers reached for hers but then drew back. His touch could startle her and she would drop her spoon—and possibly her oatmeal—into her lap. It had happened before and her cheeks flushed with embarrassment when Jamison hurried to wipe her skirt clean.

"Cora, please," he said instead. "We haven't walked to the shore in weeks. Would you like to go before I join my brothers for the day?" He and Cade had completed the rope guide long ago, but even with their enthusiasm, Coraline hadn't taken advantage.

She didn't take advantage now either. She shook her head and slurped another spoonful.

He tried another avenue. "Would you like a visit from Anwillik? I can ask Martha to fetch her on the way over this morning." The Chinook woman was one of few able to draw more than two sentences out of Coraline lately. Martha being the other one. Perhaps if the two women arrived together their teamwork would find success.

Again, Coraline shook her head. "Not today."

"Tomorrow?"

"I don't think so." Two bright tears traced down from her empty eyes and Jamison couldn't stand to sit there. He pushed his chair back and carried his full oatmeal bowl to the wash tub. Prudence, however, made him swallow it down before dunking the dish in the two-day-old water. He scrubbed any last traces away, then dried and set it back on the wall shelf.

"You should go." She still stared at that same spot on the wall, nowhere near him. "Martha will be here soon."

How he wanted to. Lately, he lived for the weeks he traveled to Stella Maris and left Coraline in Martha's care. To remove the pressure from his chest and pretend like nothing wedged within it. He craved those trips as much as he hated their time apart.

He settled his hat upon his head and retrieved his coat, one hand clenched around the fabric still caught upon the hook. "Cora, it doesn't have to be like this. I want to help."

"You do. You help others every day. You're an excellent physician and a wonderful homilist. You've saved many people, but you must give up on trying to save me. It cannot be done."

His fingers dropped from the hook. It was more words at once than she had expressed in a week. Despite their empty tone, it gave him confidence.

"Cora, I understand you say you don't need saving. You're a strong enough woman. Even without your eyesight, think of what's still out there to experience. Get to know the natives. Speech does not require sight. Use the Gift God has given you."

She shifted her face, no doubt believing she looked away, when in fact her hollow stare now drove straight through him. "I would prefer you ceased preaching. I don't even believe in God."

"You mean you don't trust Him?" It was what she admitted before they were married. That she believed God existed, but that He didn't care.

This time, however, she shook her head *no*. "I mean I don't think He ever existed. I'm sorry."

For a man who based his every fiber on God's word, it was a requirement for his wife to do the same. An ever-present hope that one day he would be able to win her over. How could he preach the Lord's unfailing love while his wife claimed He had none to offer?

"Are you leaving then?" she asked.

His boots were stuck to the floor, his hand like glue upon his jacket. How could he have landed in such a place as this? This wasn't how their life was supposed to go. For a year, marriage had been wonderful. He could remember every perfect moment...

Her high-pitched cry jolted him into motion. The pretty picture vanished into the real-life image of his wife tumbling upon the floor. Her attempt to navigate the table edge had failed. Instead, she nicked her hip against the wood and stumbled. One hand connected with the chair and it toppled down upon her.

Jamison flew to her side. He grabbed her arms and helped her stand. His eyes roamed over her for injuries. "Are you hurt?" he asked.

She shoved him away and unprepared for the force, he backed into the table himself. Whirling, she spun in several tight circles without comprehension before falling into a heap on the floor. She covered her face with her hands. "Leave me alone!" she shouted. "I don't need your help and I don't want it."

"Cora..."

"No, Jamison! I don't. You don't want me and I don't want you and we never wanted any of this."

"Cora, that's just not true." He squatted beside her, but when he touched her shoulder, she scrambled away. He was left with his hand outstretched. "I'm sorry, Cora."

"Don't be sorry. You did nothing wrong."

"Then why won't you talk to me? It sure feels like I must have."

A violent knocking shattered whatever sentiment they might have said as Clinton stomped into the room, his spurred boot heels clanking. He pushed right past Jamison and swept Coraline to her feet. As she had done with Jamison, she tried to shove him away until he spoke. "It's Clinton Reed, Mrs. Lark. You don't need to be alarmed."

She went still and Jamison wanted to punch the living daylights out of that man. He had never liked him much anyway, even if he did help save Tobias's life.

"Why are you here, Clint?" he ground out.

"I heard her scream." Clinton's glare could have cut glass. "Why was she on the floor? Did you hurt her?"

"No. Leave her alone." Jamison straightened to his full height which was about even with Clinton's. "What's happening here doesn't concern you."

"Maybe not right now," he sniffed, "but you'll leave town tomorrow or the next day. Head off to that mission to give a sermon or convert an Indian, anything to avoid being a husband. Some God-fearer you are. You can't even keep to your vow to honor and cherish your wife."

"Get out."

"Gladly." Clinton tipped his hat, a foul smirk lining his lips in a move only Jamison could see. The door slammed behind him.

Coraline didn't speak again until Martha arrived and Jamison left to meet his brothers in the fields. Even when he returned home that evening, he didn't mention Clinton's accusations and neither did she.

Two days later, Jamison was on his way to Stella Maris.

28

To Coraline, all she seemed useful for was as an interpreter between the "Boston men" and the Chinookan. She couldn't read, she couldn't sew or cook or even entertain her nephew or niece. The littlest Harper children were afraid of her and her "empty eyes." She could either speak for the tribe or speak for Larksong and then walk the rope path to the beach and back again. She could sink her toes in the sand and listen to the waves and pray they might drag her out to sea and never spit her out again.

Jamison was away more often than not. Gone at the mission for weeks at a time. When he was home, he spent most days in the fields with his brothers and at night, he cooked supper and ate in cold refrained conversation. After a few months, he stopped asking how she was. By November, their meals were silent and their bed even more so.

He never reached for her. Not that she would have let him.

Often in the evenings, they heard Levi pick up his fiddle and play a ditty outside his lodge. They could hear Marie's bright singing and their children's laughter mix with conversation as the rest of town emerged. It reminded Coraline of the dances on the wagon trail and the beautiful engagement party the week before their wedding. She remembered Jamison folding her into his arms and refusing to let anyone else take her from him. His smile held such adoration that day and for so many after. She had been his world and he became hers. How she loved him in those moments. Now, she forgot what the word meant.

Perhaps incapable of faith, she had made him incapable of love. Blind to emotions and blind to the world. Oliver would be ashamed of her. Her parents would be ashamed of her. She was ashamed of her. Only Alice Ann had the courage to admonish her to her face.

But she couldn't make it any other way.

"Would you like to join me outside?" Jamison asked one night after supper. They hardly ever ate with the family anymore. She heard the clatter of supper dishes as he stacked them on the wall shelf. The muffled pad of boot heels against the dirt floor drew beside her. "I don't have to dance," he told her. "We could sit together and listen to Levi play. You used to love his twaddle."

Coraline wanted to smile with the familiar term Oliver used to use, but it only made her eyes swell with tears.

She shook her head. "No, you go on ahead. I'll listen from here. I'll likely head to bed soon anyway."

Her fingers itched to reach out to him. She wanted him to scoop her up and hold her while they wept together. Instead, he left the house and she wept alone.

For six months, it seemed the tears never ended. No matter how lively Levi's tunes, they always played a serenade to her sorrow.

Sometimes, instead of crying, she would scream inside her mind. Yell at the nonexistent being her husband insisted would use everything for good. But good never came. This was hers forever now.

"I hate you!" she screamed. "Why would you do this to me?" Counting her steps while also attempting to run, she rushed toward the bookshelves, her hands out before her until she misjudged the direction and slammed painfully into the bedpost. Grabbing the quilt, she dropped on the floor in a heap.

Christmas swept by in a frenzy of excitement, felt vividly by the new Chinook converts and ignored by the remainder of their tribe. Gifts were exchanged by all, the type which would have been considered insignificant back at Larksong Plantation and relatively scoffed at by Jamison's father. Here in the wilds of Washington, however, they held more meaning than any other Christmas morning. Trinkets crafted from wood, stone, and shell. A collaborative feast which showcased the best talents of either side, even from those without Gifts.

Christmas Mass was exchanged for a simple prayer service until Father Lionnet could visit the week after the New Year, and then they celebrated in proper style with prayers, hymns, and a jubilant nature which Jamison wished could extend to every reach of his life.

Even at his worst, the holidays always reminded him of how blessed he was, but this year it felt more difficult to remember. His wife's hand lay cold against his arm, her expression solemn and voice silent. Not even the soft rabbit pelt he asked Quea'Quim to help him tan brought her any joy. He intended to lay it across her lap and entice her touch, but she approached its reception with little enthusiasm.

"Thank you, Jamison," she said, her tone as wooden as ever. "Being as I am, I wasn't able to make anything for you. I'm afraid I'm not much use here."

Once outside the lodge, he leaned against the door, despair a cravat which threatened to strangle him at every hour. A nightmare he tried to wake from and never could. His head fell back against the planking as his hands covered his face, tears rolling unchecked down bristled cheeks. Slowly, he slid to the ground and buried his grief in folded arms. Thankful for the night and that their door faced the woods rather than the open space used for merrymaking.

Levi's fiddle spurred up memories of happier times, when his wife still loved him and he knew how to be a husband. When he wasn't questioning God and having his faith tested at every turn.

It was no wonder his success at the mission had been only mediocre. He knew his personal feelings were circumventing his ability to provide believable testimony to any potential converts. How would they come to know the Lord if he wasn't even sure how much he knew anymore?

God was still good, right? Even in the midst of sorrow? He had to be; otherwise, what was this all for?

Had Coraline been right when she said that Jamison would regret marrying her? Sometimes he did feel like their marriage—or lack thereof—held him hostage. Maybe he did resent her for what their life had become. Or was it entirely his fault? He had loved her for years, been so thankful to marry her, and then in the face of adversity, lost all devotion. As her husband, maybe he should take her to the Willamette Valley or to California like Clinton suggested, but as her physician, he worried over the wisdom of indulging such fantasies. Her disappointment was bound to be great and grief could turn her head to madness. He could only imagine the anguish which already consumed her.

"Jamison? I'm sorry to bother but..." He raised his head as Martha knelt before him, her brown eyes round pools of compassion. "...is there anything I can do?"

He ran the back of his hand across both eyes, but knew the damage was plain to see, even in the twilight. Coraline's weeping continued from the other side of the door. "Martha, I...I just don't know. Was I wrong to marry her?"

"You love her. How is that wrong?"

"Because she's miserable. All the medical knowledge in the world and there's nothing I can do. Would she have been better off back in Charleston? Or somewhere else? They have doctors specifically for the blind, institutions she could attend. People to care for her who don't have other obligations."

"She wouldn't have you."

"Precisely. Even with my Gift, I can't help her. Clint keeps mentioning to me how he knows of these healing places and he won't leave it be. He keeps cornering me in the stable and telling me how he could take her there. The worst part is, I think he may be right."

Martha shifted back on her boot heels, speculation laced upon her expression and her tone. "Do you really think Mr. Reed would be a better companion than you? You're her husband."

"I told you. I have other obligations here. My brothers already lost Daniel and Garrett. I can't leave them short again nor leave Larksong without a doctor or a spiritual guide. Father Lionnet still only visits monthly and my letters to the Archdiocese for a permanent assignment have gone unanswered."

She frowned. "It sounds like you have everything worked out then."

"I think I do." The more he considered it, the solution seemed viable. He had prayed for a way to help his wife, and now he had one. She missed her parents, and she needed more care than he could provide. Going back to Charleston meant she could have both and finally be happy again. He wouldn't be, but after a time, life would move on, and so would he. He could dedicate his time to sharing God's word and become a priest of sorts, even if he could not become one in actuality.

"I'll ask Clint to wait until spring to leave. Winter's no time to trek through the mountains. That gives us enough time to tie up all the loose ends between us and divide our belongings. Please don't tell her. I'd like to be the one to share the news."

For a moment, it appeared Martha wouldn't agree. Then she nodded. "Of course. You should be the one." Her frown sank low as her fingers slipped across her skirt, hesitated, then dropped feather light upon his. "Might I, however, offer another option?"

He nodded.

"Don't. Stay together and fix things."

"Fix things?" He stood so abruptly, she fairly fell off balance, almost into the dirt. He reached a hand down to help her up and quickly released it. "I *can't* fix things. That's why we're having this conversation."

"Be with her. Pray with her. Isn't that what you always tell me?"

"She doesn't want that. She doesn't even believe God exists. Whenever I mention it, she only hates me more."

"She doesn't hate you, Jamison. She loves you."

She has a strange way of showing it, he thought. When was the last time they held each other's hand, much less a meaningful conversation? When was the last time she said the words, "I love you" in that order and in reference to him? Probably the day she went blind. Nothing had been the same between them since.

"Maybe she doesn't hate me," he conceded, "But if not me, then she hates God and how is that any better? At least now I'll give her something to believe in."

Back in the lodge, Coraline cuddled the rabbit pelt against her cheek, running her finger pads along its soft length. She could admit the thoughtfulness of the gesture. Jamison had given her a gift she could enjoy whenever she wished. She wondered what color it was. She should have asked, but that would require engaging him. What, truly, was the purpose in engagement now that he planned to send her away?

She figured she would have wept at the news that her husband didn't want her, but surprisingly, she hadn't shed a tear. Her focus had been on the rabbit and a mind blank as a slate fallen in the winter's snow. And as numb as the fingers which drew it from the ice.

When a knock sounded at the door, she ignored it. If it was Jamison, he would give himself leave; if anyone else, they would depart in time.

As such, neither was the case. Without another knock, the door opened and closed. Multiple footsteps tred across the floor toward her.

"Merry Christmas!" Martha called. Her cheery salutation was followed by Anwillik's sweet wishes in the Jargon.

Before Coraline could speak, both ladies arms were around her, wrapping her in a blanket of chilled appendages and warm mint-laced breath. For several solid minutes, the women sat together and even when Coraline wriggled against them, they refused to let her go.

"It's Christmas," Martha said. "You should be outside celebrating with us."

"I can't participate."

"Have you lost your hands, your ears, your tongue? Are you unable to sing and clap? We can see that you have not."

Finally, the women drew away, yet their presence didn't drift far. Martha laid a hand on Coraline's hand, still splayed upon the rabbit pelt. Anwillik's boot slipped against Coraline's to show that she was near.

"What good is Christmas without seeing everything you love?"

Coraline asked. "Most of our town doesn't even want me there."

"Of course, we want you there," said Martha.

"Not all of you."

"Who?" A slight edge ringed her tone. Coraline wanted to shout that she heard Martha's confidences with Jamison outside their door. She wasn't eager, however, to let others know how easy eavesdropping had become since her blindness. Nor did she want to implicate her husband or her friend.

"Quea'Quim," she deflected. She spoke directly to Anwillik, knowing her words would translate. "He used to follow me like a wolf on the prowl. Now, he can visit in the open, yet he never seeks me out."

"You have a husband now," Anwillik chuckled. "He is your protector, and my brother knows his place. Yet, do not doubt that he is grateful. You restored life to him. He is a leader of our people. And I have my brother beside me, even if our spirits remain apart."

Her words should not have bothered Coraline, yet they did. "I understand."

"No, Coraline, you do not. My brother and I grew alone in our tribe. We did not have the flattened brow and we did not have the tribe's support past living in the village. My husband accepted a great risk to marry me. When he died, it drove me to Christ and my own tribe turned even further against me. A wedge formed between me and my brother. But I had my faith and I had Tleyuk, and eventually, I found a way to move forward. You returned Quea'Quim to me and created this new home for us. You too lost a husband and look how far you have come."

One step forward, two steps back. She wanted to be happy as she once was, but how? Every day she drifted farther and farther away from the life she knew. It felt easier to let the current take her than to fight against it. According to Anwillik, Jamison was supposed to be her protector, but he simply couldn't protect her from this. No one could, but he at least, could admit defeat.

"Come along, Cora," Martha said. "It's time to join the others."

She clasped Coraline's hands between hers and without warning, lifted Coraline to her feet. She could visualize her friend's steady smile, those russet lips turning up on either side. Martha had always been her source of comfort. She missed living in the same place together. Martha helped her every day, but she shared her time between Marie's children and Anwillik and her son. Bless her then, for trying to convince Jamison to keep Coraline near. Martha deserved a good man like Jamison. Coraline supposed after he sent her away, her friend would be free to have him.

Fresh sobs lodged in her throat and she desired nothing more than to curl into her bed and weep until dawn. "Thank you for coming," she told her friends, "but I don't feel up to merriment this year."

"Of course, you don't," Martha said. "We, however, have arranged everything."

Coraline felt her crisp wool cape wrap her shoulders, the one she hadn't worn since Christmas last. That night, she had dressed in her best and celebrated with spruce bough trimmings and a fat cooked goose. "What have you arranged?" she asked.

"A surprise," Martha told her. "One which requires no eyes to enjoy."

Looping her arms through theirs, they directed her out the lodge's front door into the midst of chatter and carols upon Levi's fiddle. The fire's heat wafted upon her face in contrast with the chill at her back and her friends' warmth at either side. Another few paces and their footsteps must have reached the townspeople for their conversation ceased and Levi halted his rendition of "Hark the Herald Angels Sing" mid-twang.

The entire town stared and it didn't take eyes to recognize it.

Martha's hand tightened around Coraline's fingers. "Our friends and family are all here. No one is in fancy dress or decoration. No one is dancing. Tonight, there is nothing festive to see. It is only us, Levi's music, and good conversation."

An entire evening where Coraline could remain seated in one place, not worried about tripping over anyone or anything, and all participants making a concentrated effort to include her. She longed to feel gratitude, joy, relief. She wanted to believe this could lead to happier days. One step forward and then another. No steps back.

"You planned this?" she asked Martha.

"Indeed, I did. Anwillik helped, although it was difficult at times when our languages clashed between us. Despite living together, we're still learning. Tleyuk knows rather a lot of English now, did you know? He's been translating for us."

Coraline hadn't known that about Tleyuk. Even when she could see, she rarely saw the boy. He was focused on making friends with Marie's children and tagging after the Lark brothers whenever he could. Life continued on.

Martha and Anwillik led Coraline across the gathering, the fire's warmth shifting to her left as they lowered her to the ground. Anwillik moved away, but Martha settled into the space beside her. She deposited Coraline's hand into someone's on her opposite side.

"I'm glad you came," Jamison said softly. He squeezed her fingers inside his cold grip. Without gloves, his palm sat flush with hers, his thumb tracing a line along her own. She recalled the night he held her hand to stitch her wound. All she had needed back then was one touch to send shivers up her spine. They had loved each other, but she had tricked him, and now that trick meant he wanted her gone. One night would not change that. Tomorrow he would remember and all would be the same as the day before.

Perhaps for tonight, however, through the mirror of her tears, she could pretend that everything was as it had been before.

"Oh, Levi?" she called. "Do you know 'Silent Night'?"

"Why yes'm," he replied. "I's sure do."

He drew his bow through the first lines of the carol and Coraline sang her soul as high as the stars above her.

Lord, I'm still waiting, she thought. *I'm offering you one more chance. If you're up there, it's time to let me know.*

December 10, 1855
San Francisco

Jamison,

Sorry this letter and the packages arrived late. No doubt

they'll be there far after Christmas. Maybe you can have a second celebration.

After your last letter, I didn't know how to reply. It sounds like life hasn't treated you right and there's nothing I can do to change that. I'm not good with sympathy, never have been, and I doubt I'm much better now. But I've been encouraged to try so here I am, trying.

I'm sorry to hear about Coraline's vision. After everything else, that truly is a kick in the pants. She's Gifted for pity's sake! The only female Gifted! How fair is that? I can barely handle it; how can you? I know you have your God and your prayers, but are they strong enough for this?

Your letters have gotten me thinking and I don't like thinking like that. I've been wondering about my own life. I still haven't figured out why I was sent here and I'm starting to think I'll never know. What if I have to wait forever to find out? There are things I've been considering outside of San Francisco, but how can I leave before I know for sure?

I probably shouldn't even send this, but I don't have a lot of paper left and I don't want to waste what space I've already used. I suppose writing that wasted more space.

Wishing you a merry Christmas. Enjoy the presents.

Garrett

29

Outside the lodge, a wild whoop jolted Jamison from an already anxious slumber. Tangled in the blankets, he half-rolled, half-stumbled from bed and reached for his Colt pistol along with his boots. The call from outside escalated in ferocity until individual words could be distinguished. Unfortunately, not one was in a language he understood.

Deep charcoal sky reflected back through the open cedar ceiling, an indication that dawn had not yet arrived. The embers which burned brightly upon their sleeping lay cold and dark in the firepit. It couldn't be any later than half past five.

He tripped over his boot laces on his way around the bed and shook Coraline's shoulder. "Cora, wake up. I need your help."

"Mhmmm," she mumbled. He shook her again with more force this time. He didn't want to startle her into a panic, but the unfamiliar cries continued and he could hear Larksong's Chinook residents calling in reply. Both sides used the Jargon, but spoke in such a rush that he couldn't translate more than a few words in his own broken fluency. Another shout arrived from practically on their doorstep. It sounded like Quea'Quim.

"Cora!" he hissed. He yanked the blanket down to her feet and she recoiled into herself. Her eyes popped open as her wiggling toes tried to find refuge beneath her nightgown's hem.

When her hand reached for him, he grasped it, remembering the last time she willingly placed her hand in his: Christmas night, nearly a month ago. For that one night, he thought perhaps there was hope for them, then everything simply went back to the way it was. This moment, however, wasn't the time for such deliberation. "Come, Cora. We have visitors. Will you translate while I help you dress?"

With her sleepy nod, he helped her to sitting and reached for her boots.

"They want to see the chief," she yawned. "They don't realize we don't exactly have one here. Quea'Quim is telling them he will speak for the Chinook. Tobias for the Boston men."

Kneeling, Jamison laced her boots as she continued to rub her eyes. "Who are 'they'?" he asked.

"A tribe from up north. They call themselves Winedafez. I hear four voices, but there could be others."

"Do they mean us harm?"

"I don't know. Quea'Quim is calling us to the main lodge." With another great yawn, she accepted her skirt and jacket and slipped them on over her night clothes.

"Jamison!" Tobias yelped as he rushed through the door, shirt half untucked beneath twisted suspenders. His rifle was gripped between both hands. "Get your wife. We need to go."

"What is it you think I'm doing?" Jamison placed Coraline's fingers atop her coat buttons so she could clasp them. He shrugged into his own coat before taking her hand into the crook of his arm.

"What's happening out there?" he asked Tobias. "Cora said there's another tribe visiting?"

"Yes. I'm not familiar with the customs, but it appears they're not on a social call. I insisted Sarah stay home with the baby. Despite Alice Ann's usual grumblings, she and Marie brought their children over too, and thank goodness Martha and Anwillik arrived, or there might have been war between them too. Quea'Quim asked for only men to attend the talks—at least I think that's what he asked for—but we need Coraline or we'll never be able to negotiate. None of us know enough of the Jargon."

"You really should learn," she said.

"We're trying, but it's impossible for you to teach us when everything sounds the same to your ears."

He had a point. Anwillik could provide slight translations, but her English wasn't improved enough for more than a rudimentary lesson.

Cade, Levi, and Clinton waited for them outside, their own pistols properly holstered. Together, they made their way to the main lodge where smoke already billowed through the roof from the central fire.

Upon entering, they found Quea'Quim stationed at the center of a distinct divide, hands folded behind a wide stance as the firelight flickered over his firm features. To the right of the fire stood Larksong's Chinook population, every man of age in symmetrical rows. To the left, the newcomer Winedafez met their speculative gazes in stony silence. Ten strangers in total. Strong lines of navy war paint ornamented either cheek and upon the nose up to the hairline.

Like the Chinook, their dark hair parted in the center, half drawn back with a leather strap against the scalp. Each wore pressed cedar leggings, a tan leather shirt, and a cape formed from lengths of twisted cedar strands. White howqua shells lined alternating strands and clattered together at the slightest movement. Clearly, stealth was of little concern when devising their military plans. An act of confidence or foolishness? Their stone-tipped spears and quivered arrows seemed to indicate the first. Other than facial identifiers, there was little difference between them. Even the man standing opposite Quea'Quim, assumedly their chief warrior, bore a similar demeanor.

Ash and sparks curled into the air as Tobias directed their group to stand beside the Chinook, then took Coraline's hand. As Jamison relinquished his wife, he struggled to form some piece of comfort and assurance where he knew there was none. The opportunity passed unanswered, however, and Tobias led Coraline to stand between him and Quea'Quim. Jamison moved to the side with Cade, Levi, and Clinton, as close as he could be to Cora without drawing attention to himself.

Quea'Quim spoke and Coraline translated, "Let us begin."

The Winedafez leader barked back a response and his swift head shake made the shells upon his chest rattle. He jabbed a finger at Coraline. "He doesn't want me here," she translated. "No women are allowed."

"Unacceptable," Tobias said. "If they wish to stay, they will accept this condition." Coraline translated to Quea'Quim who stepped forward. A log popped hot in the fire, sending a flash of flame into the air.

"We welcome you, chief warrior Senequa, and the Winedafez to our village," he said, "but we do not welcome your hostilities. This woman is our interpreter. She remains or you must go."

Murmurs rose among the Winedafez, most unsettled, some accompanied by nods. All in deference to their leader's decision, however.

Finally, the chief jutted his chin upward. "Agreed. Listen carefully, Boston woman." A shift of his bare foot sent a spray of dust into the fire and sparks swirled upward like a hot tornadic wind. That day on the prairie, almost consumed by a tornado, was a memory Jamison did not desire to recall. Especially not here, where his wife could not see her steps and he lately found uncertainty in every task. A glance at Coraline's expression revealed little about her emotional state. While she could hear the sparks pop, she could not see their direction, nor could she recognize the angst on Tobias's lips or the suspicion in Quea'Quim's narrowed gaze. She may understand some of the bitterness exuded by Senequa, but the fierce set of his jaw eluded her knowledge.

"Tell us, chief warrior Senequa," Quea'Quim asked, "what brings you to Larksong?"

The stranger's shells jangled with his response. "Have you not heard of the treaties on the Chehalis River? Nearly a year has passed."

Quea'Quim nodded. "Those of our tribe on Shoalwater Bay attended the councils. They found the terms unacceptable and refused to sign. I cannot imagine any chief freely offering all tribal lands in exchange for the meager sum the United States government offered."

"You do not need to imagine it for it has happened. Governor Stephens has convinced several of the northern tribes to surrender their territory for reservation life. He has promised money, schools, and other trappings they are unlikely to receive and unwise to accept. They are handing over our culture for a life of degradation."

Tobias half-raised a hand as though asking a question from the front seat of the classroom. "If I might defend us, the American way is not one of degradation simply because it is different. For two years, we have lived here amicably with the Chinook, they in their way and us in ours."

Senequa's lip curled. "We do not mind living and working beside the Boston man when our ways are respected. But when they remove us from our homes, steal our wives, and destroy our way of life, we are no longer generous."

"Is that what Governor Stephens has done?"

"Tribes east of Puget Sound have encountered soldiers by the dozens, who steal their weapons and imprison their people. Nearly five thousand native men, women, and children have already been forced from tribal lands. They are treated as prisoners, not even as well as we treat our slaves. The land now bleeds from war along the Sound and into its farthest reaches. The governor's men against every tribe and every tribe against the governor."

Quea'Quim met Senequa's gaze through the smoke and fire. "This village was abandoned once already due to death, and I sought my entire life to bring restitution to my family. The Chinook do not live near the Sound and have not survived this long by aggression. Take this up with your own people. "

"Your peace will be a memory!" Senequa shouted. His white shells clanked with furious trembling. "Your children will be told of your ways rather than live them. You invite these Boston men into your village and believe you can live as one, but you cannot. Harmony with them is as smoke departs a fire. Meant to fade. Heed my warning: today they come for us, but tomorrow they will come for you."

His anger simmered in the open lodge, its heat sending both a trickle of sweat and a tingle down Jamison's spine. Could Senequa turn the Chinook against them? Surely not Quea'Quim. He had been on their side since before there was a beginning.

Quea'Quim's position didn't change. He moved neither closer to Coraline and Tobias nor farther away. He maintained his consideration of his native brother from across the fire, lips pursed so fine they nearly disappeared. All while Coraline stood straight as a wrought iron fence post and Tobias's complexion faded ever paler in the firelight.

Finally, Quea'Quim spoke. "These men are my brothers. I trust them. However..." He looked to his people in wait for their leader's response. Then to Tobias. "Perhaps there is some truth to what they say. We cannot completely ignore what is happening in the north. If you are my brother, I ask for your support."

"How can we?" Tobias asked. "You are our brother, but my brothers and I cannot declare war on the American government. The South is already in dissension and if settlers in the Northwest were to also call foul, it would only encourage a secession."

A valid argument. Were the Larks willing to risk their lives, their town, and perhaps the state of the Union to support this cause? The imprisonment and violence against the natives wasn't just, but the massacres performed against the soldiers and settlers could be equally horrific. Who was more in the wrong? The one who instigated the duel or the one who tossed back the glove?

"There is more!" Senequa's shout initiated the reverberation of a sea of stomps and shellclaps from his tribe. The clatter rose to such a frenzy and then with a wave of his hand, fell to silence.

"The governor," he said, "plans to leave the Sound in two weeks' time. It is then we will steal Seattle from his clutches. Control will be returned once he releases our people." His feet changed pattern now, sliding along the dirt into curves overlapping other lines, similar to those marked in paint upon his face. The howqua shell clatter softened along with his vocal intensity.

Despite the passion poured into the arguments, Coraline's translations rather fell farther and farther into an emotionless blanket. As though the person behind those pale pink lips had vanished inside the message and only words remained. Outside the situation rather than a part of it. Exhaustion weighed her slumped shoulder with the effort of rapid translation. Her Gift taxed her just as Jamison's sometimes taxed him, but he couldn't end the conversation without a resolution. Without her Gift, they stood at a linguistic impasse.

He almost missed Senequa's next words. "Other tribes do not agree with our plan. Seattle is small and unprotected. Rather than negotiate, these tribes plan to raid and slaughter. Many Boston men will die, many more taken as slaves. There will be innocents. If you do not help for our sake, help for your own people." Senequa returned to his stationary stance, eyes blazing through the fire.

"I don't understand what you'd have us do?" Tobias asked. "We're not an army. We're not trained and we have minimal weapons. The talents we do possess are not meant for war. I grieve for lost innocents, but I will not risk my family."

"We have Coraline," Quea'Quin said. "She has the Gifted ear. She will go to Seattle and convince our northern brothers to stop this war."

As though Jamison would allow *that* to happen. He moved past the Chinook lines and stood in view of everyone. The fire and the moon above shone like spotlights at the theatre, shifting the attention of every eye. "We are not taking a blind woman into a war."

Translating for two tribes within the familiarity of their own town was one thing, battle in an unknown city quite another. If he sent Coraline anywhere, it would be to Charleston where she could be safe and happy, not in danger or dead.

He turned his attention back to their visitors. Quea'Quim's expression showed concern, but Senequa's only impatience. "I apologize for my dissention. This is not a decision we can make in a single moment. You must allow us time to consider, to discuss."

Quea'Quim nodded. "The Chinook agree. A request of two days' decision."

Senequa crouched within his circle of tribesmen, all speaking in hushed, yet rapid tones. Coraline could likely understand much of their discussion, but chose to say nothing. Jamison admired her respect even in the face of crisis. He wanted to reach for her but restrained himself.

Finally, Senequa stood and his tribesmen rose behind him. "We will allow you time, Boston man, but one day only. By this time tomorrow, you must make your decision."

Without waiting for consent, as one, the strangers moved into the blue-grey Northwestern morning.

30

"Five boats, four scows, nine canoes," Coraline heard Alice Ann rattle off. The line of her fishing rod whizzed by with the plunk of the bob swallowed by the waves. The shore had been their distraction for over an hour while the others discussed how to respond to Senequa's request. Alice Ann had no interest in the "stupidity of men," as she called it, and Coraline saw little importance in attending. No one wanted a blind woman on a war trail, even if she could translate every language. Quea'Quim might be convinced of her usefulness, but he was the only one.

Never had she been more keenly aware of all she now missed out on. Without physical cues to guide her thoughts, every scene was set like a book with no description. One line of dialogue after another without any physical reference. She could feel the heat from the fire, but not see the sparks which may have singed her skirt. The Winedafez spoke of their reasons for joining the Puget Sound battles, but did not share the emotions borne behind their eyes. A novel was not a novel without its details. Her life was a play on a dark stage and Coraline had never cared much for the theatre, besides.

If anything positive had been gained from her affliction, it was that she finally understood her sister's nautical enchantment. The shore had become one of the few places where Coraline almost felt like herself. The landscape might be different from Charleston, the air certainly cooler, and in January, perfectly cold, but the ocean was the ocean no matter where one was. The waves here tended toward more grey than blue, but they still rolled one atop the other. The sand still stuck to her toes and the salt kissed her lips in every instance. From the Atlantic to the Pacific, she didn't need sight to know what happened when the swells crashed down.

Alice Ann had encouraged this fishing trip to check the oyster beds and fishing spots, in hopes of collecting enough to sell some when the next honest-to-goodness ship sailed by. While she worked, Coraline sat cozy between two blankets, a bundled Julep on her lap, babbling in her two-year-old way. She clapped her hands together. "Baaaf, baaf, pa, pa, pa!"

On several occasions, Jamison had noted how the toddler's vocabulary and speech weren't where they should be for her age. While her cousin, Philip, had begun to string words together, Julep still preferred incoherent ramblings to distinct syllables. Jamison claimed it could be related to something he called a "tongue tie," which of course, none of them had ever heard of. He said it was easy to fix. Alice Ann said nothing needed fixing. Unfortunately, Cade continued to side with "mother's intuition."

"That's eighteen boats," Alice Ann now groaned as the last boat passed by in the distance. "Settlers and Indians alike, out on the waves, bringing in all the best catch. The traders like oysters, but my beds are measly compared to what the others must have. How will my business succeed if I can't get out there?"

"Bla-bla, ma, ma, pfffts," Julep replied. Coraline could feel the blanket pull taut against her legs as the child pulled it, likely wadded between her fingers and headed toward her teething gums. She felt up her niece's back to shoulder until she located her cheek. As suspected, the edge of the fabric was Julep's new suckling toy.

Drool covered her fingers and dripped onto Cora's as she eased the blanket away. The girl released a shriek until her beloved rag doll was deposited into her pudgy fist. Slurpy suckles followed as into her mouth it went.

The fishing line whizzed by again. "I do declare I would be far happier if Cade would agree to leave Larksong for a while," Alice Ann sniffed. "We could buy a ship of our own, take it out on the sea, explore the world..." A heavy sigh followed. "But he wants to be here and only here. I suppose our last great adventure was on the westward trail."

"He's doing as a husband should. Considering what's best for you and Julep. Imagine how impossible it would be to raise a baby on a ship. She could fall overboard."

A pause, one too long. Julep gurgled around her mother's silence. "You're right," Alice Ann said finally. "The sea is no place for a child."

Such was her sister's obvious disappointment that Coraline almost asked if she regretted it all. She was sure she regretted coming west, but did she wish she hadn't married Cade, didn't have Julep to care for now? Even without sight, Coraline knew her niece was beautiful and bright. She could feel her full head of curls and her soft skin and knew she would grow to loveliness. She was indeed a blessing, but did Alice Ann consider her so?

"Fee Fee!" Julep's shriek erupted. The child strained against Coraline's arms, which had tightened around her tiny waist, holding her too close. Julep's fingernails, sharp as bone razors, scraped her aunt's hands as she tried to free herself. But if Coraline let go, her niece could crawl away into the water.

"What does she want?" she asked.

"She dropped her doll, Fee Fee." Alice Ann must have bent for it because Julep stopped screaming and relaxed back against Coraline's stomach. A quick check indicated that the doll was once again safe in its owner's arms.

"There, see?" Alice Ann said, clearly forgetting that her sister could not. "All she needed was her toy and now she's about to fall asleep. Which is a relief after she woke so abruptly this morning."

Julep's body gradually increased in weight until Coraline felt the gentle rhythm of steady slumber against her stomach. She tightened the blanket around her niece and covered her with her arms to keep away the cold sea air. Her own cheeks were also wind-nipped, but she didn't wish to return home and to whatever decision awaited her.

As somber as her marriage was, and as ignored as she felt, her despair would be complete if Jamison went to war. She did not think she could bear widowhood again.

"Do you think Larksong will decide to fight?" she asked.

"I don't know." Coraline could envision her sister's careless shrug.

"They might."

"Do you think they should?"

"Oh, I don't know, Cora. War is a complicated decision. At least, that's what Martha told me once. She said when you're a slave, peace is absolutely necessary to existence. You don't fight battles because you know you can never win. Do you honestly think they can win?"

"Quea'Quim and Senequa believe they can. Do you think Jamison will go?"

Alice Ann sighed. "You already asked me this."

"No, I asked you if they would all go. Now I'm asking if he will. I know he wants to find a way to be rid of me."

"Oh, please tell me a better story," Alice Ann snorted. "That man is positively daft over you, so don't insult my intelligence."

"I heard him tell Martha that we would be better off if I returned to Charleston or...or anywhere else." Tears clogged her throat and she blinked. Alice Ann had no respect for weepy women, so she couldn't be one now. "If I went back, there are doctors for the blind, including places where I could permanently reside. If he wants to be rid of me, I won't beg him to let me stay."

"That doesn't sound right. You must have heard him wrong."

"You insult my intelligence now? Not all my senses are broken. I can hear perfectly well. I know what I heard."

"Do you plan to go, then?" Alice Ann's voice was small, like when she was young and hadn't grown into full defiance yet.

"I don't want to, but how can I stay here when I'm clearly not good for him? Wherever I end up, I won't return to our parents. As much as I want to be with them, I don't want them to know how miserable my life became. This was what they wanted for us, to experience life and have some grand adventure. I want them to believe we did."

"But do you think we should have..." Alice Ann's voice trailed off and suddenly, she was lifting Julep from Coraline's lap. The baby released a sleepy squawk, but must have resettled against her mother's shoulder. "Jules needs a changing. I'll take her back."

"Is something wrong?" Coraline asked.

"Nothing's wrong, exactly. We have a visitor who I gather isn't here for me." Her tone grew tepid. "Mr. Reed, hello and goodbye. Be careful with my sister."

"Always, Mrs. Lark."

Mr. Reed? All Coraline could do was remain still while she waited for him to address her. When he did, his words were so full of kindness that she didn't know what to say.

"Good afternoon, Cora," he said softly. His hand rested upon her elbow and drew her up to stand. The sand sank beneath her boots. "The men have taken recess, so I thought we might walk for a moment."

"Have they come to a decision?"

"Not yet. They continue to mull it over."

He guided her hand into his elbow and away they went, the brisk wind at their backs and his warmth radiating all along her side. How she longed for Jamison instead. If only he wanted it too.

"Have you thought anymore about my offer?" he asked. "When I told you about those healing places? I meant what I said. I'll take you."

She released a breath and shook her head. "In truth, I long to go, but it's impossible."

Her confidence should rest with her husband, not with Mr. Reed. Except Jamison didn't understand. He was blind in heart and mind, as Mr. Reed had said, but he was still her husband. He would say she was foolish to even consider such dreams. Dismiss her without consideration.

Mr. Reed's warm breath lingered against her cheek. "Jamison could heal you if he really wanted to."

"He can't. He's tried."

"He could, but he has you where he wants you. Dependent on him. Doing as he wishes. Trapped while he walks anywhere he pleases. He doesn't want to try because he's afraid. He's jealous of what you might be capable of." He turned her into him as they stopped on the shore. "But I'm not, Cora. I'm in *awe*."

He was in awe of *her*? What was there to revel over?

"I wish I were gifted like them, but I'm not. All I have to offer is my arm as a guide and a pistol for protection. And the belief that you can be so much more than your limitations."

"You think I should go to Seattle then? Help as Quea'Quim asked?"

His sigh poured upon her face, as though to wash away any thought of that. "If you weren't blind, there would be no hesitation, but in your current state, it wouldn't be wise. There's no rope long enough to span that distance. How could you head for battle without being able to see what's coming?

"But," he continued, "if you were healed first, you could save everyone. We'll go to these places I have heard of, you and I. We'll heal you, and then we'll return you good as new." She heard him step forward and felt his hands light upon her arms. They slid down to clasp her fingers. "If you trust me, Coraline, you must trust me to help you."

"I..." Her throat clogged again with those horrid tears Alice Ann hated. "I..."

"Jamison wants to send you away. He asked me to take you back to Charleston as soon as spring arrives. Did you...did you know?"

"Yes," she somehow managed. "I knew."

For a minute, only the warmth of their bodies lingered in the inches between them. Their gloved fingers entwined, the splash of seawater mere feet away. She wished she could see his face. Was he sorry to bear such news? Or relieved that he had not been the one to bear it first? Were those lips in a frown or a sneer or a smile?

As he drew her closer, and his fingertips lifted to tilt her chin upward, she knew she should stop him. Except Jamison hadn't kissed her in so long. He didn't even want her in Larksong. He wanted to send her away and had no intention of going with her. If he truly thought it would help, she might go, but not without him. Not without...

Heat enveloped her as Clinton Reed's arms came around and his gentle kiss found her lips. Soft and easy, letting her guide the direction and how quickly she would fall.

With a gasp, she pushed him away. "I'm married, Mr. Reed."

"I'm sorry," he stammered. "I thought...it seemed like... Help me understand, but Jamison doesn't seem to want you anymore."

"I know, and I'm so terribly sorry. Please take me back to the house. Whatever else, you must know I love my husband."

Even, she thought miserably, *if he is no longer compelled to love me back.*

Together, they followed the rope path back to town and not another word was spoken.

31

All evening Coraline thought about the kiss between her and Mr. Reed—her big mistake. While she sat in Sarah's rocking chair listening to the sounds of supper preparation, she picked out Martha's laugh and wondered why Martha had been the one Jamison chose to confide in. If something had developed between Coraline and Clinton, why not between her husband and her friend? She was blind and always would be. He could easily engage in an affair and she would never be able to witness the evidence.

Surely not. If his morals did not allow for divorce, they would not allow for adultery either.

However, nothing lately had been as expected.

When all were seated and the meal prepared, the usual cacophony ensued. Silver utensils against wooden plates, tin cups set upon carved table tops. Toes tapped the floor amid the veritable rumble of children's laughter, unconcerned with the strangers camped outside. Usually, Coraline could handle her heightened senses, but tonight, with her scattered emotions, silence would have been a blessing. Meanwhile, discord reigned.

A hand slapped the table to her right where Tobias usually sat at the head. "Are we ever going to reach an agreement?" he spat. The Chinook may be our friends—"

"Our brothers," Levi corrected. "The title's as important to them as it's to me and Marie being a part of your family. I'd defend ya to my dying breaths and I liken Quea'Quim would do the same."

"But to incite war against a fully wrought and trained military? If we're not dead at the end of it, we'll be shot as traitors."

"Only if we lose," said Mr. Reed, his voice directly across the table from Coraline. If only he had chosen tonight to return to his solitary ways. "Traitors also start revolutions and form new countries. Thank you, Mr. Washington."

"This isn't the same," Tobias argued.

"It's exactly the same. Our government is oppressing the natives. The natives fight to retain what's theirs. If we're living on their land, the least we can do is help them."

Surprisingly, it was Alice Ann who chimed in. "The Shoalwater Chinook are growing irritated with us, you know. They feel we tricked their members into deserting the main tribe and insult them with our Christian converts. They think we're trying to commandeer the fishing trade too. It wouldn't hurt to pacify them a little."

"How do you know this?" Tobias asked.

"They know all sorts of things in McGowen and Astoria. The few times Cade and I have been there trading oysters, we listen."

"Is this why you never find any recruits when you go?" Tobias's voice had shifted, speaking to someone else. She jumped in her seat when his hand slapped the table again. "Farming isn't the way of the Chinook, Cade. They hunt, gather, and craft. They may stay in one place, but they are not used to planting. Let them have their fish trade and recruit fresh blood for us."

"We...we've be-en try-ing," Cade stammered. The last two words tripped off his tongue. "No one wants to come this far north. There's nothing here to entice them except land which they already have plenty of. Any men willing to move are headed south for gold, and all the women are afraid of the natives. They don't trust them. With us being on such friendly terms with colored folks...well, it makes them trust us even less."

"I think he's right," Sarah said. Her tone was gentle, but had that soothing tone one gives when a decision has been reached and the argument hit a wall. "Our town isn't going to grow from new settlers, but it could grow from amity with the natives. It's because of Quea'Quim that this town has had any success at all."

"James?" Tobias seethed. "Is this how you feel too?"

Jamison shifted in his chair. "I don't think we all need to go, but I think I should."

What? Coraline's chin wobbled, not looking anywhere, yet everywhere, until it settled upon her chest. Her husband was going to fight for the Chinook? They had no chance of victory. He would die and if not in battle then, as Tobias said, captured and killed as an American traitor.

"It was my decision to move us to the village," he said. "It was my decision to invite the converts here and it was due to my decisions that we are where we are today. Tobias, Cade, and Levi have children. I don't. I should be the one to go."

"Well, then," Mr. Reed said. A scrape of a chair followed and boot heels tapped. "I suppose if the criteria to play a coward is having children, I'm glad to go too. And Coraline? You'll be joining us?"

"No," Jamison answered before she could. "Cora will stay here with the other women."

"But we need her Gift," Mr. Reed argued.

"You send her to Seattle and you sign her execution. The battlefield is no place for a blind woman. All in agreement?"

After a moment's hesitation, a round of murmured ayes and Tobias's single nay closed the argument.

Coraline tried to pick more food from her plate, but her hand was shaking and she didn't want Jamison to notice her inability to spear even a morsel. She simply held it in her hand and stared ahead.

In a matter of moments, the last pages of her life's story had been ripped from their stitching and cast into the fire. Without a say. As though she hadn't even been there to witness it.

She and Jamison walked home after supper surrounded by their usual cloud of silence. Her arm through his but neither of them truly connected. Thoughts swirled visions through the darkness, first what they had, then what they lost, and now how much more they were bound to lose. Mr. Reed's words at the beach, *"Jamison has you trapped while he walks anywhere he pleases."*

But why, if he could walk anywhere, would he walk to Seattle? To war?

"That man is so daft over you," Alice Ann had said.

Was that what this was? Trying to catch Coraline's attention through foolish choices? To make what was broken between them whole again?

Mr. Reed's voice came again, mocking her. *"No, he's jealous of what you might be capable of. But I'm not, Cora. I'm in awe."*

If he only knew her like her husband, he wouldn't be. She wasn't in awe of anything anymore. Nothing brought her joy. Her lacking spirit, her nonbelief—things Jamison held so dear—had destroyed her marriage. Nothing she could say or do would fix it.

"I know you asked Mr. Reed to take me back to Charleston." The words were hardly murmured, but Jamison drew to a halt anyway. Prepared for his reaction, however, she didn't so much as stumble. By the distance already walked, they were likely right outside their front door.

"Let's talk about this inside," he said, then proved her assumption correct by opening the door. Once he settled her in the rocking chair, blanket tucked around her legs, she heard logs being stacked and flint sparked in the fire pit. The familiar kettle clatter indicated water over the flames for tea. They had run out of coffee months ago.

She heard his exhale from across the room. "Clint told you then?" he asked. "When you were at the shore together?"

"Wha-I-how did you know about that?"

"Alice Ann, of course. You honestly expected your sister to keep a secret?"

"She's done it once or twice." When Coraline asked her not to mention her worsening vision, Alice Ann kept that secret hidden for well over three years.

"Well, she didn't this time. I saw her and Julep return alone and asked where you were."

Her fingers began to tingle. Had he followed her? Did he already know? Was that why he was going to Seattle? The tightness in her chest clawed upward from her belly then separated its fingers across her ribcage until every part screamed to run away. She couldn't run and she shouldn't run. She told Mr. Reed how she loved her husband. If Jamison didn't already know what happened, he would find out soon enough. It should be from her.

"I let him kiss me, Jamison. I'm so sorry."

She reached out a hand in the direction she thought he was, but her grasp came up empty and he made no move to fill it. She heard him tug his boots back on, each one stepping hard to the floor in turn. "Where are you going?"

"I need to think...to pray," he corrected. "To decide what I'm supposed to do."

"Jamison, please." She stood, but didn't know what to do once her feet hit the floor. The rocking chair swayed behind her, the wooden seat striking the back of her knees with each creak. Never had she felt so ashamed. She pulled the blanket up and around her like a shield against her heartache. When she reached for him this time, he gently placed a garment into her hand. Her nightgown.

"Please change and get into bed. I'll ask Martha to move in tomorrow after I leave. She'll help you while I'm away."

"Don't go to Seattle, Jamison," she begged. "I don't want you to go."

"This isn't about what we want anymore, Cora."

She lunged out and this time, caught hold of his shirt, right against his hip. She had planned to grab his arm and the misjudged distance made her pitch forward against him. He wrapped his arms around her out of instinct and set her upright again.

"Jamison, I love you. Not Mr. Reed. I married you."

"Yes, you did. But did you ever really want to? Or was it only ever about survival?" A kiss pressed to her forehead. He seated her on the bed, then, he was gone.

<hr>

Jamison walked through Larksong with his hands in his coat pockets and collar flipped high against his neck. Bitter wind swept through the open space between lodges, but could not add to the chill which already permeated his blood into his bones. January or July, he would never be warm again.

The Winedafez glanced up as he passed them seated around the outdoor fire near the garden. Their eyes followed him, but said nothing, and he gave no response in return. He wouldn't be able to understand them anyway.

Coraline could.

He missed her.

Clinton Reed's somber horse-stable-turned-home reflected the disdain and fury that wound its way around Jamison's heart even now. The building's dim exterior and mud-chinked walls exuded the filth his skin felt at the thought of that man with his wife. Taking advantage when all Jamison asked him to do was escort Cora back to her parents. The double stable door winked at him with that same smirk Clinton gave whenever he wanted someone riled.

Thank goodness *"thou shalt not kill"* included all forms of physical violence because Jamison would have enjoyed nothing more than beating that irreverent rancher senseless. What pleasure it would bring to knock on the door first and then second, knock that rancher's lights out.

"'Do not return evil for evil,'" he recited, *"'or insult for insult; but on the contrary, a blessing.'"*

He did *not* feel like offering blessings upon Clinton Reed.

Even so, he turned away and walked the perimeter of town, one lap then two, until the chatter subsided and the natives began to head inside their lodges. He smacked his lips together as a gust threatened to ice them over. For a place that rarely received snow, it sure could get cold on winter nights.

A familiar squawk turned his head to Cade's approach, Julep bundled in his arms. The girl fought to get free, her chubby fingers reaching out to her uncle once they were near enough. With a dim smile, Jamison took her from her father and let her toy with the buttons on his coat. Her dark curls tickled against his chin.

"Shouldn't she have on a bonnet?" he asked his brother.

"She had one." Cade held up a yellow fabric scrap before shoving the offensive thing back in his coat pocket. "Every time I tie it, she screams and yanks it off. Seems she enjoys the cold."

Julep responded with a rapid lesson in incoherent babble and lowered her mouth to suck on Jamison's top button. "Oh, no, little one." When he pulled her away, her hands grabbed for it again and

Cade took her back with a groan. For the thousandth time, Jamison wished his brother would let him help Julep's developmental progress. She wasn't nearly where she should be for a girl her age and...really, what use was worrying about it now? He might not even be around for her third birthday.

Cade rested her against his chest, gently patting her bottom as they swayed back and forth. "She's been fussy since we came home after supper. Little bird slept all through the meal and now refuses to sleep. Her screams bothered Alice Ann so I offered to take her for a walk." He craned his neck to check Julep's progress and grinned when met with his daughter's heavy eyes. "Not asleep yet, but soon."

The picture of fatherly love constricted Jamison's heart. No man back in Charleston would be caught cuddling his child in a plantation parlor, much less out in the streets for the world to see. Childrearing was for nannies and governesses and perhaps mothers, if they were destitute or did the raising in quiet back bedrooms away from society gossip.

Alonzo Lark would have whipped his youngest son all over again if he saw what a "milksop" Cade turned out to be.

"James?" Cade asked. "Are you all right?" His brother's expression had turned sour. "Is it Seattle? You don't have to go."

"No, I should go. For Quea'Quim and all he's done for us. As Proverbs says, 'Refuse no one the good on which he has a claim when it is in your power to do it for him.'"

"I suppose I can understand that thought, but you told me not to go because I have a baby. You have Cora. She needs you too."

"She'll have Martha while I'm away."

"Take her with you. She can translate."

"Are you dotty? That's her death for certain."

Julep sputtered sleepy bubbles against Cade's shoulder, a dark spot widening on his coat as she drooled. "Jamison..." His voice trailed into the air between the spruce and cedar. He shook his head as he unnecessarily patted Julep's back. "Just...remember we're not the only page in God's book, but one of many words making up the story. Coraline told me that once, back on the trail."

When she still feigned divine belief, Jamison thought. Before he knew the truth and it all went wrong.

His choices, however, had been his own. He had decided to send Coraline away. He had enlisted Clinton's help and thereby pushed his wife into the scoundrel's arms. She may have presented Jamison with a shoulder of ice for months, but he had done little to thaw it or chip the block away.

He chose this path, not God, and he would have to accept the consequences.

32

Without anywhere to go, no books to read, or work to do, Coraline remained safely tucked in bed, awake but lost to her dreams, thoughts flickering from one to another. From under the heavy winter quilt, she ran through her twenty-six years in torturous detail until Jamison finally returned. She had no idea what time it was, but hours must have passed. She kept her eyes closed as the straw mattress sagged with his added weight, and after not too long, she sensed the shift in breathing which indicated slumber. Carefully, she placed a hand on his shoulder and shook him gently. No response, not even a change in breath. He really was asleep...or chose to make her believe so.

Would he miss her after she was gone? Even a little? Perhaps not. Assuming he returned from Seattle—a battle with many outcomes she refused to entertain—he had his ministry and the town to keep him occupied. Any grief his brothers would help him overcome. What about her friends? Sarah, Martha, Marie, who stood by her until the waves grew high and the stakes of friendship even higher. She had no doubt that Alice Ann would barely blink, so absorbed in her own life that she hardly had the time to bother. And Mr. Reed? He might be the only one to notice her absence.

She slid sideways from the mattress, careful not to tug the blankets, and let her feet find the icy floor. Slowly, she pulled on the day dress she had left beneath the bed and fastened every button at throat and cuffs. Once her heavy black boots were laced, she counted her steps to the door and wrapped herself in the warmth of her deer-skin coat. Gloves on. Bonnet tied beneath her chin.

The brisk night air brought a nip to her cheeks, but she simply rubbed her hands together and drew her coat closer about her neck. With her opposite hand, she gripped the braided rope and began her descent to the shore.

Wildlife erupted as she went, the calls of owls and coyotes playing symphony with the whir of rolling spruce and cedar needles underfoot. She imagined the tines in bundles upon the forest floor, carpeting the path she walked and floating down around her like a beautiful rainfall. Being blind, she could imagine anything she wanted. Therefore, despite knowledge of the late hour, she pictured an orange summer sun breaking through the branches. Its warmth spread over her like a good book just finished.

There were flowers too. Daffodils and posies and bluebell bonnets. Azaleas with their fragrant pink blossoms and Spanish moss so low it mirrored a weeping willow's curtained branches. Beyond opened to the long shore where dense sand absorbed her footsteps into silence, leaving only the breakwaters' crash and the wind as it whipped her bonnet strings from side to side.

Such was the portrait of a life she longed for, not the one she had, where no one knew how to approach her and Jamison's only solution was to send her away. How had her father managed to remain optimistic all those years?

Because he had Mother. He had Mercy. He had Alice Ann, and he had her.

Was he still happy now that she and Alice Ann were gone? Or was he standing on the Charleston shore, two thousand miles away, wondering the same as she?

Maybe it would have been better to have remained in Carolina, never married Oliver, never seen him die. Never had the opportunity to run headlong into Jamison's arms, no matter how much she loved him. Would have never betrayed him with someone she didn't.

Her boot heels sank and slurped as dry sand transitioned into wet surf, the terrain uneven yet its familiarity reassuring. Alice Ann had always loved the sea more than she, but even Coraline had been entranced by it from afar. Its brine reminded her of an adolescence near the water, watching her father bring in his fishing boat. In her mind's eye, she could see him enter the house after a long day, strings of fish slung over his shoulders and a smile as wide as the harbor.

"My girls!" he would cry then kiss them all. Not once had she ever heard him despair over never having a son.

She jolted as a wave smashed into her ankles, swirling about her skirts and wanting to drag them back into the sea. The chill sent a shock up her spine and set her teeth chattering. Her fingers held tight to the rope as the water reversed, forming canals beneath her boots as sand rushed away. If she walked out far enough, even if her body rebelled—and it would—she wouldn't be able to make it back. Wouldn't even know which way to turn. Her limbs would tire and eventually fail. She would go under and then...well, it would end.

Her fingers let go of the rope and allowed herself to be propelled forward. Water poured into her boots, numbing her toes. A wave splashed frigid from knees to nose.

Would it hurt? she wondered. Dying? She imagined it would. Drowning was the same as suffocating. Or would she freeze to death first?

Even as fear seized her insides, this decision felt right. She would free Jamison from a life shackled to her care, and free herself from enduring long years of solitary suffering. Wasn't she supposed to feel terrible, guilty, ashamed? She didn't. She just felt so, so tired.

"Coraline."

She straightened, standing still, listening. Only the still waters responded. Who had spoken her name?

"Is someone there? Jamison?" No answer came on the wind. She took another step.

"Coraline. Stop."

She tripped onto her hands and knees, the surf breaking against her chest and splattering salt between her lips. She sputtered and coughed as she sank back onto her bottom. Water rushed up against her again, the sand pulled from beneath her thighs. In with a whoosh, out with a slow hiss until she sat in a sand hole, her fingers clenched around thick soupy grains. A shell popped up beneath her touch. Perhaps she imagined it, but she thought she felt something nibble at her ankle.

"Coraline, you're headed the wrong way. Come back."

"Maybe there is another way." The words didn't feel like hers. They came from somewhere outside herself, from another place she had never dared to tread. Her entire world was a land unknown, each footstep upon unsteady ground, yet somehow, she knew this wasn't the way.

She had thought darkness meant nothingness, but night did not despair because it couldn't see what morning held. The waves still battered the shore and sand crumbled away beneath it. Day or night, oysters made their beds and salmon fought the river's current. Even when that fight was the last thing the salmon would ever do.

She stood as water sluiced from her skirts, down her legs, and into the surf. "Where are you?" she called.

"Follow my voice."

She turned in its direction, but another wave struck and she slipped backward, going under. Flailing and sputtering, she became disoriented. The water shouldn't be this deep yet. She should be able to stand, but another wave came, and she couldn't steady her feet beneath her.

A shout sounded in the distance. How far had she drifted? Was she going out to sea? "Help!" she shouted. "Please, Lord, help me!" And for the first time in a long time, she truly meant it.

"I'm here! Take my hand!" Fingers connected with hers and she clung to them. An arm wrapped her waist and lifted her to her feet. With every step forward, the water grew shallower until they finally collapsed onto moist sand.

Beside her came a man's labored breaths. His fingers remained in hers, slick with salt water but beneath that, calloused and worn. Hands that had seen hard labor. A carpenter perhaps? Could she truly have been saved by Christ?

Her astonishment dissolved with the man's next words. "Coraline, what happened?"

"Tobias?"

Her savior was not the hand of God after all. For a moment, she had hoped Jamison was right, that finally He had come to her aid, that finally He cared. But it appeared He was as silent as ever.

"You shouldn't be swimming," Tobias said. "Especially not by yourself."

"I wasn't swimming. I...I don't really know how to swim."

The resulting pause lay as serious as every other failure since they started this town. Tobias's lack of words punctuated the darkness like tiny arrows penetrating her skin. She felt their phantom blows, the harsh strikes of disappointment that her brother-in-law must have for her. Their lives were difficult enough, and she had chosen the easy way to escape.

"Why?" he asked.

"I didn't see another way." She laughed a low miserable chuckle at her unintended jest. "I feel alone at every moment, missing the life I should be living, hearing it pass by but unable to experience it. I am useless to the town and a burden on Jamison. He and I barely speak. I even kissed another man." She licked her lips, tasted salt, and remembered how ashamed Mr. Reed's kiss made her feel. "I figured I would provide a service to everyone and lighten your load. As I said, I didn't see another way."

"Oh, Cora..."

Here it was, she thought. The revulsion, the pity. Telling her how wrong she was, that her life was worth living and how even in her blindness, she had a beautiful purpose. She already knew she should believe those things, had even argued them with herself dozens of times, but it hadn't convinced her to seek a better way. She didn't want pity or good intentions. She wanted to know that someone, somewhere understood.

Tobias's hand left hers and slid around her shoulders, drawing her in close. As taut as his muscles were, she realized that the gesture was meant to comfort himself as much as it was to comfort her. There was desperation in that action and it had nothing to do with her.

"Tobias?"

"I need help, Cora." Only in the quiet of the night would she have been able to hear his words. "I came here to do the same thing you were."

No. Impossible. Along the trail, he had been their ever-present leader, always with a word of encouragement and sound advice. Larksong existed because of his determination. He had struggled since their arrival in Washington, but everyone assumed his moodiness was due to the town's hardships. Coraline figured this cloud would pass like any other rain shower.

Except it hadn't.

She turned into him, folded her arms around his muscular chest, and drew him near. Their wet clothes clung to them and to each other and sand scraped against Coraline's bare legs. His forehead fell upon her shoulder and between the two of them, they wept enough tears to fill another ocean. This time, she didn't weep for herself so much as for the brother-in-law she comforted and the husband asleep at home. For the sister she no longer knew and the friends she had forgotten in exchange for her sorrows. For the blindness they all suffered even when their eyes could still see.

"I didn't see another way either," he moaned. "I lost my Gift and I let it destroy me. Without it, I felt worthless and I brought our town to ruin. I failed everyone. Sarah, Philip, Mary Grace, my brothers, the entire town. I even felt like I failed the rest of the wagon train when I know they made their own choices to leave. Then Jamison stepped up when I couldn't and saved everything. I figured everyone was better off without me."

"But Sarah? You would leave her to raise Philip alone?"

"Jamison?" he countered. "You would leave him alone?"

"I felt alone." She could barely force the words from her lips. It wasn't an excuse, but a reason, and she knew the inaccuracy of her feelings now. She had never been alone; she just hadn't known that anyone cared. Asking for help seemed like another trial rather than a relief.

She thought it was love which drove her actions tonight, but really, it had been fear. Afraid of sharing herself with Jamison and being rejected as a burden. Of him and everyone else telling her to leave for an asylum because that was the only place she truly belonged. Yet, fear, what a liar it was! Her chest hurt with what she had been about to throw away because of it.

"We should get out of the cold," Tobias said, and she realized then how violently she shivered. Her teeth clacked together, and she hadn't even noticed when it started. He, too, shook beside her, although much less noticeably. All at once, the wind drove knives upon her flesh and her soaked deer-skin held no warmth. If they stayed out here, they would catch pneumonia, and then what good would it do for him to have saved her?

He guided her to her feet and gently slipped her arm through his. Together, they made careful steps toward town, her hand gripping the rope as much as she held to him.

When they finally arrived at her cabin door, she paused with her hand still in his. "Tobias?"

"Yes?"

"It feels illogical to admit, but when you saved me from the water, at first, I thought it was God calling."

She heard a smile in his voice, an expression he hadn't offered in a long time. He squeezed her hand. "I think He's been speaking to us all along. Only we forgot to listen." He kissed her cheek. "Sleep well, Cora." Only once she was safely inside, did she hear his footsteps depart.

She counted her way to her trunk, silently removed her sea-soaked clothes, and leaving them in a wet heap upon the muddy floor, slipped into bed beside her husband.

The minute she wrapped her frigid arms around his warm chest, Jamison jolted awake. She could feel his stare and could picture the dismay upon his lips when he said, "Where have you been!" His fingers cupped her cheek, his touch gentle yet also insistent. "Why are you soaked to the skin?"

"I went for a swim." Like it was so reasonable.

"You went *where*? It's January. You could freeze to death." They both knew that was the lesser of his worries, but she appreciated how he didn't mention the most obvious one.

Her hand covered his. His fingers entwined with hers. She kissed his knuckles, then kissed them again. She wished she could see his face. Nearly wept for want of it.

"Jamison," she whispered. "I love you with all my heart. Please, don't ask me to leave you. I want to be here, with you, and I'll beg you if I must."

For a troubled moment, he said nothing. Then his breaths turned staccato and she understood that he was crying. So silently he no doubt believed she wouldn't realize, but he didn't understand how blindness heightened her other senses. Emotional charges changed within its depths.

Her fingers trailed until they found the warmth of his face, the stubble of his chin, and the softness of his cheeks. Still higher until she could wipe away the tears upon his lashes.

He turned his head to press a kiss against her palm. "I thought I lost you."

"You did, but I'm back now, and there's so much I need to say."

He reached for her then and an ache pulsed deep within, a longing so deep she could barely contain it. It pushed outside her until it lay between them, right where he could hold it as truly as he held her. She had wasted time when sight was still an option, when she could have loved him more fully with every sense of herself. She had wasted the time she could have had with Oliver too. She wouldn't waste another chance.

Coraline, you're headed the wrong way. Come back.

Follow my voice.

I'm here. Take my hand.

Maybe Tobias was right. She might have stopped believing in God, but even in this darkness, God never stopped believing in her.

33

That night, Jamison and Coraline found their way back to one another. They cried and laughed as they hadn't since before she went blind. Then he listened to her plan to help the natives. To finally use her Gift for something greater than mere interpretation among their own people. To try to bring a hint of peace to a world without any.

"God spoke to me," she said. "Last night down at the water. He picked me up and told me there was another way."

God spoke to her? His heart raced and he had to swallow back every rising emotion. After all these years of doubt, the Lord had brought her hope?

She squeezed his fingers and smiled. "Please take me to Seattle. Help me convince Quea'Quim."

Oh, how he adored that smile of hers. He hadn't seen it in so long. He didn't know exactly what had happened down at the shore, but it didn't matter. *Thank you, Lord*, he prayed. *After all our prayers and questions, you have finally brought her home.*

"I will stand with you, Cora. If that's in Seattle, I will bring you with me. I will never send you away from wherever I reside. But if you want to return to Charleston, or go to California, or even to the Holy Land itself, I will find a way to take you there."

"'For wherever you go, I will go, your God will be my God,'" she whispered. "'Let naught but death separate me from you.'"

From the Book of Ruth. Even when she claimed unbelief, his sermons and incessant readings had still found their way through.

In response, he bent to kiss her thoroughly. How wrong he had been to plan to send this woman away. God help him to never do so again!

"There's one more thing," Coraline said when he finally released her. Her voice trembled and he wondered what could be so terrifying that she could not say.

"You can tell me, dearest. I meant my promise. I will not send you away."

"It is an awful thing."

"Then we will sort it out together."

Then she told him what really happened at the shore. How she went in the water because she was going to end it all. He listened dumbfounded as she tripped over her words and sent them spinning like gravel under wagon wheels. Like tiny bullets to his heart. Lodged so deep he could barely breathe.

She apologized for everything. How *she* behaved, how *she* pushed him away, how *she* ran to Clinton. As though it was entirely her fault.

"Oh, Jamison, I felt like I was drowning every day."

"I wish you had told me. You may have pushed me away, but I equally let you go. There was no way for my Gift to help you. I didn't know what else to do."

"All I wanted was someone to stand by me. To remind me that there's more to us than just our Gifts."

Jamison held her closer, let her cheek press firm against his chest. The ache hadn't lessened. "To my father, our only worth lay in our Gifts. It's difficult to forget that sometimes. But you're my better part, Cora, not my father. I'm so sorry I ever made you walk this path alone. How long must I prove my regret?"

"Are God's mercies not new every morning?" she asked.

"Of course."

"Then grieve no more, for tomorrow, so shall we be."

Come morning, they returned to the main lodge, both the Chinook and Winedafez arranged as they were the previous day, with one difference. Tobias and Coraline still stood beside Quea'Quim but this time Jamison joined them, rather than being removed at a distance.

Quea'Quim raised his hands, and all murmurings quieted. The air stilled. Jamison reached for Coraline's hand and her fingers gripped his.

"The Chinook remain firm in our decision to help our northern brothers," Quea'Quim announced. "A portion of our tribe will travel with the Winedafez, hopeful for a resolution, but prepared for war if we must."

A collective stamping of feet and jangling shells erupted from Senequa's men at the announcement, although their leader did not smile. He did, however, nod once before he spoke. "The Winedafez agree to an alliance." He looked to Tobias then. "What say you, Boston man? Will you also fight for peace?"

With a soft exhale, Tobias turned his glance from the people to Jamison at his side and smiled. "I have decided to cede this decision to my brother, Jamison Lark. He is the true leader of Larksong. He stepped to the task when I was unable and has chosen a wife who will help lead our town to a prosperous future."

"Pardon, but what?" Jamison gawked. He *had* stepped up when Tobias couldn't and made decisions when his brother wouldn't, but he never expected Tobias to simply hand over the reins. This town was his brother's dream. Jamison hadn't even wanted to come in the beginning. He had only done it in the name of family.

"You heard correctly, James. The trait of a good leader is knowing you cannot do anything without the men behind you. Asking for help when you must. Otherwise, I am no better than our father, demanding respect where it hasn't been earned and perhaps, never will be. I would rather have you respect me, Jamison, than resent me. You have always been a wiser man than I."

From Larksong's back row, Cade nodded his agreement. For a man who didn't like potential confrontation, that simple gesture said volumes.

Jamison wished Garrett were here, despite the undue complication if he were. He'd likely seek a fight and cause them all more trouble. Still, he missed his middle brother and wished they were together for this moment. Even Daniel would be welcome. It was time they put the past behind them.

He hoped they could.

"I choose to stand with my brothers, Tobias and Cade, and our Chinook brother, Quea'Quim. As we decided last night, Clinton Reed and I will join you in Seattle, along with..." He glanced sideways at Coraline. She stared across the room, but her eyes were far from unfocused. Determination simmered within them, with none of the defeat he had witnessed for so many months.

They were taking a risk, but one they both believed necessary.

"My wife, Coraline, will travel with us and act as interpreter."

A rumble of dissent rose from the Winedafez and Chinook alike. Coraline did not translate, but he could imagine their words. A woman in battle? It simply wasn't done. A blind woman would assuredly be a liability they could not afford. She would cost them this fight.

"James?" Cade said. That was all, just the one word, but the look in his eyes said so much more. Hadn't it only been last night that Jamison adamantly refused to allow Coraline to go to Seattle? He had said it was certain death for her being blind. But last night, when she actually tried to take her own life, everything changed. His view of what he thought he knew and how he knew it. Coraline might be blind, but she was not helpless. She may not be able to see, but she had vision and talent beyond her physical strength. He would be bereft if he continued to treat her as he had been, like an invalid with no future. If her own husband would not support her, why would anyone else?

Quea'Quim said something to Coraline then, words meant only for her ears. His brow furrowed and his thin brown lips creased with worry. Yet, when she replied in Chinook, her lips curved into a sympathetic smile.

She released Jamison's hand and held up both of hers, raised outward in offering, rather than upward as Quea'Quim had before. The effect, however, was surprisingly the same. Silence fell across the room, all eyes turned on the woman who could not meet their glances. For all she knew, the silence fell from their lack of attention, not because of it.

When she spoke, there was no hesitation, only assurance. This was not a broken woman, lost and begging Jamison to keep her. This was the woman he fell in love with outside his plantation home, who had been determined to make a life for herself, who remembered the dreams she once had.

She spoke first in Chinook, then to the Winedafez, then finally in English, straight to his heart.

"Quea'Quim would choose for me to stay, but I know he speaks out of love. It is not because he does not believe in my resilience. I, however, have spent far too long ignoring the true usefulness of my Gift. When people fail to understand one another, they cannot see the way forward. Being blind has, in a sense, shown me how to see what's right. I am not Chinook nor Winedafez, but I understand feeling forced out of one's own life. The loss of everything you knew, the loss of what was comfortable. Feeling alone. Hopeless. But feelings lie. We are not alone. Our combined town of Chinook and Larksong proves that. I have become one of you and I hope that you feel you have become one of us. Quea'Quim brought us together. My husband believes in him and I must stand with my husband on this matter. If we do not fight for our brothers and sisters now, then who will fight for us later?"

"I stand with my wife," Jamison said. He reached for Coraline's hand again. "She will join us in Seattle to peacefully negotiate between the natives and Governor Stephens's men. Battle will commence only if all else fails."

A combined murmur circled the group as Tobias voiced his assent, followed by Cade, and finally Quea'Quim. Although she couldn't see, his elder brother gave Coraline a knowing smile, and Jamison wasn't sure exactly what it was his brother knew. He was simply glad that they were in agreement.

At last, there was only Senequa left to vote. He did not smile. "The tribe does not agree with this course; however, recognizes its courage. We will support Larksong in this mission. May the spirits of the earth grant us victory."

Coraline gripped Jamison's hand. "May God protect us all."

34

By the next day's dawning, the Larksong-Chinook-Winedafez warriors forged the trail through the Washington forest, around the growing town of Olympia, and finally along Puget Sound to Lake Duwamish. There they would meet with the other tribes and hopefully formulate a compromise.

Coraline didn't argue when Jamison insisted she ride a mule rather than walk. It would make travel far easier for her and less worrisome for everyone else. Most of the natives had already grumbled over the inefficiency of bringing a woman at all, much less a blind one. Her Gift didn't seem to even factor into their frustration as none of them, with the exception of Quea'Quim and perhaps Senequa, believed she would amount to any help.

In direct opposition to the natives' nearly silent steps were the mule's hoofbeats and the sound of Mr. Reed's hatchet as he slashed his way through tree branches and undergrowth. His boots crunched their downed limbs, surely causing disrespect toward the native's spiritual beliefs.

"Must you be so loud?" Jamison hissed. He led Coraline's mule with reins in hand while she held tight to the pommel. "We'll lose any element of surprise."

"Quea'Quim told us we'll walk for five days, no?" Mr. Reed replied. "I have four left to be riled. Besides, Coraline never minded my exuberance before."

She could picture his smirk and that swagger which cajoled ladies into sympathy and men into aggravation. Without visual charm to overshadow his insults, it became far easier to understand Jamison's disdain. And far easier to visualize the full-bodied scowl which must have her husband's fists clenched at this very moment.

"In this instance," she replied, "I believe prudence to be the best policy. Quea'Quim and Senequa know these woods best and understand any tribal resistance we may encounter. We cannot control the mule's volume much, but we can control our own."

"I'm only trying to protect you, Cora," Mr. Reed said.

"I have a husband for that, thank you. Perhaps it would be best if you protected the rear of the line for today. Quea'Quim will likely have another task for you tomorrow."

"Very well, Mrs. Lark." As he huffed off, she heard a hard slap of fabric, followed by Jamison's stifled grunt. Seconds later, his gloved fingers wrapped hers and squeezed.

"Did he hurt you?" she asked.

"Only my ego."

She squeezed his hand back and turned her chin downward, hoping she pointed his way with her smile. "You do know I'll always choose you."

"I know it; although, it does help to hear."

Having him beside her and Mr. Reed yards away eased the discomfort in her middle. Many trials awaited in Seattle, ones they might not all return from. Those who did certainly wouldn't return the same people they once were.

Life's most beautiful and most horrendous moments were equally capable of leaving an impression. Although she could not see the landscape, she wanted to paint it in her memory. How the brisk winter wind nipped her nose and cheeks and the mare's soft hide raised warmth beneath her. The forest's woodsy aroma mixed with the natives' war paint and spiced ritual smoke. These experiences in such a combination wouldn't last. This time in history, like the stories in her beloved novels, would never be written in precisely this way again. She must be grateful for every scene in the story God had granted her.

Before that desperate night on the shore, it had been years since she spoke a prayer she truly meant. Every Mass had been a rote utterance; every psalm a praise of emptiness. She still didn't understand His ways, but at least now she believed that someone was listening and cared. She could be frail and unstable and uncertain with Him. He would carry her even when her legs gave out beneath her and she didn't know where she was.

Now that she had found her own faith, she understood the struggle Jamison endured when he decided to marry a woman with none. The same struggle that Anwillik and her brother encountered near daily, although neither probably realized how much of their conversations Coraline digested. People often forgot that being blind did not mean being deaf.

Over the next two days along the trail, as Seattle and war and their futures came closer at hand, she considered Anwillik and Quea'Quim's last conversation, overheard through the chapel window where Coraline and Jamison prayed the night before departure.

"Stay safe my brother," Anwillik had pleaded.

"I'm always safe on my own."

"This is different."

"You are right. I am not on my own this time. I would ask for one promise of you."

"Yes?"

"If I do not return, you will care for our people?"

"If you are asking me to give up my new life and my faith, I cannot make such a promise."

"Anwillik, I ask you as your brother. Do not send me to war without knowledge that your spirit is whole with our people."

"Quea'Quim..." She paused, her heart undoubtedly as heavy as her carefully chosen words. "My love for you will never change, but my spirit rests with Christ and I cannot deny that. Not even for my brother. Although, I will also never diminish the faith you have in the old ways. For at one time, I too held them in greatest honor."

"Then promise you will care for our people. I do not wish to part without tranquility between us."

"You know, if the time came, I would care for them. I will not need to, however, for you will return."

No one ever knew when the last time would be the last time.

Would Coraline ever see Julep or Philip grow up? A blind woman going to war—her odds were not very high.

At least she was walking it with a newfound love for her husband, faith in the Lord, and a hope for the future, three things she hadn't possessed even mere days ago.

There had been other farewells, nearly all tearful. Levi and Marie. Tobias and then Sarah. Her friend pulled her close, great emotion thick upon her words. "Thank you," Sarah whispered into Coraline's ear. "Tobias told me what you did for him. Never in my wildest dreams would I have imagined... Cora, he told me everything. Years worth of thoughts I never knew." Her arms tightened and a damp cheek pressed against Coraline's. "My darling friend, I am so thankful you're alive. I should have told you more."

"You've told me now," Coraline whispered back. They were back in Sarah's cabin on the day of the engagement party, laughing and crying together over Coraline's nuptials and Philip's newly discovered existence. "But, my darling friend, I'll want to hear it again when I return."

"Of course," Sarah laughed as she stepped away for Martha who pulled Coraline into the fiercest embrace they'd ever shared.

"You come back," Martha demanded. "I need you at my wedding."

"Why, Martha, what man have you been hiding?" Coraline immediately imagined her friend with one of the natives or perhaps Quea'Quim himself, the two of them with a home so near. Martha helping Coraline with her babes and Coraline devotedly holding Martha's while she worked. Not an even exchange perhaps, but one did the best with what they were given.

Then Martha said, "None yet. All I know is I can't go marrying him without you there. Understand?" Coraline nodded for that's all she could do.

Her sister arrived next and Coraline's beautiful imaginings burst like a splash upon the sea. Over their twenty-one years as family, she believed she knew all Alice Ann's worst behaviors and most controversial arguments. When one danced with a dramatic adolescent, one expected to encounter a few unfamiliar steps, but none prepared her for Cade's desperate shouts.

"Alice Ann! You cannot do this."

"Four years you're lackadaisical," Alice Ann returned, "and now, when I have a chance to do something important, you choose to assert force? We can go together or I can go alone, but I know you won't fight for anything and I'm not being left behind this time."

Coraline gasped. Did she dare assume that her sister planned to join them in Seattle?

"We have a daughter," Cade argued. "Also, I fight for things all the time."

"Yes, and then you always concede. You can stay to care for Julep. You're a much better parent than I am anyway."

Cade sounded as though he were close to tears. "That's not true."

"Yes, it is. Keeping her safe is your other Gift. We can discuss this when I return. Or rather, not discuss it, because by then you'll have seen the wisdom of this decision and decided it isn't worth the argument."

"Alice Ann, please!" But Cade's cry came at the same moment as little Julep's: "Mama, Mama!" Coraline could imagine those tiny reaching fingers longing for her mother's hold and being denied. "Mama!" The tearful cry about broke Coraline's own reserve. Was she doing the right thing by leaving? If she stayed, would Alice Ann stay too? A girl needed her mother.

"Alice Ann stays," Jamison said, firm and with no room for argument. The type of tone Tobias often carried on the trail before he resigned his leadership to his brother. "We made an agreement that those with children would remain. Clinton, Cora, and I have none; therefore, we will go."

"You expect me to thank you for saving my life when you take my sister to her death?" Alice Ann retorted. "You spoke so sensibly at supper. How did you become so brainless in a single day? You are the worst husband I have ever seen, with mine ranking squarely behind you."

"Alice!" Cora wanted to grab her sister by the arms and shake her until she remembered who she was. What she had chosen to take on when she made the choice to be intimate with Cade, to share a life with him as man and wife. Life was no longer only about her. In fact, it never had been.

But Coraline couldn't see where her sister was and Julep's tender cries had erupted into squalls. "Mamamamama!" Cade's soft shushes were ineffective. How very much would she rather take that toddler in her arms and cuddle her than leave on a warpath.

Suddenly, Alice Ann's slender arms were around her. Her sister didn't say anything at first, but she knew it was her. Twenty-one years together did that.

"Stay with them," Coraline whispered. She tightened her hold, splayed her hands upon her sister's back. "They need you and how can I do what I must if I must worry for your safety too?"

"No one really *needs* me, Cora, but for you, and only you, I will not go to Seattle."

Alice Ann walked away and Coraline did cuddle Julep then. She held her niece so close that she feared her erratic heartbeat would frighten the child. But Julep's arms wrapped around her neck, her head tucked beneath Coraline's chin, and sniffled her way even further into her "Na Na" Cora's heart.

The morning of January twenty-sixth, their journey finally ended on the shores of Lake Duwamish, just east of Seattle. A deep expanse of forest separated the town's structures from the tribal meeting place. Voices drew them along, first mere whispers and then definitive conversations. Several main speakers surrounded by a group of respondents.

"What is happening?" Coraline asked Jamison. He lifted her down from the mule and carefully set her feet upon moist earth. It sank half an inch or more beneath her boots. "Why is the ground wet? It hasn't rained since yesterday." Thankfully, the lush canopy had spared them all a soaking.

"We've stopped about a half mile from the edge of the lakeshore. The lake itself is impressive, smooth water and the trees come nearly to the shore. Another fifty meters down, there's a tight group of natives gathered, at least five tribes from what I can decipher based on clothing. Perhaps three hundred men or more."

Three hundred. She knew there would be many, but she hadn't expected needing to convince *hundreds*.

She heard him fiddle with something. "I'm tying up the mule. A loose knot. In case we don't make it back, so he won't be trapped."

"You don't think we'll make it back?"

His fingers laced through hers. "'At dawn let me hear of Your kindness, for in You I trust,'" he recited. "'Show me the path I should walk, for to You I entrust my life.' I leave everything in the Lord's hands, Cora, but that doesn't mean I am not afraid."

"I am too."

He did not reply and she felt his eyes watching her with an intensity akin to sadness. She wanted to tell him to forget this plan. To lead them back home where they could all be protected.

Retreat, however, would not bring Quea'Quim honor, nor help any of their people. The war could end today without them or it could rage like fire from a tender spark, taming the land into ashes and swallowing Larksong along with it. If they played their part and destruction won the day, at least they could say they hadn't abandoned their brothers.

Whispers passed down the line of natives until Coraline could translate that Senequa had asked for a descent to the shore. Mr. Reed announced himself as he joined them once again, although his presence did nothing to qualm her frightened spirit.

"Wait, my friends," said Quea'Quim. His long limber fingers filtered warmth through her coat as his hand came to rest upon her shoulder. "Boston men must not go yet."

"What would you have us wait for?" asked Jamison. "We agreed to help."

"You will help. Coraline will interpret for our brothers, but first must wait. These tribes have been wary of the Boston men for a long time. Senequa will call when the time is right."

Jamison led her through the brush to the edge of the clearing, only distinguishable by the frigid breeze which met them off the water. She trusted that they remained within the shadow of the trees, but could not say for certain. From here, they could now hear every detail of the tribal conference. Her fingers felt like they were breaking within her husband's grip, but she didn't dare release him.

Softly, she translated, "It is our solemn call to restore what we have lost to these Boston men! They imprison our people, our women, our children, without reason. They starve them, rape them, kill them. Take them for their own families. What can we do to stop them?"

"It is precisely why we have come," Senequa said. "We bring a treaty from the Boston men and a special gift."

"A treaty like the others? Gifts we have received only to be turned upon our backs. We will not surrender to Governor Stephens's men. He threatened to kill us on sight!"

"We do not ask you to. If a war must come, we will help to fight it."

"We have your loyalty then?"

"Yes."

A pause followed this with whoops and hollers among the tribes. Something wasn't right.

"Quea'Quim," Coraline whispered, "What are you not telling us?" Her world was always dark, but this...this felt different.

His voice shook, that perfect, always determined Chinook accent now broken. "If there is danger, go to Seattle and warn the people. Make sure the women and children are safe. Tell the men to take their arms. If the northern tribes do not know you are here, they will not know to stop you. Quea'Quim does what he must to keep you safe."

"I understand the risks, Quea'Quim. You are part of my family too."

She would have liked to have written the ending to her story right there. To say that they walked hand in hand down to the shore, explained themselves to the tribes, and everyone left full and satisfied. An epilogue to tell how the war ended by her Gift's intervention, the captured natives released, and the massacres extinguished. What a lovely way to end a tale.

As too many good tales end, however, this one was to take a similar dreadful turn.

"We cannot allow any of them to live!" the tribal leader shouted. "There are no innocent white men. Their children are tomorrow's oppressors and their women birth more of them every day. The more of their blood that flows, the more they will fear us!"

Jamison squeezed her fingers so hard, three of her knuckles popped.

"There is a ship," the tribal leader continued. "In the bay. It is carrying American supplies, food, and weapons. Let us capture this for our own and burn every house along the way. It is the only way our message will be heard."

Coraline jolted as Mr. Reed spewed hushed expletives into the morning air. "Some fine geese you've chosen to defend. Why the devil are we here? To protect a tribe of monsters?"

"They're not all monsters," Jamison said. "And we're not all against them. We have to find a way for there to be peace. That's what we came for."

"It is too late," Quea'Quim whispered. "The Boston men must go. Now."

Jamison's hand crushed hers. "But we haven't had our chance to speak."

"They will not give you one. You must go, now, or they will come for you first."

What had they missed while Mr. Reed and Jamison argued? Coraline wondered. What had been said? "Quea'Quim—" she began, but he stole her words with his own.

"I know these tribes. You hear their words, but I see their expressions. I love my tribe, but I am loyal to my family. It is you I choose to protect. If you remain here, you will not survive."

Even through her glove, she felt the warmth of his hands cover hers. "I will hold them back as long as I can but you must warn the people."

"Are you willing to fight your own people?" Jamison asked him. He waited for Coraline to translate. "Or the other northern tribes?"

"They will not negotiate," Quea'Quim replied. "Their hatred has run them as hostile as the governor's men. Now, you must run."

His touch disappeared, and he moved away with his ever-silent footsteps, the same as the day they met across the stream.

35

Jamison carried Coraline toward Seattle, his eyes set on Clinton's back at their lead and his ears focused on his rhythmic boot heels. The cold air penetrated his lungs and made each step more labored than the last. He believed they maintained a significant lead over their potential pursuers, but if they stopped, according to Quea'Quim, they would wind up dead. The people of Seattle, rather, had no idea the danger coming for them.

Swampy terrain extended from the forest, and across that, a central dirt road ran down the center of what could hardly be called a town. Wood-planked homes and trade lodges were arranged at seemingly random intervals along the main line and five side streets. Hardly larger than Larksong and to be honest, probably with a far lower residency.

As they skirted the marsh and moved into the town's center, people turned from their morning chores to stare. They must look rather a sight, he supposed: a group so disheveled from crashing through the trees, with mud splattered up and down, and leaves in their hair.

A townsman stepped from the shadow of a house to cut them off, rifle at the ready. "Where did you all come from?" he demanded. He squinted past them to the woods. "We don't want trouble here."

"There will be no trouble from us," Jamison said, "but there is from what's coming."

"You brought trouble with you then." His trigger finger twitched.

Jamison set Coraline down and eased her behind him. "No, sir. We came to assist your negotiations with the natives, but our attempts have proved futile. We must warn your women and children to find shelter and the men to take arms for danger is close behind us."

The man's eyebrows hitched. "That so?"

"It is, and this conversation is wasting precious minutes."

Although the man still didn't appear convinced, he did finally lower his rifle. One thumb hitched over his shoulder. "A'right, this a way. I'll take ya to Woodhouse." His turtle-like amble, however, suggested an impressive lack of urgency.

"Oh, for the sake of the president and all his cabinet." Clinton pushed past Jamison and rattled the man's arm. "You may not care for your life, but I do mine. Which way to this Woodhouse fellow? We'll go ourselves."

The Seattleite scowled at him, his thick jowls swaying. His spindly finger pointed down the main thoroughfare. "Across from the docks."

Clinton released him with a grunt. "Let's go then."

Andrew Woodhouse's residence lay on the eastern side of the main thoroughfare, which they learned was actually named First Avenue. A mist descended as they trudged through mud and around horse droppings. Through the saloon doors, a drunk stumbled, despite the sun barely showing nine o'clock in the morning. At the sight of them, every stranger settled a cautionary hand on his revolver, necessitating Jamison and Clinton to create a guard around Coraline.

Woodhouse was mid-breakfast when they burst through the door without invitation. His young wife and toddler son were seated beside him and the child screamed at their entrance.

"Mama! Strangers!" The boy tumbled off the bench and hid behind his mother's skirt as the same time Woodhouse shoved back his chair and stood with pistol drawn.

"Who are you?" he demanded. His brown beard twitched with each word.

Jamison threw up both hands in surrender. "Please, sir, we are friends. I am Jamison Lark, this is my wife, Coraline, and our friend, Clinton Reed. We've come to warn you."

Woodhouse's brow creased. "Warn us? From what?"

"The natives, sir. They plan to take arms against you."

Woodhouse finally lowered his weapon and set it on the table. "There have been whispers of an Indian uprising certain to arrive any day. I've been waiting for it. Tried to square up a militia, but Seattle's a town of loggers, not soldiers. I assume you want to join us in the fight."

"No, sir. We came to compromise with the natives, but our negotiations did not occur as planned. We have a Chinook friend who remained behind in an attempt to ward them off, but believes his chances are slim. You must secure the women and children."

As though to punctuate his statement, four strong knocks sounded on the front door. "Woodhouse," a man shouted. "Open your door! They're coming!"

Woodhouse cornered the table, but he never reached the door before it opened. Ten townsmen, all carrying rifles, swarmed in and at first sight of the strangers in their disheveled dress, pointed every firearm in their direction.

"Men, halt!" Woodhouse ordered. His wife huddled behind him, their son shielded between her skirts. "These people have come to help. They will not be harmed unless they withdraw their loyalty." He side-eyed Jamison. "Let us hope our trust in you is not misplaced."

He passed a rifle to his wife with a brief kiss, then reached for their son. The boy sobbed as his father claimed him. "Be good for mama, David. She will protect you. Rachel, barricade the door, and allow no one entrance unless I come. Flee for the boats only if you have no other choice."

"Boats?" Clinton asked.

"There is a path to the north along the sound which leads to a dock. About a half mile from here are two rowboats which the Pucketts use for fishing. They are not much, but enough to help the women and children escape if it comes to the worst. Now, take arms, men! Form the barricade as we discussed." David screamed and wailed as his father handed him back to his mother and followed his men out the door.

With an anguish Jamison hadn't time to contemplate, he took Coraline into his arms. "Stay with the women," he said, while knowing what her answer would be.

231

"No. I'm coming with you. I may not be able to shoot, but I can translate. It may buy you time." Moisture threatened the edges of her brown irises and she wiped them away. "Those are our friends. I don't believe I could shoot any of them even if I were able."

"I don't know if I can either."

Out there, somewhere in the forest, were Chinook he had known for years, and he had no idea if they had joined the assault or fled back to Larksong. He simply couldn't imagine the caring folk he worked and prayed and laughed alongside turning on him. He also couldn't imagine having the strength to kill one of them if it came to it. Both the Chinook and the Larks believed in protecting family. They were his "brothers." How could so great a divide suddenly stand between them?

"Jamison," Coraline gasped. "Quea'Quim..." Anguish dwelt behind those dark eyes, and no words needed to explain it.

As word passed from ear to ear of the imminent battle, Seattle radically changed from daily life in a logging town to a mismatched battlement. Soldiers whose training consisted of little more than hunting skills and a few basic courses from an old war hero now slopped up the muddy hill they were prepared to die on. Cries came from inside homes, perhaps of children, perhaps wives. Profane shouts of "Kill those fool injuns!" and worse bombarded them. Equally troubling was the singular cry of a hunched over old man, "'Whoever sheds the blood of man, by man shall his blood be shed, for God made man in his own image.'"

Oh, Lord, what are we doing? Jamison wondered.

The foursome paused between buildings, near enough to view the first natives spill through the trees, Senequa alongside their other leaders. From across the marsh approached the storm of three hundred natives ready to defend their land and destroy any white man who stood in their way. War shrieks and foreign words blurred with face paint and mud. He did not spy any of the Chinook, including Quea'Quim. Had they died or fled?

"Perhaps there is still a chance to change their minds," Coraline offered. She clung to Jamison's arm. "Let me talk to Senequa. If we prove they can live in peace as Larksong does, they will lay their weapons down."

"Have you lost your senses?" Clinton practically exploded. "That will lead to nothing except our deaths."

"Please, Mr. Reed, we have to try. I need to know I did some good in my life."

Jamison loathed that his wife had succumbed to desperate pleading and especially that she was pleading with a man who openly vied for her affection. He hated that he disagreed with her plan, while at the same time wanting to try again. Tears rolled down her pale cheeks from eyes that couldn't see and her hand kneaded empty air searching for Clinton to take it. Which he did. He kissed her knuckles and Jamison wanted to drown him in the marsh.

"Cora," Clinton said. "To me, you are perfect. You don't need to risk your life to be better. *I've* always known how wonderful you are."

She released a shuddered sob, and Clinton's eyes locked with Jamison's. Such malice in that stare. His words had been tender, but his expression challenged Jamison to defend himself and his authority as her husband. He should have either let the moment pass or dragged Clinton into the main thoroughfare and demanded a duel. Anything to move them away from that specific spot upon which they stood. But he didn't. Neither did anyone else. That single moment's hesitation allowed for an outcome none of them foresaw.

"Jamison! *Ni'-ka ka'po!*" a strangled cry erupted in some of the few Chinook words he knew. *Jamison! My brother!*

He spun as Quea'Quim crashed into him, the native's body wrapping Jamison's like a shield as they fell. They sank into the mud together, Quea'Quim sprawled across Jamison as a moan of anguish echoed from his lips.

"What happened?" Coraline screamed.

"God, our Father in heaven..." Clinton rasped and for once, he didn't seem to utter it as a curse.

Jamison rolled Quea'Quim off of him and immediately discovered the source of his friend's anguish. An arrow lodged deep and high in his left side, its tail feathers quivering. In a crimson creek, blood trickled from the wound and coated Quea'Quim's white howqua shell necklace like the fallen leaves of autumn. Even without close examination, Jamison knew the arrow head had broken through his friend's rib cage and lodged directly into his heart. Quea'Quim had been shot, not by the enemy, but by his own alliance. An alliance which, in the beginning, he hadn't even desired. He had chosen Jamison's life—a Boston man and a Christian—over his own.

Perhaps Quea'Quim had thirty seconds more to live. Not long enough for Jamison to do...anything. Quea'Quim's hand shot out and he held it with the realization that his friend's last movement was more nervous reflex than conscious intent. He was already gone.

Time slowed for a single second. Gunfire and war cries muffled. How would he explain to Anwillik and to the tribe? To his own family? To his wife who, thankfully, hadn't seen any of it, but now stood behind him in confusion.

Her terrified shout broke the time barrier as another assailant tackled him away from Quea'Quim. A flash of tangled copper-skinned limbs flew at him with a rock-hewn knife raised to strike. Thankfully, he recognized neither Chinook nor Winedafez in his attacker's war paint or his dress. No amenity reached out from those dark pupils, nor offer of negotiation.

Jamison rolled away and struck out his boot, pitching the stranger forward. Leaping to his feet, he stomped on the man's hand until the knife fell from his grasp. Brandishing it at him, Jamison gestured the warrior back toward the marsh. "Leave, before I change my mind!"

With a final curse which required no translation, the man released a terrifying cry and raced away, as two townsmen headed in pursuit.

Quea'Quim's body now lay an inch deep in the mud. His limbs had crumpled in on themselves and his wide eyes stared up, unseeing. Nausea climbed Jamison's throat like Joseph of the Old Testament, trying to escape the well after his brothers pitched him into it. Blood, paint, and mud flooded into a perverted kaleidoscope behind the tears rapidly filling his vision.

"Your people and ours are meant to live as one," Quea'Quim had told him once.

Then Coraline: *"I need to know I did some good in my life."*

"Coraline," he croaked. "We need to stop this." Silence. "Cora?" He spun in a circle and saw not a flash of her tan skirt or brunette curls.

"Cora!" he shouted. "Cora!"

In every direction he turned, she was gone.

36

"What's happening?" Coraline shouted as an insistent grip dragged her away. She stumbled into the man's back as he halted. She yanked her arm from his grip. "Who are you? Jamison?" She knew it wasn't but had to ask.

"No, Cora, it's me."

"Mr. Reed?" She latched onto him before she lost track of his position. "I thought you were one of the warriors. Where's Jamison?"

He seized her arm again and pulled her forward, but she dug her heels in. "Where is Jamison, Mr. Reed?"

"You won't like that answer. Please, we have to get to safety."

She clutched her skirt and as nonsensical as it seemed, swore she could feel the darkness closing in on her again. How was it possible for pitch black night to be even more pitch and black?

Mr. Reed turned her in another direction and she let her steps move wherever they cared to trod. He laced her arm through his to keep her steady as they hustled out of the fray. Tears desired her purchase, but she refused. Somewhere nearby a woman screamed, and an Indian shouted words Coraline wished she wasn't able to translate.

Dear God, help us!

"Mr. Reed..." she whispered. "Is my husband dead?"

"No, he's alive." He didn't halt, but he did loosen his grip a bit. "It's Quea'Quim who's dead. Another native killed him."

He had been right. She didn't like that answer. Not at all. It was more than she could comprehend.

"Quea'Quim can't be dead. Jamison would have been able to help him—"

"He tried, but it was too late. Then, he turned his pistol on us. Told us to leave him."

Get out of here before I change my mind! She had heard Jamison shout those words right before Mr. Reed dragged her away. She hadn't thought he meant her...that couldn't be right. Could it? He had promised they would remain together. *Where you go, I go.* Except he had wanted to send her away before. Send her away with Mr. Reed. Perhaps under duress, he realized he made a mistake by their reunion. Now, he intended to carry out the plans already begun.

She didn't want to believe it of her husband, or what happened to Quea'Quim, but at this point, she had little choice but to follow Mr. Reed's lead.

More shouts rang out, closer, although too far to be translated. Mr. Reed tugged on her arm. "Quickly!"

They were running, tripping, falling. Her leg hooked onto something across the path, whether a wayward log or a city trapping she couldn't tell. Everything mixed into the confusion of gunfire and war cries. Her hip connected with a solid object and down she went, a mouthful of dust sending her sputtering. She spit it out and coughed, but there was hardly time to catch her breath. Mr. Reed's arms were around her waist, then under her knees, her slender body cradled against him as he sprinted toward...what only heaven knew.

Unlike the seashore, there were no ropes here to lead her home and the steps impossible to count.

Farther away they drew until the forest's natural ambiance surrounded them and battle lingered at a distance. Some creature scampered through the brush and pattered away. Mr. Reed's footsteps pounded louder with each labored exhale. Yet, on he went.

"How far must we go?" she asked.

"Just a ways more. We're headed to the dock."

Of course. The dock the Seattleites mentioned in their escape plan. They would wait there for the others.

When he set her down at last, her boots landed upon a hard surface, wooden from the sound, and confirmed when her fingers wrapped around the raw plank she sat upon. As she shifted her feet, granules scraped beneath her soles, no doubt sand from the boat's previous occupants' climb in from shore. On either side, water lapped against the hull in steady rhythm.

"Hold on," he ordered her. With a jolt, he stepped into the boat and maneuvered his way to the opposite end. Although the vessel set to rocking, her steady grip upon the seat held her secure.

A moment later, she heard a familiar clack as the oars dropped into their locks and splashed into the water.

"Where are we going?" she asked.

"Someplace safe."

"Shouldn't we wait for the others?"

The swoop of the oars didn't slow. As they went farther without any indication of where they were or where they were going, memories of the last time she entered the ocean swam through her mind. This time, however, neither Tobias nor Jamison were there to help her. She had to trust that Mr. Reed did what he thought was best.

Eventually, however, gunfire crept back into her hearing, then shouts, and finally the dense odor of sulfur which meant a return to that which Jamison meant them to escape.

Fear rose beneath her sternum, tight and smothering like before, but this time from a completely different type of terror. If Jamison told them to leave, why were they headed back?

"Where are we going?" she asked again. Her tone rose and there was no concealing her anxiety.

His tone rather was as calm as stagnant waters. "Do you remember the battleship the natives spoke of, the *Decatur*? It sits directly off Seattle's coast. They'll take us where we need to go."

"Where is that?"

Cold and distant laughter met her ears. "Where there is a bounty on your head so large, I will never need to worry about my future ever again."

"Bounty? What are you talking about?"

Panic swelled. She pressed a hand against it, while the other clung to the edge of the boat, praying for rescue. *God, I believe you're there…*

"I'm under employ as a bounty hunter," he explained. "You better believe I deserve a tidy sum after living in your filth hole town all this time. The *Decatur*'s law-abiding men will never help you when I tell them you're a fugitive."

"But I've done nothing wrong!"

"You, no. It's your Gift they want. Think what power one would hold to have every language at their grasp."

"You've known for two years. Why wait all this time?"

"Up 'till then, I'd only been assigned to gather information on you Larks. With Jamison constantly sending letters, it was easy to have him post mine. Then 'bout a year ago, I received your assignment. I knew if I got caught, there'd be no pay and Tobias'd probably shoot me besides. I tried to make it easy on you. If you'd only gone when I asked you to go with me. I even had Jamison wanting you gone, but eventually, Cora, one gets tired of waiting. A war will provide the perfect cover for your disappearance."

Her tongue felt like dust, rough and tangible on her throat as she swallowed. "What does this man plan to do with me?"

"He didn't say and I never ask."

He *never* asked? That meant he had kidnapped for this man before.

"Is that where you sent Gabriella?" she asked. "Or did you murder her? Was that why Garrett couldn't find her?"

"I don't know why he couldn't find her," he said. "It wasn't my plan to lose her, but I definitely didn't murder her. Nothing about my job is ever personal enough to constitute murder."

It was personal to Coraline though. She had offered him her vulnerability. In a moment of weakness, she even let him kiss her. Under the guise of healing, he had tempted her to let him take her away from all she knew. Now she recognized that his kindness was only to lure her away without causing suspicion.

She wondered how much he was being paid.

Without warning, an explosion rang out from much closer than expected. A shockwave tossed the boat low on one side and she grasped the opposite edge with both hands to keep from going over.

The oars splashed back down as the boat righted itself, rocking from side to side.

"What was that?" she cried.

"The *Decatur*. She's firing on the Indians. Taken out a fair number from what I see through the smoke. They're fleeing into the woods." His steady rowing continued, this time distinctly in the direction from which the explosion sounded. "Well, good riddance to them all," he spat. "Traitors every one."

"Who is the traitor, Mr. Reed? You betrayed us all of us."

His mission wouldn't stop with her. If his employer wanted her Gift, in time, he would come after the others. Jamison, Tobias, Cade. Even Julep or Philip, although they were too young to determine yet what their Gifts may be. They were in danger from much more than the natives or a misguided government.

Without thinking about the consequences, she threw herself forward, hands outstretched until they connected with his chest. Having pegged his location, she thrust again, shoving him toward the side of the boat. She heard his body thud against the wood, but as his grip loosened from the oars, one swung forward. It rammed into her middle, throwing her in the same direction he had rolled, before the entire vessel shifted. She grappled for the boat's edge or the bench seat—anything—but determined fingers latched onto her ankle. A scream escaped her lips to match his snarl as the world upended and sent them both into the dark waters of Puget Sound.

37

"Coraline!" Jamison screamed. "Cora, where are you?"

Everywhere he turned was chaos. Bullets passed on one side only for him to narrowly avoid arrows on the other. Smoke and dust clogged his senses and, filtered through the daylight, made everything feel like a surreal dream. Weren't they supposed to be well organized in lines of troops like the paintings he had seen of the Revolution? Then why were townsfolk and natives running haphazardly without a commander to lead them?

Where was Coraline? Where was his wife? Bringing her hadn't even accomplished anything. They had no time to even try. If she died, it would be exactly as Alice Ann said, his fault. He had barely come to terms with his part in Oliver's death—finally felt he could forgive himself—and now he would be forced to battle his heart yet again. That was a battle he didn't know he could win this time.

Where was Clinton? He had disappeared about the same time Coraline did, or so he thought. He wasn't sure. Had Clinton taken Cora somewhere? Was he keeping her safe?

He could only focus on one thing at a time. Coraline was blind and alone in an unknown place. He had to find her.

Lord, I need you!

A man ran by, one of the Seattleites, with a shotgun in hand. A dribble of blood ran from a wound on his cheek. "Sir!" Jamison shouted. He grabbed the man's shirt sleeve and threw his hands up in surrender when the Seattleite swung the weapon upon him. When he caught sight of Jamison, he lowered it a few inches.

"Please, sir, I lost my wife. Have you seen her?"

The man's eyebrows raised a solid inch. "The blind woman? What kind of husband are you?"

Jamison was saved from answering when an explosion crashed from the *Decatur*. The impact tossed them both into the air and slammed back to the earth, where he lay with his ears ringing like a kettledrum. Dense smoke hovered above him. Hazy clouds which lazed about a gun silver sky.

Slowly, he moved every appendage, relieved to find everything intact. He rolled onto his side and pushed himself to stand with a groan. He hurt, but he wouldn't feel it until the adrenaline wore off or he died, so he needed to use the reprieve to his advantage. Thankfully, the man he spoke to was coming to his senses and seemingly unharmed as well. As he reached to help the man up, more cannon fire exploded, except farther away this time. They held onto one another as the ground shook beneath their feet.

When the smoke finally cleared, the last of the natives were fleeing into the woods across the marsh. Several trade lodges had suffered damage and flames erupted from the roof of at least two homes. Bodies of the dead—almost exclusively natives—scattered the area from the flames to the forest. In the eerie calm which followed there pierced a feminine scream.

Jamison's gaze drew in the direction of the *Decatur*, from where it seemed the sound had emitted, but the soldiers on deck peered instead into the sound. About one hundred paces off the *Decatur's* bow, a man and woman fought over control of a rowboat, the vessel sloshing low and nearly tipping. Although he couldn't see clear details, he would know his wife anywhere.

"Cora!" He took off like a shot toward the shore, then dove in without hesitation.

Years had passed since he swam and never with this many clothes on. His deer-skin coat weighed heavy and his boots sought to drag him to the bottom, but he couldn't stop to shed any of his garments. His arms plowed through the water, only halfway to the rowboat when he lifted his head and saw no one. The boat floated upside down and neither Coraline nor her assailant were visible.

His scream garbled as water splashed between his lips. He spit it out. "Cora!"

"Ahwhah!" The cry was indistinct but enough to judge a direction. He rounded the boat and found Coraline about ten yards off, arms flailing as she disappeared beneath the surface.

He dove after her, but the water was dark and it felt like the devil himself assisted with the speed of her descent. Her arms trailed above her, her legs limp, with one boot missing. No bubbles sputtered from her lips as they ought to do. Pushing onward, he grabbed ahold of her around the chest, but she was akin to a bundle of rice sacks before separation. He gasped as they broke the surface, great heaves while wondering if he inhaled enough water to drown later in his sleep.

He cast a glance for the boat's other passenger and saw no one. A split second of sorrow racked his soul before he remembered that the man had been trying to harm his wife. If he could only save one, he would save her. A great splash sounded and seconds later, two soldiers heaved the rowboat upright and hauled Coraline inside.

"Send the physician!" one of them shouted up to his comrades on the *Decatur*. "We have an injured woman!"

"Move! I'm a doctor!" Jamison shoved them aside and knelt over Coraline's still pale form. She wasn't breathing.

Gruesome memories wouldn't stay at bay. Ephram Tull's broken body beneath the wagon wheels, Oliver's swollen snake bite wound. Geraldine Lark's broken neck high in the attic rafters and Jamison's father, still smirking even in death. Coraline wasn't dead yet but he couldn't think how to help her. What was he supposed to do? Did he have any skills at all? It felt like when he knelt over Tobias's bleeding form without recollection of any of his talents.

But he *had* saved Tobias. He *had* stitched up Coraline's arm.

For the gifts and the call of God are irrevocable, he recited.

God had gifted him with these abilities. He could do this.

The soldier shouted up to the ship again, asking them to send down a sling. The other soldier reached for Coraline, trying to flip her to her stomach, probably to slap her back and the water from her lungs. It wouldn't work; Jamison knew that much. He knew more too; he simply needed to remember how to do it.

He shoved the soldier away onto the other side of the boat. It rocked with the movement, threatening to capsize them again.

"What are you doing?" the man shouted. "We have to help her!"

"I am! I'm a doctor and she's my wife and you're in my way!"

The man backed off, but continued to peer anxiously up at the ship. Like Alice Ann, he would hold Jamison responsible for whatever happened to Coraline, which was no less than the account to which Jamison would hold himself.

The laws of the Gifted reasoned that she should die beneath his hands. But who made those laws? Were they true or had the Larks never tried to overcome them because their father said it couldn't be done?

"All I wanted was someone to stand with me," Coraline had told him. *"To remind me that there's more to us than just our Gifts."*

He still had his brain and everything he had learned.

Lord, help me. I know I have been selfish and scared. I know I have neglected Cora in times of desolation, but it was You who brought her to me. You gave me this Gift of healing. Let me use it to keep her a little longer.

Clasping one hand atop the other, he placed them together into the center of her chest and struck downward. Then again. Five...ten...fifteen...

"What are you doing?" the soldier shouted. "You're going to kill her!" He tried to rip Jamison's arms away, but Jamison shoved him back and reached for Coraline again. He tilted her head back and lifted her chin while his other hand pinched her nose. Covering her mouth with his, he breathed deeply, twice.

The soldier tried to push him away again. "Stop right now!"

Jamison drew his pistol, clearly waterlogged and worthless, and pointed it at the soldier's chest. He would be arrested for this and he didn't care. "You don't let me save her and I will shoot you."

He dropped the pistol with a thud and went back to his chest compressions. Halfway through the third set, water spewed from Coraline's lips. He turned her onto her side as violent coughs wracked her body several times. Finally, she lay gasping, her body limp but alive.

"I don't believe it!" the soldier cried. "Men!" he called up as a sling finally made its descent. "She's alive!"

Jamison barely heard the words. He wrapped her in his arms, both of them shivering beneath the wind pummeling across the waters. "Thank you," he whispered. The words were stolen, lost in the activity of soldiers and slings and waves upon wood.

But he knew the One they were meant for always heard.

38

Forearms propped on the *Decatur*'s starboard rail, Jamison observed the small town of Seattle as she tended to her wounds. The morning after the soldiers' cannon ended the battle, the fires had also been extinguished, leaving half-charred ruins. In a town of only a few streets, the loss of even one building would be felt mightily.

Would the citizens remain with her through another year or would they take advantage of the coming summer and return east while they still could? Supply ships arrived in port every few months. Plenty of time to gather supplies, pack belongings, and secure passage back to wherever they hailed. Rumor had it that storms around Cape Horn were no pleasant affair, but a family might risk it for the security of established civilization. He himself had considered that very option.

Of course, the Seattleites were not the only victims of the battle. What of the Indians? In the end, an untold number of natives had been killed, but only two settlers. Jamison could justify the natives' anger toward the United States government, but what had they accomplished by their attack? It felt like they were right back where they were before. Or perhaps even worse off.

"Mr. Lark?"

He turned as a sailor approached, the insignia on his uniform indicating an officer's status. His eyes slid in the direction of Seattle and grew pensive. "Shame what happened yesterday, isn't it? If only those Indians would go where they're told. It would solve all our problems, really."

Jamison wanted to lash out, grab him by the lapels, and shout how he had called one of those "Indians" a friend and brother. How that "Indian" had saved his life. Quea'Quim had a sister and a nephew who admired his courage. He had a tribe who turned to him for leadership, and a town of "Boston men" who owed him their survival. He had been someone, not just anyone, and Jamison didn't know how he could tell Coraline that Quea'Quim was killed by his own kind.

Alas, assaulting a military officer, one obviously at odds with his beliefs, would only land him in jail or dead. He was lucky enough not to be there already.

"How is my wife?" he asked. They had placed her in the first mate's cabin after drawing them both up from the water. Once settled, he had asked to return to shore and help minister to the wounded, but the soldiers insisted the ship's physician would tend to the injuries. Jamison should remain near his wife in case she needed him. As a result, he didn't know what happened to Quea'Quim's body. He despised the idea of his friend prone to carrion, but there was nothing he could do to help him right now.

"The ship's doctor says she's awake and recovering well," the officer told him. "She's lucky to have a physician for a husband. Not even our doctor had heard of that procedure you did on her. You must have impressive schooling. Harvard?"

"South Carolina, actually."

"Oh, I suppose that would explain the accent. Never met anybody from there. Did you own slaves?"

"Slavery's outlawed in Washington and how about we see to my wife?" Thankfully, that was the end of the inquiry.

When they entered, Coraline sat up in the single berth bed; a two-drawer dresser and wall hooks being the only other items in the room. Both furniture pieces were bolted to the floor without any visible personal effects. A single port window shadowed speckled light across the room.

"I'll leave you with privacy," the officer told them. He ducked out the door and closed it behind him.

"Your husband's here," Jamison said as he strode toward her. Her eyes, as usual, stared past him, but her hand shot out, searching for his grasp. Claiming it at once, he pressed a kiss upon her brow and lowered himself to sit beside her. She immediately snuggled into the crook of his shoulder, her arms slipping beneath his coat to wrap his middle. Her steady breathing rose and fell against his chest. There was still life in those lungs. Life he replaced despite every logic telling him it wasn't possible.

Coraline's arms tightened, bringing him back. "You're quiet. Where did I lose you to?"

He smiled, knowing she could hear it. "You'll never know how glad I am to see you alive and well."

"You told me last night."

"Well, it's still true this morning. How are you feeling?"

"Tired. My chest hurts. Right here." She tapped a fingertip to the exact place where he had resuscitated her.

"Sorry. I had to."

"I know. I'm glad you did."

They eased back into silence, and let the ship's rocking ease them toward the conversation he didn't wish to have. But some wounds must be caused eventually, and a disused sword still remained sharp. It was strange to think Quea'Quim wasn't out in the woods on the edge of Seattle, waiting for them.

He ran a palm over the scratchy wool blanket scrunched between them. "Coraline, I'm afraid I need to tell you some unfortunate news about Quea'Quim."

Her breath hitched. "I already know and I don't understand. He waited his whole life to be respected by his people and he finally was and now, he's...gone. It's so senseless and poor Anwillik. She loved her brother." She rubbed the moisture from her eyes with his shirt. "Will we have to burn the town again?"

"No, but the rest of the Chinook may decide to rejoin the tribe on Shoalwater Bay. Assuming that yesterday, they didn't abandon us altogether."

"Quea'Quim wanted us to live as one. So did Tobias."

"I did too." Everything was moving so quickly. Life and death. Him becoming the leader of Larksong in the blink of an eye. Almost losing his own life and then Coraline's in another.

"We did our best," he assured her. "We wanted to help and we tried. They wouldn't listen."

"They didn't give us a chance. The battle would have ended up the same with or without us."

She wasn't wrong. He wished she was.

A swell caught the underside of the *Decatur*, raising the hull an inch, before settling it back into the water. "What of Mr. Reed?" she asked then, her tone timid. "How is he?"

How is *he*? Unwelcome jealousy flared inside Jamison. His ears puckered beneath its heat. It had been enough of a struggle when the man was around. After having that no-account desert them in battle, his prayer no longer consisted of "heal my jealousy" so much as "Lord, keep me from tossing him out of town and to the wolves."

Four deep breaths allowed him enough time to calm his words, and be thankful that Coraline couldn't see the grimace upon his lips. There were few advantages to her blindness, but never having to worry about facial emotion was one of them.

"Cora, Clinton abandoned us during the fight."

Her nose wrinkled. "Perhaps he abandoned *you*. He tried to kidnap *me*. He was in the boat with me before it capsized."

Four deep breaths were not enough. Jamison drew another four.

Clinton kissing Cora in a moment of missing his Gabriella could be forgotten. Stealing her was another matter entirely.

The Christian task would be for him to forgive, and he would. Over and over until he actually felt it become true. Seventy times seven times.

Clinton Reed had been a thorn in their town's side and most of the time, a loafer, but he had also saved Tobias under threat of gunfire and helped Sarah transport him back to the wagon train. He had provided the cattle which supplemented their food stores through times of low supply. Eventually, Jamison could allow that goodness to help him forgive the wrongs. Especially now that the man's soul needed more prayer than his life.

"We didn't find him," he told her more gently than he felt inclined. "Assumedly, he drowned when the rowboat tipped." A mix of emotions flitted across her face. Surprise, grief, a sense of justice, perhaps. "Did he say what he wanted with you?"

"He said he had been hired. His employer wanted my Gift and was willing to pay high to get it. He said he's been spying on you and your brothers for years."

So, those letters Clinton had been sending weren't to his relatives after all. Had his employer known about their Gifts before hiring Clint, or did Clint tell him in hopes of turning a profit? Was Cora's abduction his employer's idea or was Clint the mastermind? Had it been one of the natives? They tried to be careful with how much they shared, but if they knew about Cora, they could have figured out the others as well. Without the culprit there to ask, they likely would never know. One thing was for certain: their world was apt to grow much larger and perhaps further complicated.

According to Garrett's last letter, he still resided in San Francisco, the last known destination of Clinton Reed's letters. Which meant that if any danger were to befall them, Garrett would be closest to the blast. As soon as they were back in Larksong, he would pen a letter and take it to Father Lionnet himself for posting.

"Jamison?" Cora's tone told him he had wandered off too long again. "Do we need to worry? Could someone else come for us?"

He squeezed her protectively within his grasp. "We must be cautious, but I have no desire to uproot our town and flee. It wouldn't guarantee protection. What we have is based on standing together, and trusting our family as we have since Charleston. Believing that we have the strength to hold on. I promised to stand beside you, Coraline, and I intend to. Everything will right itself in the end." He hoped.

"I am glad to hear you affirm it. Mr. Reed told me you wanted him to take me away during the battle, and I worried that it might have been true."

"Of course not. I tried to find you. I had no idea where you were and I was terrified."

"Then why did you say...oh, it doesn't matter. Let's put all that behind us." She smiled. "Besides, this mysterious employer might not be as bad as we think. Perhaps he's Gifted too and simply wants to find others like him. He just needs to go about it a different way."

"How I would love it if that were true." And how he loved that her innocent optimism was returning.

"It could be."

"You're right. It could be. If I'd believe anyone, I'd believe you."

A light rap sounded at the door and when Jamison called his acknowledgement, the first mate's tall form followed. "The Captain says that everything's in order for us to make way. We'll take you to your shore, then we must return straight away. The townsfolk have provided travel clothes for you and the lady." Onto Jamison's lap, he placed a bundle wrapped in what appeared to be a hand stitched quilt. Such an offering felt too generous on the part of the Seattleites; however, since their traveling bags were lost in the woods, he remained certainly grateful.

"Thank you," he told the officer. "Please extend our thanks to the town."

"Of course, sir. We'll be shipping out first light tomorrow."

Once they were alone again, Jamison offered to let Coraline rest, but she only held him tighter.

"Please, won't you stay? I don't want to be alone."

How could he refuse? He could still remember a time when he felt so unworthy of this woman's love, yet it had been there as real as this moment was now. Two moments of many in a life he would do everything he could to keep. Even unto heaven.

"I won't leave you for a moment, my love. Not until we're safely home."

39

Over a month had passed since they arrived back in Larksong, and one would never know that Coraline had almost lost her life in Puget Sound. The pain in her chest vanished within a few days and her semi-labored breathing returned to normal a day after that. Any other doctor would have called her recovery miraculous, and it was, but only the Larks knew the source of the miracle.

As the new leader of Larksong, Jamison's responsibilities continued to grow, requiring a supportive wife to stand beside him. For now, however, she was content to walk arm in arm with Alice Ann along the shore, enjoying a rare obligation-free Sunday while Julep toddled along barefoot beside them. Cade had warned of rain showers overnight, but evening still lay hours away.

Every so often, Julep screeched with laughter as a wave came close and she leaped out of the way. Alice Ann would announce her silliness for Coraline's sake and continue on. But her daughter's uneven steps eventually sent her stumbling face first into the sand and screaming for an entirely different reason.

"Mama, mama! I ga sod! Et sod!" she yelled.

"Oh, Jules..." Alice Ann lifted her up, dusted her off, and after swiping sand from the inside of her cheeks with a now slimy finger, sent her off to do it once again.

"That girl," she sighed as she took Coraline's arm for the sixth time. "She's always falling down and getting hurt or trying to eat things she shouldn't. She screams about nothing in particular and

Cade mollycoddles her for it. Ugh. Listen to me, using words like 'that girl' and 'mollycoddle.' I'm practically an old woman."

"Oh, biscuits, you're far from it," Coraline chuckled.

Alice Ann's voice grew soft. "It's been a rather long time since you used the word 'biscuits' and laughed about it. You are happy again, aren't you?"

"Wouldn't you believe it, but I am."

"Even blind?"

Of course, her sister would put it so bluntly. "It is not without difficulty. I don't like being blind. I wish I wasn't. I cry about it all the time, but I have Jamison and we have our prayers, and we know they'll come to good someday."

"Well, I couldn't do it—oh, for Pete pity's sake, Julep. She's eating the sand again."

A shrill cry sounded on the tail end of Alice Ann's statement and she released Coraline for the seventh time. "Would you mind holding her?" she asked. "She needs her nap and you're so talented at rocking her to sleep. We'll sit on the sand just up there."

"Of course." Coraline held out her arms and Julep immediately snuggled into her aunt's neck, sand dusting from her curls onto Coraline's skin.

Holding her sister's elbow, Alice Ann led them to a dry patch of ground settled well away from the water. Julep curled up tight upon Coraline's lap and as she stroked the little girl's crown, she heard the soft suckling of a tiny thumb between toddler lips. For a while after, the women allowed the silence, broken by the waves and the cool March breeze through the distant branches. The occasional gull squawked as it passed overhead. Not too long after, Julep's steady breaths were only broken by the occasional adorable thumb suckle.

"She's asleep. Shall we take her back to the house?" Coraline asked.

"No. I..." Alice Ann's substantial inhale was followed by a sharp release. "I need to be honest with you, Cora. I brought you here to say goodbye."

"*Goodbye*? Where are you going?"

She heard her sister shift and grains of sand showered down as she shook out her skirt. "I'm leaving Larksong. I'm heading out on the high seas as soon as I can afford it. That was always my dream and it's time I followed it."

Coraline must have heard her incorrectly. "You mean that you and Cade and Julep are all leaving on a ship."

"No. I am. Just me."

"But you're married."

"Yes, and Cade will move on. He'll find someone better. More suited." Coraline had a sudden flash of her sister at seventeen, bare feet and no stockings, under a trail wagon tempting the youngest Lark brother with her untamed braids. They hadn't been suited then nor suited now.

"I think he would prefer you," she said.

Alice Ann snorted. "Cade's such a ninny. He cried the first time we made love. What an embarrassment." There was sudden silence followed by another sharp intake of breath and another exhale. "No, actually, honestly, he wasn't. He was...very kind to me."

"He loves you."

"I know he does."

"Then why are you doing this? Do you not love him? What about Julep?" The girl slept on in blissful ignorance, unaware that her mother wanted to shatter her world.

"Julep's better off without me, too. Honest, Cora, did you ever think I'd be a mother?"

No, she hadn't. She never thought her sister would be responsible enough, although she had hoped... "But you are a mother, Alice Ann. You have to give this little girl what she needs."

"I am. She needs a kind and loving mother. Someone like our mother. I'm not that, but you are. So are Sarah and Marie and Martha. You'll give her all the maternal care she needs."

"But—"

"This decision isn't whimsy. You know how much I've wanted to sail and have a life of adventure. Cade doesn't want that. He can predict the storms, but he never wants to weather them. He runs out on our arguments and agrees with me rather than try to win. I don't want stillness. I don't want to be trapped here for the rest of my days."

"Where will you go?"

"Wherever the first ship I can afford is going. Maybe I'll return home, take up Papa's business."

"How would that be an adventure?"

"I suppose it wouldn't."

Did Cade know how deeply this weighed on Alice Ann? Surely, he would fight for her if he did.

"You need to give Cade another chance. Tell him what you've told me."

There was a rustling and Coraline jolted as Alice Ann's cold fingers touched hers. A folded bit of parchment was forced between her fingers. "Give this to Cade once I'm gone."

Coraline turned her hand so she gripped Alice Ann's, the note wedged between their palms. "I won't. You can't do this to him."

"Everyone's always said he didn't deserve someone like me. You said it. So did Jamison and Tobias and Sarah. Name anyone. You were all right."

"He'll follow after you. He'll catch up to you before you get even a mile away."

"No, he won't, because you won't have an opportunity to tell him until I'm long gone. You're holding Julep and the rope path is at least ten yards away. You would never risk walking the wrong way and hurting her. So, you'll wait right here until, in about an hour or two, Jamison or Cade will come looking for us. They'll see you sitting alone and that's when you'll tell them. But you won't know which direction I've gone or who I've enlisted to help me. You'll return to town and you'll have supper and tomorrow, you'll convince Cade to continue his life without me."

Coraline couldn't understand this. How could she? "This is selfish, Alice Ann. You have a daughter."

With those words, her sister yanked her hand away. Alice Ann's next words came from above rather than beside her. All sympathy had driven away from her tone, leaving only bitter resentment.

"No, Cora, this is the *least* selfish thing I've ever done. All my life, I've only looked out for myself, and you looked out for me. I was a bad sister, bad daughter, bad wife, bad mother. I'm the only one in our family who deserved to go blind, but I didn't. You're going to let me do this one good deed and take a little of the burden off your shoulders, since I know I placed so much of it there. Tomorrow, hopefully, I'll be the best of everything everyone wanted."

"This isn't what we want," Coraline begged. But her only response was the whisper of the wind, the roar of the waves, and the ever steady suckling of a now motherless little girl.

40

May 1856
Four Months Later

Coraline's bare feet dug into the sand, its miniscule granules cool between her toes. The tiny rocks scraped her skin as she followed the rope down to the water's edge and let the surf slip just over her toenails. As expected, like the breeze which fluttered her loose curls against her neck, the water was cold even in mid-May. Her lungs filled with the brine of her childhood and that of her adult home, and the thrill of wave crashing upon wave finally brought her comfort rather than despair.

Somewhere out on that water were her Chinook townsfolk, their canoe paddles slicing through the deep blue mirror, their muscles taut as they pulled in the first salmon of the season. Tonight, they would all dine together—Chinook and Boston man alike—celebrating another year of Larksong's unity despite the continued disquiet all around the Northwest region. Five Chinook warriors remained unaccounted for; whether due to desertion or death was unknown. The rest had refused to fight and returned home after being separated from their leader. It was only later that they learned of Quea'Quim's passing.

Although the Puget Sound battles had ceased in March—at least according to official government records—the war never truly ended. The native tribes continued to sign treaties, move onto reservations, and lose their tribal lands. After Seattle stole the lives of nearly every Winedafez warrior, Senequa quickly surrendered his tribal lands in order to save their meager population.

For now, the Chinook were free to remain as they were, but they all wondered how long that would last.

Just as the Larks wondered how long until their Gifts were sought out again. They agreed it best to remain in the shadows for now. No new members would learn of their talents, nor the Chinook, past those who already knew of Coraline's translations. Even Anwillik was sworn to silence. If one of their own had already turned against them—someone carefully selected by their own hands—what outsider could be completely trusted? If resistance did arrive, they had a family and a tribe standing strong in protection, even if that family was now one fewer.

Coraline swiped a tear from her cheek. Quea'Quim had been her protector, like an older brother she never had and never knew she needed...until he was no longer there. He hadn't deserved death after finding his place in life so soon before.

When they left Seattle, Jamison had asked for the *Decatur* to retrieve Quea'Quim's body. The captain was skeptical, of course, but Woodhouse's personal testimony was enough to convince him. The soldiers carried Quea'Quim from the dinghy down the path to Larksong Cemetery where he received a raised canoe ceremony per Chinook tradition. Next January, they would bury his bones alongside little Mary Grace in a Christian funeral as Anwillik asked. Her brother never understood or agreed with Christianity, but when she begged Jamison to provide her this one request, he obliged. She clung to her faith with a fervor Coraline hadn't the strength to in her sorrow but deeply admired. In many ways, to her, it felt like Quea'Quim had died for nothing, but to Anwillik, her brother had given his life for something greater. To her, he was a warrior worthy of every honor.

Yet, despite all that, or perhaps because of, Coraline now found more meaning in her life than she ever had.

She placed a hand on her swollen belly. "Not too long until we get to meet you. I bet you'll be beautiful." As usual, she was rewarded with the firmness of her child's happiness, a flutter of movement which required no sight to cherish. How blessed she was to be granted such a miracle.

The clouds likely parted then, for warmth passed upon her face. She raised her chin to the sun, in the direction of the sea, remembering its beauty. How the waves curled white foam against her toes, their color as grey as the sky, the evergreens of deepest emerald, and the majestic mountains capped in lamb's wool. The opalescent sunrise, singing its joy, and every evening the sky set ablaze. She still pictured every detail in her mind's eye.

Her father had indeed been wise in his decision. As he predicted, the West had been an adventure. If only it had been enough for Alice Ann. Whenever Father Lionnet delivered the mail, Cade always asked if there was anything for him. She knew he would never stop asking. Julep grew bigger by the day, her dark hair a match to her father, but her wide-eyed curiosity so like her mother. It wouldn't be long before she understood why her cousins and friends still had mothers, but she didn't. All they could do was pray that one day soon Alice Ann's restless spirit might lead her home.

Tears pricked, but this time, Coraline managed to blink them away. She wouldn't dwell in longings. She had the blessing of her husband's affection and soon, the joy of her child's laughter. The welcome scent of the sea and the flavor of each salmon the Chinook brought for supper. A family who loved her even at her lowest and a God who never left her, even when He appeared to be silent.

"Au-tee Cora!" Her nephew Philip's sweet call floated on the wind, his hand likely clutched tight in his momma's. "Suppa Time!"

With a smile, Coraline lifted her skirt in one hand and followed the rope with the other, turning the page on a new chapter and leaving the old ones behind.

41

MAY 1856
SAN FRANCISCO, CALIFORNIA
GARRETT

Dear Garrett,

I pray this letter finds you alive and well. Tobias told me not to bother you—he seems convinced you're never coming home—but Cade thought it better if you knew. Let me assure you that we are all well, but you need to be cautious. It appears Clinton Reed may have sold our secrets, to whom I do not know. Unfortunately, our last encounter resulted in his untimely death when he tried to kidnap Cora for a bounty. He did not say what his employer planned, but I am assured it was nothing decent.

Please come home soon. Josiah too, whatever it takes. We are stronger together than apart.

Your niece and nephew send their love.

Your brother,
Jamison

Garrett lowered the letter.
Their Gifts were in danger? Coraline had almost been kidnapped?

By *Clinton*? Who was now dead?

He read through the letter again. *Come home. Josiah too, whatever it takes.*

Perhaps he should listen to his brother. Even with near empty pockets, maybe it was time to honor his promises and head back to Larksong. He could help protect his remaining family from whatever threats may come their way.

Not yet. There was a reason he was here and he had to know what it was. If he didn't, he would always wonder what he missed. He would discover his purpose here by the time he turned thirty-five, or he would consider the opportunity forgotten.

He added Jamison's letter to the one in his breast pocket, full of delicate words penned by a woman who deserved more consideration than he could give.

Wait for me, Martha, he thought. *Two more years. I promise that's all I need.*

Larksong Legacy continues with Martha and Garrett's story in *Sparks Fly Upward.*

AUTHOR'S NOTE

Like the characters in *Dusk Shall Weep*, anxiety and depression affect millions of people worldwide every day. If you, or someone you know, live with these conditions, you are not alone. Hope is only a call or click away.

Focus on the Family Christian Counselor Assistance
1-855-771-HELP (4357)
https://www.focusonthefamily.com/get-help/

Substance Abuse and Mental Health Services Administration
1-800-662-HELP (4357)
https://samhsa.gov/find-help/national-helpline

National Suicide Prevention Lifeline
1-800-273-8255 or Text "TALK" to 741741
https://suicidepreventionlifeline.org/

Did you know that a comprehensive eye exam can help detect a number of different diseases? For more information, visit:

National Eye Institute
https://www.nei.nih.gov/

American Optometric Association
https://www.aoa.org/healthy-eyes

There are many additional resources available in addition to those listed. While the organizations listed above are United States based, similar organizations are available in other countries.

Have faith. Have hope. You have beautiful purpose.

HISTORICAL NOTES

Behind Coraline's Eyes:

The medical term for Coraline's degenerative blindness is retinitis pigmentosa. Symptoms usually begin in childhood and one's field of vision gradually narrows until familiar tasks such as reading, facial recognition, and even walking can become difficult. Progression can take from years to decades. Although retinitis pigmentosa was originally identified in 1857, the concept of diseases passed via heredity was not fully understood until 1863, which left only one "logical" conclusion: inescapable sin.

For a character who spends most her story doubting God, however, Coraline's creation was full of Biblical influences:

The blind man at the Pool of Bethesda
In John Chapter 5, Jesus comes across a man near the Pool of Bethesda, who had been blind and lame for 38 years. This pool was known for its healing properties, but the man had no one to lift him into the pool. Instead, Jesus tells him to take up his mat and walk and he is healed.

The women with the hemorrhage
Both Mark Chapter 5 and Luke Chapter 8 tell of a woman who suffered from a hemorrhage for 12 years. She spent all her money on doctors and prayed every prayer, but nothing helped her situation. Then she sees Jesus and in an act of pure faith, reaches out to him. When she touches his cloak, she is instantly healed.

Jesus's apostles speak in multiple languages
In Acts of the Apostles Chapter 2, Jesus's apostles have gone out to preach the Word after Christ's resurrection. Through the power of the Holy Spirit, they are found to miraculously speak in multiple languages, so everyone listening understands. Today,

people who can easily learn many languages are called polyglots. One of the more famous spiritual polyglots was Saint Pope John Paul II, who could speak eight languages fluently and perhaps up to four more conversationally.

I wanted Cora to be someone who used to have faith, but her faith dwindled as she lost hope, similar to how the blind man and hemorrhaging woman felt. Can you imagine being considered "unclean" for all those years, kept outside the community, and even outside of temple worship? Coraline too felt like an outsider, trapped inside herself and away from all she loved. In her darkest hour, she uses her last bit of strength to finally reach out to God. It is only through faith that she can truly find healing, although it is not in the way she expects.

For more details on the background of the Gifted, please see the Historical Notes in *For a Noble Purpose*.

No Victors in War:

As written in *Dusk Shall Weep*, the real-life Battle for Seattle ended without a definitive outcome. Often in life, there are battles we can't control and in which no one wins. Such was the case with the Battle for Seattle, the culmination of over a year of failed treaty negotiations and unrest between Governor Stephens's men and the Northwest tribes.

On January 26, 1856, several tribes gathered near Lake Duwamish (now Lake Washington) to arrange an attack on the small town of Seattle. As described in the story, they planned to take control of the battleship *Decatur* which was anchored in the harbor undergoing repairs; however, they did not realize that the ship was full of soldiers. The natives tore through the town, burning several buildings, until they reached the harbor where they were fired upon by the *Decatur*. In the end, up to 28 natives died with 80 to 100 wounded and only two settler fatalities. Their plan to massacre the townspeople had been foiled by a native who brought warning to the "Boston men" and gave them time to prepare.

Some readers may not enjoy that the Chinook/Winedafez war councils included only men, with the exception of Coraline who attended due to her Gift. To a modern sensibility, this seems sexist, but back then, it would have been standard practice. While the men of Larksong took their wives' opinions seriously, fighting the natives on their inclusion in a war council could have bred unnecessary hostility. It should be said though that many of the Pacific Northwest tribes did have great respect for their women, often including them as leaders and confidants, but my research indicates that war was still very much a man's world. Even having Coraline speak as she did was a risk.

Finally, although there are many similarities between tribes in the Pacific Northwest, each tribe has its distinct culture. Therefore, it would be impossible to give every tribe its place within the complexity of the Puget Sound War. I chose the Chinook as the central tribe due to their known peaceful nature and willingness to work alongside the "Boston men." When they were asked to participate in the Battle for Seattle, they actually declined.

The Winedafez tribe is entirely of my imagination.

Speaking the Jargon:

In the 1850s, if you asked someone if they spoke the "jargon," they were referring to a special trade language used between the settlers and the Pacific Northwest tribes, in particular the Chinook.

Much of my research of the Chinook during this time came from James Gilchrist Swan's 1857 book, *The Northwest Coast; or, Three Years' Residence in Washington Territory*. He discusses the area around the Querquelin stream (aka Mouse River) where a real Indian village had been abandoned due to the chief's death and fear of evil spirits, whom only "Boston men" could tame. Once the settlers moved into the village, the natives quickly returned to trade with them. My description of the new Larksong comes from this village. The Chinook customs of head flattening, slavery, spirit quests, funeral customs, howqua shells, and salmon fishing are also factual, as are the names Quea'Quim, Anwillik, Tleyuk, Spaärk, and Senequa.

The Chinook legend of the sea monster destroying the earth was taken from a true event in January of 1700 when the Cascadia Fault shifted, resulting in a horrific earthquake and tsunami. Most natives near the shore lost their lives and one Ozette tribal village was buried under a mud slide. Excavation of the site began in 1970 and continues to this day.

Finally, the Stella Maris (Star of the Sea) Mission on Point Ellice, where Coraline and Jamison marry, was established by Father Joseph Louis Lionnet as a Roman Catholic mission in 1848. Between 1848 and 1860, he baptized, married, buried, and evangelized to an untold number of both native and white residents. St. Mary's Catholic Church now stands in its place and provides Mass during the summer months.

Acknowledgments

As always—and I can't say it enough—thank you to my readers! God has blessed me with an audience I couldn't have even imagined at the start.

To my husband, Scott, and our children. You put up with my excitement over historical events of which I know you have no interest. Thank you for sometimes acting like you do. I love you!

To my parents, Ken and Ruth, and my godmother, Mary for teaching me that faith is always first. I couldn't have written Jamison's character or Coraline's conversion without you.

To my fellow historical fiction author friends: Jennifer Q. Hunt, Susan Laspe, Rhonda Ortiz, and Tanya E. Williams. Because of you, this novel is completely different from my original outline and so much better. Thank you!

To my beta readers: Ann, Jennifer, Ken, Mary, Mindy, Rhonda, Ruth, Sarah, Sharon, Susan, and Tanya. For your many comments, suggestions, edits, and hours of discussion and debate. Thank you!

To my advance reader team, the Catholic Writers Guild, the

Christian Mommy Writers group, and the wonderful bookstagram community. Thank you for your advice, reviews, posts, interviews, and well wishes!

To the many organizations who helped make my historical information accurate and believable, especially the Missouri Historical Society, St. Charles and St. Louis County Libraries, Middle Village Station Camp McGowan (U.S. National Park Service), Chinook Indian Nation (chinooknation.org), Washington State Historical Society, Washington Grown, Seattle Municipal Archives, Oregon National Historic Trail (U.S. National Park Service), Oregon Encyclopedia, The Metropolitan Museum of Art, The National Gallery of Art, and all those real-life pioneers and Native Americans whose stories were left behind. I hope you found the dreams you were searching for.

Most importantly, to my Lord and creator, Jesus Christ. Every good and perfect gift is from above. Without You, none of this could be.

ABOUT THE AUTHOR

Kelsey Gietl is the author of the early 1910s Over the Atlantic duology, the WWI War Across Waters duology, and the 1850s Larksong Legacy series. Combining faith, family, and lessons from our past, her books provide inspirational stories with a dose of romance and a dash of intrigue.

She holds a Bachelor of Fine Arts in Theatre Design and Graphic Design and has made a career in fields from event planning and proposal writing to product management and communications.

She lives in Missouri with her husband, two children, and two dogs. She is a member of the Daughters of the American Revolution and the Catholic Writers Guild.

You can connect with her online at:
kelseygietl.com